AF616505

City of Diamonds

City of Diamonds

ROSALIE LAMET

TARGUM/FELDHEIM

First published 1996

ISBN 1-56871-097-6

Published by:
Targum Press Inc.
22700 W. Eleven Mile Rd.
Southfield, MI 48034

Distributed by:
Feldheim Publishers
200 Airport Executive Park
Nanuet, NY 10954

Distributed in Israel by:
Targum Press Ltd.
POB 43170
Jerusalem 91430

Printed in Israel

CONTENTS

DEDICATION

I dedicate this book to the memory of my beloved, never-to-be-forgotten mother and my oldest sister and brother, who were deported from Antwerp and brutally murdered by the Nazis. Needless to say, there are no graves, no stone monuments to remember them by.

May this book be a memorial that bears testimony to their lives and to the tragedy of their cruel, untimely deaths.

ACKNOWLEDGMENTS

I am grateful to my teacher and mentor, Kristin Lauer, Ph.D., head of the writing department at Fordham University, who thought I had a story that should be told. Her belief in my ability motivated me to write this book. She never let me lose my courage.

I wish to thank my niece, Barbara Rotenberg, and Bea Young, for their help and good counsel, as well as Esther Shafran for her comments, keen perceptions, and encouragement.

I also wish to thank Goldie Berger, my dear friend and advisor, who gave so generously of her experience and expertise.

Much thanks to Ruchama King-Feuerman, whose professional skill was pivotal in enabling me to complete this work.

I am deeply grateful to my editor at Targum, Libby

Lazewnik, and to the proofreader, Suri Brand, for their valued help in producing this book.

I am indebted to my beloved husband for his patience and understanding.

To my wonderful children and family, to my good friends, I express heartfelt thanks for your interest and support.

FLIGHT

On May 10, 1940, at six o'clock in the morning, I was awakened by the sound of Stuka dive bombers roaring through the sky. The radio soon confirmed, "Hitler declares war on Belgium, the Netherlands, and Luxembourg!" I sat up in bed, looking about me in shock. Though I had known war was imminent, I could not believe the news.

Our family immediately focused on a plan of action. A car with a chauffeur was ordered. To avoid the Germans, our family would flee Antwerp and head south. We expected to reach Uncle Henri's house in Paris sometime tomorrow.

Mama was emphatic. "Naomi! Boys! Each of you can take only your most essential belongings. We must leave room in the car for bags of sandwiches, fruit, and other provisions for this long trip."

I quickly opened the closet in my bedroom. I packed a blouse, a skirt, my housecoat, and medium-heeled shoes. A navy Shabbos dress, trimmed with red, Swiss-dotted silk, caught my eye. After a moment's hesitation I put the dress in, too. Maybe I would need fashionable things in Paris. Then I packed my toothbrush and some cosmetics, as well as my leather-bound prayer book.

I zipped the small suitcase shut and looked around the room. My eyes rested on the familiar blue wallpaper. Would I ever see this room or this house again? Just in case, I wrapped my photo album in a towel and stuck it between the clothes.

In the hallway, my brothers' luggage stood ready to go. Like myself, Leon and Benny didn't seem particularly scared. If anything, they seemed excited.

Mama locked the front door. I peered at her sideways, half expecting to see her wipe a tear from her eye, but her expression was composed and resolute and her movements as she locked the door quick and efficient.

I wasn't too surprised at Mama's stoic calm. Our family was not a demonstrative one. We found it difficult to show warmth and affection or give compliments and kisses. Long ago, when my father was still alive, we kissed our parents' hand every night before going to bed. Then, as now, we would hug and kiss our parents or one another only on birthdays, certain religious holidays, or other special occasions.

However, should one of us fall sick, the most loving and tender treatment was lavished on the patient. As a child, I had frequently suffered from throat infections. At once, a bed would be set up for me downstairs in the salon. All day long Mama would be in and out of the room, making sure I was comfortable, taking my medicine, gargling as prescribed, and drinking the hot tea she'd prepared. She even found time to sit at my bedside and discuss the foods that would restore my strength.

These thoughts flashed through my mind as I sat staring out the car window, scenery whizzing past my face.

Presently, Leon pulled out a small volume of the Mishnah. Aha! So he had brought something extra along, too — that which was closest to his heart. I had always admired my older brother's religious devotion. He had set his heart on going to the Mir Yeshivah in Poland, and in our town such a move was practically unheard of.

But while I looked up to Leon, I also feared him. On Shabbos he watched me with penetrating eyes to make sure I didn't accidently violate any law. Although I was brought up strictly religious, my education had been neglected. At eighteen, I knew only how to read Hebrew and the very rudiments of our history. No wonder Leon was always watching me to see that I got things right.

Benny was completely different. He was the youngest, playful, and mischievous. I peeked over his shoulder; he, too, had brought something extra — a miniature chess game. He practiced opening strategies on the tiny board positioned on his lap.

At one point, Leon looked up from his studying and recited Tefillas HaDerech, the prayer for a safe journey. I thought of my other brothers and sisters. They were older; my sisters were married with children of their own. We had made plans to meet them in Paris at Uncle Henri's.

Mama kept her eyes on the scenery, her lower jaw set. She wore her usual short, dark-brown wig, as was customary among the religious women in our neighborhood. Mama's skin was still white and smooth, and her eyes shone a clear violet-blue. In her handbag, I caught a glint of some sparkling object. When she reached over to give us sandwiches, the bag moved just a bit. There it was — Mama's diamond brooch. This is what she treasured and had chosen to bring. It was the first piece of jewelry Papa had given her from his flourishing diamond business.

Many years ago, my mother had lost her beloved husband. Now she might be losing the home that meant so much to her. I felt Mama's pain behind her stoic façade and a bit of shame at my teenage anticipation of the adventure ahead.

"We're coming to Malines," Louis, our chauffeur, announced cheerfully. "There's hardly anyone on the road. I think we're going to reach the French border in record time."

"Great!" Benny exclaimed. Louis winked back at him. This chauffeur knows what he's doing, I thought to myself, leaning back in my seat. He gave me a sense of safety and stability.

We soon arrived in Brussels. Once there, we unexpectedly learned that because of troop movements the main highway was off-limits to civilian traffic. Forced to make a detour, our chauffeur drove for hours through a maze of back roads.

"Are we close to France?" Leon asked.

"I sure hope so," Louis answered. "No need to worry. I'll find the way."

By now we were overtired and getting anxious. Yet Louis was still in good spirits.

Finally, in the dead of night, we landed in Grammont. Our chauffeur parked in front of the town tavern where, in spite of the hour, we were taken in. Our family was allotted one room. I shared a bed with Mama, and the boys also doubled up. Although it was a tight squeeze, we all slept like newborns.

Early the next morning, we heard a knock on the door. It was Louis. He kept his head low as he walked into the room and didn't look at any of us directly in the face. "I just listened to the radio," he said. "They sent out a warning. A shortage has already set in, and soon there'll be no gasoline available." My brothers groaned.

Our chauffeur went on. "I am very sorry, madame, but I must return to Antwerp." He shrugged. "Or I risk getting stuck here with my car."

Seized with apprehension, I looked at Mama, who simply nodded. She took out the money she owed Louis and paid him. He doffed his chauffeur's cap, wished us *"bonne chance"* — good luck — and left.

I stared at the door with disbelieving eyes. We had been relying on this man to take us past the border. I had felt so secure with him at the wheel. Now he was gone.

Over the next few days the war escalated. Refugees flooded the town. Soldiers appeared with bandaged arms and legs and ripped, blood-encrusted uniforms. All trains were stalled; all roads were cut off. We were stranded in Grammont! As I looked at the wounded soldiers, my former excitement about the war changed to horror.

The situation was serious. We had to get out of there.

Armand, a local young man, had befriended Leon at the tavern where we were staying. On Thursday, Leon introduced him to my mother. "Mama, Armand's father has an old Minerva parked in his garage. He thinks — for a price — his father might be willing to drive us closer to the French border."

The young man explained, "My dad hasn't driven that car

for a long time, but it is in running condition. I can't promise anything before I speak to him, though."

"Please, tell your father we would be ever so grateful and I will pay him handsomely," Mama said eagerly.

Within an hour, Armand returned with his dad. We could hardly believe our good fortune when Gaston, Armand's father, agreed to drive us to Courtrai — the nearest border town. We had no choice but to start out on Friday, before noon.

A most welcome Gaston appeared with his big, old Minerva. Again we loaded our luggage into the car. The trip took one and a half hours. When we arrived in Courtrai, our driver stopped the Minerva on a side street and rang the bell of a two-story house. A middle-aged woman opened the door.

"Gaston, my friend! What a nice surprise to see you here. Come in," she exclaimed.

"I'm not alone, Emma."

"I see. You've brought a carload."

"That's right. And these people need a place to stay. Can you possibly accommodate them?"

We had all stepped out of the car. I looked at the red-roofed Flemish house before us. The May air felt warm on my cheek. I stared with hopeful eyes at the woman.

She shook her head. "I'm sorry, all my rooms are rented out."

Mama held on to her luggage tightly. Although she always kept a firm grip on her emotions, I could feel that she was nervous. Shabbos was coming, and we had to be settled. There were no two ways about it.

Gaston said, "Who might take them in? Maybe your —"

"Wait a minute," Emma interrupted. "One of my boarders, a student, left the other day and hasn't come back." She turned to Mama. "I could let you have his room if you want. Come upstairs and have a look at it." We filed after her, hardly knowing what to expect — though at this point we would gladly have taken anything.

On one side of the room stood a bed. A chaise longue extended along the opposite wall. In addition, there was a desk, an armoire, a chest of drawers, and an easy chair. Mama discovered a sink and a two-burner gas range in the small alcove. She smiled at the landlady and said, "We'll manage just fine here."

We were left to ourselves. "This is great!" I cried out. "Now we have a sink with running water! That sure beats using the pump in the backyard of the tavern in Grammont."

"You're so right, Naomi," my mother replied cheerfully as she opened the window to air out the musty smell. "With no privacy, we could never wash ourselves properly over there."

We unpacked our suitcases and found the armoire full of clothes belonging to the student. The drawers of the chest were crammed with photographic material. "Look at this! It's a Leica," Benny said, admiring the sophisticated camera.

"He also has a box full of unused film," Leon announced. "Must be a photography buff."

Gaston came up to check on us. He saw each of us walking around, busily unpacking. Mama rummaged through her purse and handed him some bills. "All of us will remember your kindness," she said.

"It was nothing," Gaston told her, and then he left.

Just before leaving Grammont, Leon and Benny had

managed to buy bread and rolls, an assortment of canned fish, fresh eggs, and fruit from a supplier at the tavern. Mama had already bought spoons, forks, knives, and a few unbreakable dishes in town. These, together with a small frying pan and a tea kettle, made up the sum total of our household goods.

We considered ourselves lucky. For days we had gone without proper kosher food. "How I wish we could have a real Shabbos," I said with a sigh.

"Crowded in this small room? With barely enough to eat?" Leon scoffed. "How could it feel like Shabbos without —"

"We do have privacy here," I broke in. "Let's see. There's still time to look for a grocery. We must buy candles. Maybe we'll find other things we need, too."

Benny's face perked up. "Yippee! I'll go with you!"

"Me, too," Leon said.

The three of us were running down the stairs before Mama could say a word. It took awhile, but we shopped well. We even found a bottle of grape juice for Kiddush. On our return, we were utterly surprised to find a dining table and chairs in place of the desk and easy chair in our room.

Mama seemed elated. "Emma accommodated me at once. And graciously, too," she said. "Look, she even lent me this white tablecloth and a wine glass."

At sundown, Mama lit two candles in improvised candlesticks — carved from potatoes. For lack of challos, two rolls were laid on the table and covered with a white napkin. Leon proudly recited Kiddush, holding the glass of grape juice in his right hand. I wore the navy Shabbos dress that I had packed with visions of Parisian fashion.

An aura of peace prevailed, and all of us were relaxed. Our

mother beamed. "It feels so good to usher in the holy Shabbos with my loved ones. Even in a rented room."

We enjoyed our cold dinner of canned salmon on lettuce and a tomato salad. For dessert, there was canned peaches and applesauce. Between courses, Leon and Benny belted out Shabbos songs, and I joined in. The singing released our tensions of the past few days. We were all in a joyful mood.

It was time for bed. Mama removed her wig and placed it on top of the chest of drawers. My brothers and I retired soon after. While lying in bed, I heard my mother cough repeatedly, a little, nervous cough. There were sighs, too.

"Mama, what's keeping you awake?" I whispered.

She whispered back, "I'm still excited about our dinner tonight. It turned out so lovely. And I feel like we haven't slept in such clean beds in ages. Here one feels far removed from the war, from the turmoil outside. In this house we found a safe haven. We will all sleep well. Good night, Naomi!"

We both fell silent. I wondered if Evelyn, Daniel, and their two little girls had reached Paris before us. What about Claire and Julius and their children? Where were they and Charles and the rest of our family? At least here the Belgians were kind people. How graciously they had lodged us. It was comfortable here. A safe haven, just like Mama said.

I snuggled deeper under the covers. The pattern of my mother's breathing revealed that she had fallen asleep. Eventually I, too, drifted into sleep.

In the middle of the night, we were abruptly awakened by shouts and pounding on the door. "Open up! Police! Open up, or we'll break the door down!"

With eyes half-open and groggy with sleep, I called out,

"Just a minute. We're coming!"

Leon shuffled toward the door and unlocked it. As the door was flung open, he jumped aside to avoid getting hit. Two men armed with rifles stormed into the room. To our surprise, they were not in police uniforms. They wore black leather jackets and boots. The taller one was obviously the leader. His dark eyes exuded flashes of hatred as he glanced around the room. When he spotted Mama's wig, he grabbed it and cried triumphantly: "Aha! Here's the first piece of evidence! Spies are known to disguise themselves. My partner here has been observing you since you first arrived. He got suspicious right away. And we heard you singing in that foreign language — German, I'll bet!" He glared at us and thundered, "You will not get away with spying for the enemy this time!"

The second man ransacked the armoire and every drawer of the chest. He pulled out the Leica and shouted, "That's the camera they were going to use! It's additional evidence. And we're not finished yet!"

Then the leader found Leon's phylacteries. He turned them over in his hands, staring at the black leather cubes attached to their straps. "Radio transmitters," he pronounced.

We were stunned. Gaping, we listened to the ominous words without taking in their meaning at first. A smirk settled on the leader's face, and the evil glint in his eyes grew even more menacing as he said, "We've got all the evidence we need. You are spies, and you are coming with us to the gendarmerie!"

Mama stood as straight and tall as she could. In a trembling voice she said, "Who are you accusing of being spies? Your accusations are insane! We can explain everything."

"You'll do your explaining to the authorities who will decide your fate," he answered in a mocking tone.

Both men held their rifles at the ready. The leader threw open the door and said, "All of you — *en avant!*"

Flanked by the two thugs, we were marched off to the police station. It was 2:00 A.M. In the street, the darkness was total. A blackout had been implemented, and not even a cat was to be seen.

I rubbed my eyes. There was a nightmarish quality to our traipsing through the streets in our nightclothes. The hem of my robe dragged along the cobblestone road. My slippers kept falling off my feet. I felt shame for Mama, who had to walk with her hair uncovered. She had tried to grab a scarf to cover herself, but the thugs stopped her. Were these our kind Belgian neighbors? Suddenly I remembered something I had always heard: some Flemish people hated foreigners of any kind.

"If the moon were shining it wouldn't be so pitch black," Mama moaned.

The leader answered, sneering, "It'll get lighter at dawn. That's when you can expect to be shot by a firing squad! You're not the first spies to be executed in wartime. And I'll just love to watch your execution!" He laughed.

I gasped and stopped to draw breath. "Keep moving — and fast. Faster!" he snarled. Mama and I accelerated our pace.

Suddenly, there was a scuffle behind us. I cried out, "What's going on?"

"Cut that out!" Benny screamed.

Leon yelled, "Stop it!"

Hideous laughter — like the cackling of a witch. "Don't slow down! Keep marching!" the leader shouted.

"This sadist keeps poking us with the butt of his rifle," Benny groaned. "I must be black and blue all over!"

The second man gave Leon a forceful shove, which nearly knocked Benny down. The two of them banged hard into mine and Mama's backs. I grabbed hold of my mother before she lost her balance. The second man cackled again. The leader guffawed.

I fought the tears welling up in my eyes. In all my life I had never been so afraid. I prayed with fervor, "God Almighty, please! Oh, please don't forsake us in this time of need. Protect us and give me the strength to withstand this ordeal!"

We finally reached the gendarmerie. The officer behind the desk looked up and frowned at the two armed men. "It's 2:30 A.M. What's the meaning of this?"

"They are spies and we caught them!" the leader of the thugs replied with bravado.

"Couldn't you have waited till daybreak?"

"They're dangerous! If we'd left them, they would have flown the coop. Wait till you see the evidence. In the end, you will congratulate us on a job well done."

I shuddered. He spoke with a venom that exuded authority. Perhaps the officers would believe him.

Mama said, "Please, *Monsieur le Gendarme.* If you let me explain, you will see that these accusations are unfounded. They are absolutely crazy!"

"You will get your chance, madame. In the meantime, you can all sit down on the bench against the wall."

Martial law had been declared in Belgium, and the military had jurisdiction over the courts. The gendarme conferred with his colleagues and then addressed the two armed men. "We will have to get *Monsieur le Commandant* out of bed. If I know Jean Le Duc, he won't be thrilled. It had better be for a good reason!"

I looked at Leon, who sat withdrawn at the corner of the bench. Fright was written all over his face. Leon, who had such strong religious beliefs and whom I looked up to for guidance, was cringing under the malevolent gaze of the taller thug. I stared at him without comprehension. What had broken his bold spirit? We were innocent! I resolved to fight and let no circumstances defeat me.

Once again, I moved my lips in prayer. "Dear God in Heaven, help us. Please!" While we waited, I repeated those words again and again, praying as I never had before.

At 4:00 A.M. the commanding officer arrived with his aide. Before long, the two armed men and our family were beckoned to approach Jean Le Duc at his desk.

"Let's hear from you first," he said to the accusers.

"*Monsieur le Commandant,* these people are dangerous spies!" the leader declared. "In their room we found the tools of espionage: the wig they use in their disguises and a camera with loads of film. They even have a radio transmitter."

"Did you bring the evidence?" the officer asked. He was a tall man with angular features and a deliberate air. He leaned slightly forward as he spoke.

"We were sure that *Monsieur le Commandant* would order a thorough search. So we left everything in the room."

The officer seemed to ponder this. He turned to Mama. "Well, madame," he said after a long pause, "what have you got to say?"

"These charges are ludicrous! Believe me, monsieur. We are

no spies! We are Belgians from Antwerp on our way to France."

The commandant raised a brow. "What about the wig, the camera, and the radio transmitter, all of which incriminate you?"

"We are Orthodox Jews, and the wig is mine. I wear it for religious reasons." Mama went on to describe the phylacteries.

The officer leaned back in his leather chair and listened attentively. "I know some Jewish people and am rather familiar with their customs," he said. "This still does not explain why you have a camera."

Mama responded, "The only room we were able to rent when we arrived in Courtrai yesterday belonged to a student. Evidently he dabbled in photography and was equipped for it. The camera is his. It was left in the room along with his other belongings."

Jean Le Duc nodded. He paused for a minute, then spoke. "I am quite satisfied with your explanation, madame. I regret that you and your children have been subjected to this harrowing experience and had to spend your first night in our town filled with anguish."

We looked at each other with immense relief. Leon mopped his forehead with his pajama sleeve.

The two men in their black leather jackets were nervously pacing the floor. The officer called them over. "You idiots!" he roared. "Where do you get the audacity to harass decent people like that? The Auxiliary Police Force of Courtrai has no use for brutes like you!" I could not help but grin at the sudden change in our accusers' demeanors. Their heads hung low like chastened pups, and they appeared to have visibly shrunk.

The two ruffians answered meekly, "We're sorry. We only

wanted to do our duty. We were convinced they were spies."

Jean Le Duc thumped his hand on the table. "You'll do a better job or you're out! Is that clear?"

"Yes, *Monsieur le Commandant.*"

"Now get lost! Both of you!" He gestured imperiously toward the door.

The officer turned to Mama. "I am sending two gendarmes to escort you back. Only for your protection, you understand."

"Thank you, *Monsieur le Commandant.* You are very kind," Mama told him. Benny, Leon, and I added our own fervent thanks.

The corners of his mouth curled upwards. With warmth in his eyes, Jean Le Duc said, "I wish you a safe journey from here on. *Bonne chance* to all of you!"

We walked through the town, a gendarme on each side, and talked quietly. Leon had emerged from his earlier despondency and walked with a sprightly step. The darkness gradually lifted and gave way to a soft, pale light. How beautiful Courtrai appeared, with its small, red-roofed houses, its beech trees and cherry laurels, and its winding roads.

Leon said, "That Jean Le Duc... Now there's a first-class gentleman for you. We're lucky we met up with him."

Back in our rented room, we fell limply onto the beds and chairs, too exhausted to utter a word.

Later, as I rose to dress, I reflected, we've met all kinds of people on our journey so far — Louis, Armand, Gaston, the ruffians, Jean Le Duc — some average men, some evil ones, and some truly good human beings.

My glance fell upon the candlesticks carved from potatoes

and the wine glass on the table. They looked as if they had arrived from another world. It was still Shabbos. No thugs could take that away from us, no matter how hard they tried. At that moment Shabbos appeared like two strong and loving arms, holding me and embracing my entire family.

Here was the safe haven — not the student's room, the tavern, or even our beautiful home back in Antwerp, but Shabbos! It would always be there to envelop us, to comfort and inspire, no matter where circumstances might lead our family in the danger-fraught days ahead. This thought filled me with such peace that I lowered my head to hide my tears.

Leon stood up and washed his hands. He recited the morning prayers with extra feeling, and soon Benny joined him. I took out my prayer book, and, slowly, with great thankfulness, I began to pray, too.

THE BATTLE

It was time to leave our little student room in Courtrai. Belgium was falling fast. We had to reach France, which was believed to be well protected by its Maginot line and by the French and British armies.

But the route to the nearby French border was cut off. By early afternoon, my mother, brothers, and I had joined a stream of refugees on the West Flanders highway. We began our trek toward the North Sea, hoping to enter France near the coast.

We had put our belongings on a cart, leaving space for Mama to sit on top. Leon and Benny pulled the vehicle amid the throngs of refugees also fleeing south. I walked beside the cart. Families with children, young and old people, formed a column on both sides of the road and kept treading at a steady pace. It was a balmy day, and the sun beamed in a cloudless sky.

Suddenly Benny cried out, "Look what's coming!" I glanced skyward. An enemy airplane, a *Messerschmidt*, was coming right at us! With a long, shrill whistle, the plane swooped down and sprayed the ground with machine-gun fire.

There was no time to think. I darted for cover and found myself cowering in a rain ditch. All around me people dove, tumbled, or rolled into the ditches that lined the highway. From my hiding place, I spotted Leon and Benny hurriedly helping my mother off the cart. They huddled underneath the two-wheel, wooden contraption. I stared at them in anguish. Dangerous as my position was, theirs was even more precarious.

I should have stayed with them, but I had run without a second thought. I was overcome by shame and a longing to be with my family, whatever might happen.

Suddenly the plane wheeled, climbed, and took off, sputtering a few last bullets as it went. Heads lifted with caution. Slowly, everyone returned to their belongings, and the straggling caravan resumed its walk.

I rejoined my family. Mama was ashen. Even Benny looked shaken.

"It's sheer luck that no one got hit in this section," Leon said in a husky voice.

In an uncharacteristic display of emotion for our family, we all hugged each other.

"Look at those cows and horses in the field. They got it all right!" Benny exclaimed.

Along the way we passed the dead livestock. Cows, pigs, horses, and sheep lay on their backs with bloated bellies, their skins stretched tight as if about to burst. As soon as rigor mortis set in, their upward pointing legs made each of the animals appear grotesquely wooden.

Whenever we came to a village or hamlet, most of the wanderers stopped for a rest. A sort of camaraderie had evolved between our family and the refugees walking near us. During the last break, one young man offered to carry my bundle, but I declined his offer. A Hollander who was a student at the University of Leiden gave us some oranges. I ate mine with relish.

Someone offered me a scrumptious-looking chunk of cake, but — not without a pang — I turned down the offer. I had been overweight for most of my childhood and only recently, through intense dieting, had succeeded in slimming down.

Actually, as a child I was scrawny, and Mama was forever worrying about me. As a result, she constantly plied me with cakes, rich dishes, and chocolates to fatten me up. By the time I was seventeen it was misery to look at myself in the mirror. My face was puffed up, and I looked like a bloated, middle-aged woman. But the full impact of my appearance didn't hit me until this one incident:

I was taking a stroll, after buying groceries for Mama, and had turned down a street where construction workers sat eating their sandwiches. When I came into view, they all stopped munching, and, as if on command, their faces broke out in mocking grins.

"Look what's coming," one of them said.

"Well, well, did you ever?"

"That's some fat cow. Ugh!"

I tried to hurry past, holding my head up high. A chorus

of laughter followed, probably in response to another caustic slur, though this time, thankfully, no longer within my earshot. I wished I could die!

Tears of humiliation flowed freely as I walked doggedly on. When I arrived at the house, I dropped my purchases on the kitchen table and ran upstairs. With the door closed behind me, I burst out crying.

Finally, I wiped the tears off my cheeks. I decided right then and there to see Dr. Lahay, a nutrition and dieting specialist Mama had been urging me to meet.

At Dr. Lahay's office, I was given pills to activate my thyroid gland and certain vitamins. My prescribed food intake was twelve hundred calories a day — a downright starvation diet. The hunger pangs, which began in the pit of my stomach and spiralled outward, were almost more than I could bear. But even more difficult was Mama offering me cinnamon buns, fresh out of the oven, or plying me with pralines, fried potatoes, and omelettes. "Your diet is too drastic," she'd say, looking anxiously at me.

I realized food had always been Mama's way of expressing affection and concern for me. She was not a demonstrative person, and I was taking away her sole means of showing her love. I felt torn refusing her, but I somehow found the strength to do so.

Gradually, after months of intensive dieting and daily exercises, the distorted contour of my face turned into a perfect oval, and the shine returned to my eyes and complexion. My sense of accomplishment — and satisfaction — made all sorts of gastronomic sacrifices well worth the price.

We passed Zonnebeke and Poelkapelle, and the trek continued. At night we slept in inns or, lacking that, on straw and hay in big, draughty barns. We kept walking and walking among the masses on the road leading to the North Sea. The *Messerschmidts* harassed us periodically. After five days of dodging live fire and stepping over dead bodies, we finally arrived at La Panne. Following the crowds, we were soon at the French border, where a multitude had already assembled. To our shock, a red and white barrier had been erected to prevent anyone from crossing over.

Had we come all this way for nothing? This was our last chance to enter France. Our desperate aim to avoid the Germans seemed all but smashed. The mob strained against the barrier, attempting to break through.

"We've been sitting here for twenty-eight hours, waiting to get into France," a woman cried above the tumult.

"Nobody goes across!" a guard bellowed back. "Those are our orders — military orders. If necessary, we'll bring armed reinforcements to keep you out!"

The crowd kept shouting. "What's going on? Why aren't we being told what's happening? Tell us the reason for this!" The guards fell silent. The refugees had no choice but to calm down and wait further.

Hundreds were already camping on the site. They'd spread bedding on the ground, where most of the women and children stayed while their men went to buy food. In the second week of war the country's food reserves were just about exhausted. The two bakeries in La Panne posted signs, announcing the hours they would be open. Bread lines formed long before that time.

But Mama couldn't be stopped. "Now that we've come this far we're not just going to give up," she decided. "We'll stay here, ready to walk across as soon as that barrier goes up."

I could not help raising my eyebrows. "Stay here? I think we'd be better off finding ourselves some lodging. We can come back to check on the border situation."

Leon shook his head. "We've got no chance of finding any accommodations in La Panne."

"Then we'll walk back to the next town. That's Coxyde, I believe," Mama replied, jutting out her chin. And that was that.

In Coxyde we procured the brightest, most inviting rooms that any summer home could offer. In addition to a picture window, the spacious living room had a domed roof set with glass panes. The upstairs bedroom had an adjoining bath and a den that opened onto a sun deck. "At last! We'll be able to shower, to live like human beings," I exclaimed.

We bought food, obtained milk from a farmer, and dined on bread and jam. All of us had a restful night and slept well into the morning.

The next day, while Leon and Benny were reciting their morning prayers and Mama and I were still in our nightgowns, we heard the whir of an approaching airplane. Accustomed to the sound by this time, we thought nothing of it. But the bomb blast that followed was deafening. The house shook to its foundations, and large cracks appeared in the walls. A deluge of glass came crashing down, narrowly missing us. Nothing less than Divine intervention could have prevented us from being slashed and punctured by the shattering glass.

Stairs descended from the living room, ending at a blank

wall. Somehow, Mama, Leon, Benny, and I found ourselves there. None of us recalled making a dash for this shelter. When we stopped shaking with fright, we came to believe that something extraordinary had happened, leading us to safety.

The stillness in the narrow stairwell became oppressive. Cautiously, we climbed back up. Leon opened the door at the top, and we gaped at the living-room floor, which was covered with metal strips from the roof's framework and a million fragments of shattered glass. The upholstery of both couches had erupted to spew masses of stuffing onto the chaotic scene.

Mama and I were still waiting on the steps barefoot, in our nightclothes. Leon and Benny had to carry us into the upstairs bedroom, where we found every window blown out. It took us quite some time to dress and gather our belongings.

After leaving the house, we stood gazing at a wide, deep hole in the ground. Just one villa separated us from where the bomb had exploded. The structure had its roof sheared off, and only part of one wall remained standing. The rest was rubble.

I gasped. "It was really that close!"

Mama exclaimed, "Our Father in Heaven shielded us, letting no harm come to us! Leon and Benny, you're obligated to offer the special prayer of thanks for this."

"The blessing of thanks should be recited in shul, in front of ten men," Leon answered. "But who knows when Benny and I will be able to pray in a regular shul again?"

"I'm sure that day will come," Mama said. "Meanwhile we must not delay our thanks to the Almighty for having spared us."

Leon seemed deep in thought. After a short pause, he reflected, "I remember a debate on the subject. According to one opinion, in a situation like ours it is all right to say the prayer of thanks by ourselves."

Back in the villa, Benny managed to retrieve his prayer book from the shambles. I listened to the Hebrew words as my brothers' voices rose in unison: "Blessed are You, our God, King of the Universe, Who bestows goodness upon the guilty, Who bestowed every goodness upon me."

Although I remained silent, inwardly I prayed along with unprecedented fervor. My gratitude for being alive and well could not have been more profound.

It was imperative that we find new lodgings. My mother, Leon, Benny, and I walked toward the center of town in search of a place to stay. By chance, we met Shimon Brodt, a former Hebrew teacher of my brothers. He invited us to move in with his family.

Coxyde seemed overrun by British servicemen. Obviously something was up. Benny and I ran through the streets looking for information, hoping to find out why no one was being allowed to cross into France. It all remained a mystery.

The following day, refugees and natives of Coxyde alike waited with apprehension for the imminent invasion of enemy troops. We were informed that they were practically at our doorstep. Mama admonished Leon, Benny, and me to stay indoors and, even then, to be on our guard.

She told us the story of a young girl in Antwerp at the time of the German invasion in the first World War. The girl had been sewing and wore a thimble as she stood by the window watching the enemy troops march by. Sun rays — intensified by the glass — struck the metal thimble and made it glisten. One soldier saw the flash. He aimed his rifle, fired through the window, and killed the girl. The story imprinted itself strongly on my mind.

However, in spite of Mama's warning, my brothers and I continued to roam the streets. We came upon a crowd gathered near some parked lorries. Standing on top of one vehicle, a couple of Tommies — British soldiers — shouted down at the people, "Everything must go! Whatever's left will be smashed to pieces. We're leaving nothing behind for the Nazis!"

Next we heard, "Anybody want a brand-new adding machine? And here's an Underwood typewriter. I see a hand go up. Yes, it's all yours!"

"I don't believe this," Benny muttered. "Look at what these Belgians are carrying off with them."

We watched people walk away with cases of cognac and Scotch, as well as blankets, field glasses, and other valuables.

"I guess we don't need any excess baggage to drag along, right?" Benny remarked somewhat ruefully.

"Right!" I said.

A Tommy approached me. "Mademoiselle," he said, "my buddy and I have been driving a small gray Austin. Where we're going we can't take it. Rather than leave it for the Germans, we'd like you to have it."

I was flabbergasted. A car would transform our journey. We would be able to travel with ease. The offer was tempting. Then a thought occurred to me.

"No thanks," I said. "My family and I will be accused of being spies. Anyone with an English car would most probably be stopped by the Nazis."

"You've got a point there," the soldier admitted. "Please

forgive me. I meant no harm by the offer." He smiled his apologies.

"It's quite all right," I said matter-of-factly. Though I knew the decision had been right, I was regretful. How much simpler our situation would have been with a car of our own.

Leon, Benny, and I drifted off. On approaching the street corner, we could hear the sound of axes hacking away. We listened to the cracking and snapping of wood and the outcries of Tommies hewing furniture and other equipment into scrap. Walking on, we reached the main boulevard leading to the sea and witnessed a most moving scene. A row of lorries packed with British troops stood the length of the avenue. As a fleet of anchored ships came into view, the Tommies whooped and hollered. Shedding tears, they hugged and kissed each other and cried, "We're going home! Home to Mother England! Hip hip hurrah!"

Their cheers ended in song. As we left, the sound of "Hail, Britannia" followed us. They were intoxicated with the hope of crossing the Channel and returning to their loved ones.

The next day, we woke to the pounding of shellfire nearby. The scream of airplanes was followed by blasts of bombardment. A bomb landed in the vicinity, and for interminable seconds our villa shook dangerously. Everyone ran down to the basement, where the two families huddled together. After dashing back up to fetch their prayer books, phylacteries, and Mr. Brodt's prayer shawl, the men began praying with relentless fervor.

Meanwhile, the shrieking rain of bombs continued, to the accompaniment of a thunder of artillery fire. With each nearby detonation, the building tottered and the walls threatened to tumble. I recited the Shema, as did everyone around me. I was sure this was the end. If the villa caved in, God forbid, we would all be buried alive beneath the ruins.

Beside me, my mother sighed deeply. As though she had read my thoughts, she turned to me, squeezed my hand, and said, "As long as the battle is raging, this basement is the safest place for us."

Waiting in the dark basement, images of my home in Antwerp flashed through my mind: the lilac flowers in the garden, the exquisite ecru lace curtains that hung in the salon, a crystal chandelier Papa had bought at an auction.

I stood listening to the bombs exploding, some at a distance, some close by, and felt the precariousness of life. Suddenly my memories became precious to me. I recalled how Papa had loved beautiful things. There was an oil painting he once bought of a reclining child simply because it appealed to him. Then came our gleaming, black, lacquer piano. Soon he had his three daughters taking piano lessons, to the disapproval of his fellow Gerer Chassidim.

Mama was more careful about money and would become angry when he brought home these lovely — and, she felt, unnecessary — objects. In this respect she was strict. But in other matters, she was soft-hearted and Papa the disciplinarian.

Papa made all nine of us children line up each night of the winter to take our spoonful of cod-liver oil, which I would gulp down while holding my nose. When we finished the bottle, though, there was always a franc for each of us. When the boys became too wild, he pulled them across his lap and spanked them with a leather belt. Just the threat of a spanking was enough to make my brothers behave, so he rarely had to use the belt.

How he pampered Mama! She was so different in those days. Her main responsibility was running the household and managing the servants; it was Papa who liked to dress the younger children and say the Shema with us at night. I wondered why he spoiled Mama so. Sometimes I thought it was his gratitude to her for having borne him nine children. After that, what more could he ask of her? Other times I thought it was his simple desire to spare our elegant and graceful mother any hardship.

When Papa died, Mama was only forty-two. She, who had depended on her husband so utterly, suddenly had to become a tower of strength for her children. She succeeded admirably. But many times I longed for the gentler mama of years ago.

Through the long hours, as the bombs exploded around us, I sat sunk in my own thoughts. Eventually, I became aware that the interminable noise had come to an end.

Only after we finally emerged from the cellar did we learn of the clandestine sea operation — the brilliant scheme the British military had put into effect. Against all odds, they had succeeded in evacuating the majority of their forces. Not in any war had a tactical withdrawal of vanquished troops on a scale of such magnitude ever been recorded.

Craft of every description had arrived from England and taken aboard the battle-weary Tommies, not only from the French Channel ports but from the Belgian coastline as well. Numerous vessels were manned by civilian volunteers. A concentration of the Royal Air Force protected the entire operation.

As soon as this maneuver was detected by the enemy, the *Luftwaffe* entered the scene. Field Marshal Kesselring's air fleet attacked with a nonstop hail of incendiary and high-explosive bombs. The docks and quays of Dunkirk were blasted into rubble, and, in the ruins of the town, one thousand men, women, and children were found dead. Our family and those praying with us had been spared.

All along, none of us had an inkling that we were within the battle zone of Dunkirk — or that a memorable page of history was about to be written at the shores of the North Sea and the English Channel.

For three days and nights we stayed underground. The dawn that followed greeted our two families with silence. Total silence.

"Does it mean the war is over?" I asked.

"Looks like the fighting's stopped. Let me find out for sure." Excitedly, Leon rushed out of the basement and into the street.

Eventually, he returned with the somber news: "Belgium has capitulated! The British wanted to continue fighting, but King Leopold III asked the Germans for an armistice. He signed an unconditional surrender."

"Who told you that?" we wanted to know.

"People on the street heard it on the national broadcast. It's official! But guess what? All British troops have vanished. No Tommies around to be taken prisoner by the Nazis. How do you like that?"

After the dimness of our basement, I welcomed the return to daylight. Thick black smoke arose in the distance from the hellish explosions that had ignited the oil tanks of Dunkirk.

Orange and red flames kept leaping skyward from the petroleum refineries that burned out of control. When the sea breezes wafted to the north, the pall of smoke drifted toward Coxyde.

That same morning, my brothers and I felt drawn to the seashore. We knew instinctively that a human drama had unfolded there. We expected to find some evidence of what the retreating troops had had to withstand in order to embark at sea. However, not one of us was prepared for what we were about to see.

The beach, at ebb tide, presented us with the unreal vision of a nightmare. Bloated and twisted bodies of Tommies who had drowned or had been hit by gunfire made that stretch of sand a sight of infernal devastation. Countless helmets, boots, and other objects lay strewn among the corpses. Wrecked motorboats and whaleboats could be spotted inshore amid drenched military cars and other motor vehicles.

The three of us stood, transfixed by what we saw. I gasped, "Oh, oh!"

"They always tell you war is hell. But look at this. It's going to haunt me. Give me bad dreams," Benny groaned.

The next instant, Leon caught himself and said, "Say, Benny, we're *kohanim.* Even though there's the prescribed distance between us and the dead, we mustn't stand here and look at them."

I, too, shook myself. What were we doing here in the first place? The Germans were probably coming.

Sure enough, the warning spread throughout Coxyde like a gust of ill wind that drove people off the streets: "The enemy troops are at the outskirts! They're practically here!"

If the approach of Hitler's *Wehrmacht* instilled fear in the general population, how much more powerful was the foreboding that gripped the two Jewish families in our villa? Who knew if the Nazis in Belgium would treat the Jews any better than they had in their own country?

Once again, Shimon Brodt put on his phylacteries and prayer shawl. With a catch in his throat, he cried out, "This is a tragic moment. Foremost, regarding our people. We must implore the Almighty not to abandon us." Everyone joined him in reciting the Psalms of King David.

My mother stood to the side, her head tilted in the way I'd come to recognize as one of deep thought. Finally she said, "It's best that we return to Antwerp. We must look for transportation as soon as it's safe to go outside."

Leon, Benny, and I nodded gravely. What other choice was there?

Then it struck me. That's why the crowd at La Panne had been prevented from crossing into France. We had thought that France was safe, and all the while, the Germans had been invading the north of France, making it the most dangerous place to be. I could not help sensing the irony of the situation. We had been rushing right into the arms of our captors. Now, balked of our original plan, we had to return to Antwerp.

Who knew what awaited us there?

THE RETREAT

It was time to leave Coxyde. But how? Gas rationing ruled out our hiring a car. The only solution suggested to us was hitching a ride with a German vehicle departing from Coxyde.

The idea was far from appealing to any of us. We were convinced we'd feel uncomfortable as passengers in an enemy truck with a Nazi driver at the wheel. But we were assured that the *Wehrmacht* had received orders from their high command to help all refugees return to their homes.

After thinking it over, Mama decided, "This may be the only chance to go home. Since we have no other choice, we'll take it."

Soon after, we were able to board a *Wehrmacht* truck departing for Brussels. Much to our surprise, the German soldiers were exceptionally courteous and helpful. Mama and I were even given the privilege of sitting up front with the driver, while Leon and Benny shared the back of the truck with other refugees and three Germans in uniform. Perhaps all the horror tales we had heard of German savagery were simply made up. At least, I hoped as much.

I sat staring out the window, too lost in my own thoughts to be struck by the irony of our situation. Now that the war had ended, I was anxious to track down the whereabouts of all our family members. My brother Michael and his wife, Sabine, were still in the unoccupied zone in France, which gave me some relief. It was probably much safer there than in Belgium. Last I'd heard, Claire and Julius and their children were in Free France, too. We had hoped that Evelyn, Daniel, and their two girls had crossed the border into France but heard no word to verify this. Thank God, Nathan and Eugene were in New York. And Charles? He had been drafted into the Belgian army, and we didn't know when we would next hear from him.

Finally we arrived in Brussels. The *Wehrmacht* truck let us off in front of the *Gare du Nord,* where train service to Antwerp had been restored. It was a half-hour later when we arrived in Antwerp's Central Station.

Clutching our last remaining suitcase, we got off the train. I looked around me. Uniformed German guards were now posted on both sides of the marble staircase in the railroad terminal. These Nazis stared intensely at all the passengers going by. I watched as they picked people at random and interrogated them on the spot:

"Your identity card, please? Where are you coming from? What were you doing there?"

They spoke in civil tones, yet immediately I began to tense my shoulders as if I were guilty of wrongdoing. When it was our turn to walk by, I felt the guards' eyes piercing me from beneath their steel helmets, and a tremor ran down my spine. What would they do if they discovered we were Jews? So far, we hadn't experienced any distinction in their treatment of Jews; there was no reason to think we would be singled out now. Still, I was frightened.

I regained my composure only after we were no longer in their line of sight. With a sigh of relief, we made our way down to the splendid domed hall of the Central Station. There, in the middle of the hall, hung an oversized flag. We stood, gaping at the fiery red cloth, with the black swastika printed on a round white background. Everyone's eyes were drawn on it in fascinated horror. I shuddered to see the Nazi banner displayed in Antwerp for the first time. My fellow townspeople seemed equally horrified.

"Please, let's get out of here," I pleaded.

With every step we took in our city, the reality of occupied Antwerp began to dawn on me. Military trucks, small gray cars, and motorcycles manned by Germans in uniform were racing to and fro. German soldiers were everywhere.

On the way to our house, we walked through the Pelikaanstraat — the nucleus of Antwerp's diamond industry. Concentrated within a few blocks were the Bourse, the Kring, the Diamond Dealers Club, the Fortunia, and some smaller, restricted meeting places where trading was conducted.

I remembered how, on a regular weekday, it had been virtually impossible for passersby to move on the sidewalk in the diamond center. Dealers and brokers scurried from one building to another, waists bulging under their suit jackets where they bore portfolios filled with diamonds.

But on this day, there was no trace of the hustle and bustle that had invariably prevailed in the Pelikaanstraat. A pall had descended on this section of town. A lone bicyclist rode by. I saw a few civilians on foot, but that was all. We soon discovered that the gloom extended to virtually every street.

Before long, we would learn that the *Kommandantur* was located inside the Bourse, and that the Gestapo was setting up their headquarters in an adjacent building.

Benny and Leon, faces alive with indignation, pointed out the various changes that had taken place in our town. As for me, I found myself retreating deeper and deeper into a strange numbness. While I had been on the road, everything seemed like an exciting adventure, but what I saw before me now was bleakness and alienation. I did not want to accept this new reality. I glanced at my mother. Her head was bowed stoically. I sensed a deep sadness emanating from her.

When Mama, my brothers, and I rounded the corner of the Milisstraat, we came face to face with Louisa, a girl who lived next door to us. She had always greeted our family with a warm smile, as we were on friendly terms with our neighbors. But now Louisa turned her head abruptly, giving no sign of recognition as she walked on, her nose in the air.

"How do you like that?" I exclaimed. "The day before the war broke out, she rang our doorbell and asked if she could have some lilacs from our garden. We let her help herself to a huge bouquet."

Leon added, "Every spring she came for flowers. So did all the other neighbors."

Mama shook her head and said sadly, "How this girl snubs us at a time like this. As Jews, we'll soon find out who our true friends are. Let's not become disheartened at the first sign of rejection from so-called former friends."

Within minutes we reached the house and unlocked the front door. We had been absent for three weeks. Our home seemed like a forbidding and unwelcoming stranger. Inside the murky entrance hall, I saw at a glance the wilted brown leaves of the potted palm in its brass planter. On the day we left, it had been thriving.

"Look! The palm is dead!" Mama cried. "It's been standing here for so many years. In a way it's like losing an old friend."

The wall clock in our family room had stopped. A chill enveloped me. In an attempt to dispel the dimness and musty odor, I rushed from room to room, pulling up blinds, opening windows, and fluffing up the pillows on our chaise longue. Then I plunked down on a chair and burst into tears. It was one thing to feel like a foreigner in your own city, but to feel alienated in your own home was something else entirely.

Mama put her hand on my shoulder. "Don't worry, Naomi. I'm sure all the Flemish won't receive us like Louisa. Soon this place will feel just like home again."

But I did not share my mother's optimism. I said, "What about Maria?" Mama fell silent. Maria had been our beloved Flemish housekeeper for many years. One day, she abruptly gave notice without indicating any reason. Soon after, we found out from Maria's cousin that her father had forbidden her to work for "Jewish vermin." He had adopted Hitler's ideology to the fullest.

Benny and Leon nodded their heads vigorously. Leon said, "I doubt the Nazis will have too much difficulty finding collaborators among the Flemish people."

But Mama tried to maintain her usual positive attitude.

"Let me put up a pot of split-pea soup," she said. "You'll see. Everything will be fine."

Through my tears, I felt the beginnings of a smile. That was Mama, always trying to remedy a situation with food. I wondered, rather irrelevantly, whether now that I was back at home I would gain back all the weight I had worked so hard to lose.

The next few days we all waited for news from the rest of the family. We were greatly relieved to learn that some of them were in the unoccupied French zone. Clearly it was safer there than in Belgium.

Meanwhile, other people returned. Every day Mama welcomed back friends and acquaintances, and we listened to their stories. Most of them had crossed the French border and headed south. After the fall of mainland France, everyone talked about the *Wehrmacht*'s amazing rescue job. Besides being competent, these German occupation troops helped individuals in need of personal assistance. They treated all passengers courteously and got them home safely. I nodded as I listened to these accounts. They certainly confirmed our own impression of the Germans as benign.

In the days that followed, the diamond trade picked up considerably, and once again the streets were teeming with business. How quickly life had returned to normal!

Antwerp's Jewish boys' school, Yesodei HaTorah, had reopened its doors, and Leon resumed his teaching position there. The principal of the school, Mynheer Van Looveren, told all teachers, "The *Wehrmacht* does not concern itself with civilian affairs outside its province. We will be allowed to function as a religious institution without interference." A great sigh of relief went up from the audience.

Judging from the appearance of things, the Jews were not going to be singled out for persecution. Everyone, ourselves included, wrote to relatives of the safe conditions in Antwerp and encouraged their return.

Life had returned to normal — except for the food situation. Strange how things always came back to food. In the days that followed, my fears of gaining weight were dispelled.

When we first arrived back in Antwerp, food rationing was well underway. Without delay, Leon and Benny went to the Gemeente Plaats, a square where a somber and squat town hall loomed in its center. They waited in the windowless structure for over an hour and were finally issued ration cards for each family member, with food stamps to be renewed each month. With these stamps we could buy staples such as flour, potatoes, sugar, rice, and beans. There were special stamps for soap, shoes, and other items.

When the boys brought home the food rations, I stared in shock at the meager offerings.

"That's supposed to last us a month?" I exclaimed. "Why, any adult with a normal appetite would finish this off in two weeks!"

"They can't mean for us to starve, can they?" Benny asked.

Mama, too, peered at the scant supply of food. "Somehow we'll have to make do," she said, but I saw doubt on her face.

This is a test, I told myself, like all the other tests we've had to endure so far, and I will pass it. I will be brave. Truthfully, though, I didn't think I would be able to manage at all. Much as I wanted to be strong in the face of adversity, I was used to the comforts of good living. I was spoiled.

I couldn't stand eating our rationed, clay-like black bread. It had a pasty consistency and tasted just awful. It required an effort to swallow each bite.

"Here, look," I told Mama the next morning, pointing at red splotches on my neck and arms. "I've broken out in hives all over. I think it's from that horrible bread."

Mama heaved a sigh. "That wouldn't surprise me. I heard it's made of ground potato peels. And who knows what other garbage gets mixed in?" She paused. "If you have an allergic reaction, you shouldn't be eating this bread."

"But how else am I going to stop my hunger pangs?" I asked plaintively. "Those 225 grams of black bread are the mainstay of our daily diet."

Mama said nothing. She just bit her lip and turned away.

But a few days later, Mama told me in a confidential tone, "Leon is working on something — a black-market connection with a farmer from the Polders. It must be kept quiet, of course." She gave me a meaningful look, and I nodded.

A story had just begun to circulate of a man who'd been caught working in the black market. I happened to know him — a big, burly fellow with a pleasant smile. He disappeared for a while, and when he returned, I saw him on the street and could hardly recognize him. His face was bruised and pulverized; his body seemed shrunken, as though half of him were missing. This is what might happen to Leon if he were caught! Or even worse, perhaps, being a Jew. He might be sent to a camp in Malines. I shuddered to think of the possible sacrifice our brother was undertaking for our welfare.

And so began Leon's stint in the black market. One day, I came upon a whole shelf stacked with chocolate bars, wafers, bags of caramels, and nougat. My eyes widened as I recognized the finest Belgian chocolates, which had completely vanished from stores. When I spotted my favorite, Cote d'Or milk chocolate with hazelnuts, I couldn't help licking my lips.

To my chagrin, Leon locked the doors of the buffet with a key, while I looked on. "If I tell you what it's going to fetch on the black market, you won't believe me," he said gleefully.

"You mean it's right in our house, and I can't even have one?" I wailed. Suddenly I was reduced to the level of a six-year-old.

"C'mon, Naomi. This is purely business. What we've got here — it's gold!"

Sure enough, the following week deliveries arrived at our house. I watched as they unloaded a sack of rice, another of kidney beans, and a smaller bag of flour that was not white. Potatoes, carrots, and turnips from the Polders came on a different day. They were stored in the cellar together with the wood kindling. The other provisions, cans of sardines and herring in tomato sauce, were kept in the buffet with the sweets. Watching all the nutritious food come in, I felt mollified.

Then bad news struck. Parents could no longer afford the tuition fees at Yesodei HaTorah, and Leon was now teaching without pay. With one source of income gone, it was necessary to develop the black market even further. Leon began to sell and deliver to more customers. We thought it unwise to have buyers coming and going, since vigilant neighbors might suspect illegal trading and denounce us to the authorities. During the weeks that followed, there was a continuous flurry of activity that made me believe that Leon had, indeed, hit upon a way of acquiring "gold."

Benny helped Leon with errands and deliveries. One day, Leon made contact with an Orthodox slaughterer who could, on occasion, supply kosher meat. Benny was entrusted with the pickup of a huge roast and brought it home safely. We stored the meat in our icebox, making sure there was always sufficient ice available. When the High Holidays came, we celebrated *yom tov* with a sumptuous roast. We felt truly blessed.

As I watched my brothers actively engaged in their business, I envied them. Leon was the seventh child out of nine, but now, with Michael, the oldest, gone — and all the others as well — it was as though he had become the man of the house. Benny, the youngest, had also taken on a position of responsibility. They had a job to do. They were productive; they were earning income and providing for the family. All I could do was dream about Cote d'Or chocolate bars.

I approached my brothers. "Do you need any help with the packing and ordering? Could I help with deliveries?"

Leon dismissed me with a wave of the hand. "It's not for girls," he said flatly, and that was that.

I wanted to work, to do something. But what? A religious girl I knew worked in a lovely clothing shop and had already been promoted to buyer. Would Mama even let me go out of the house if I found a job?

I approached her one day while she sat on the patio outside the kitchen. I explained my predicament and ended, "Please, Mama, could I try to find work?"

My mother stared at me. "Naomi!" she exclaimed. "Why would you want to leave the house if it's not necessary? You have a job to do here. Why, there's cooking and cleaning, and you have other things to do besides." She stopped and thought for a moment. "What about your knitting? You've always enjoyed that."

It was true that I liked to knit. I had opened up all my old sweaters and knitted new ones with the yarn. Still, it was not what I had in mind.

"But Mama, that's busy work!" I told her. "I want to really help, to be useful, like Leon and Benny."

Mama folded her arms and shook her head. "Outside the house is not for you," she said. Then she picked up a book that was lying on her lap and began to read. I left the patio and went inside the house feeling terribly deflated.

How could I explain my emptiness? Again I could not help comparing our present situation to the weeks our family had spent fleeing to France. During that ordeal I had been tested in various ways, and I had felt myself growing — religiously, emotionally, and in my ability to deal successfully with the outside world. Here, at home, the walls hemmed me in. I felt stagnant. All my recent gains in maturity seemed to have fallen away. Well, perhaps Mama might change her mind when she saw how unhappy I was.

A few weeks later, the weather turned colder, and Yesodei HaTorah had to close. Conditions had deteriorated so badly that the parents could not even afford anthracite, a coal substance used for heating. All the students were dismissed. Leon had to give up his teaching job. As a result, he took full charge of the black-market business. Benny was discharged from his position as helper.

One afternoon I came across him languishing on the chaise

longue in the family room, listening to the radio.

"Hey, Benny, turn off that radio. Don't you know? It's the death penalty for anyone caught listening to the BBC!"

"Aw, Naomi, who's gonna hear it except us?"

"You never can tell," I cautioned. "All those collaborators spying for the Nazis. How do you know who to trust these days?"

Benny grimaced. "What else am I supposed to do with my time? Ever since Leon stopped teaching, he's running a one-man black-market business. I don't know what to do with myself!"

I nodded grimly. I knew exactly how he felt. Suddenly a thought occurred to me. "There's a rumor that the yeshivah in Heide may be opening again. Would that interest you?"

Heide, a hamlet close to the Dutch border, was a rustic plain with a growth of pine woods. The region attracted Jewish families, who spent their summers there. Mama claimed that inhaling the intoxicating pine fragrance strengthened the heart muscles.

Before the war, two successful businessmen decided to build a yeshivah in Heide. Upon gaining the support of Antwerp's Orthodox community, they traveled to Lithuania and engaged a prominent Torah scholar to head Yeshivas Ohr Torah. Thanks to the outstanding personality of Rabbi Aaron Freigut, the student body had increased from a handful of boys to 150 within a short period of time.

With the outbreak of war, the yeshivah had been closed. Lately, though, there was talk that the place was reopening. I wondered how Benny would take to the suggestion. While he liked to study Torah now and then, he did not have the same passion or religious zeal I saw in Leon.

Benny propped himself up on the couch. There was a reflective look on his face. "Maybe it's not such a bad idea," he said. "Do you think Mama would let me go?"

Truthfully, I didn't know. She seemed to take comfort in having her children close by. I said, "I will speak to her."

I found my mother in the kitchen, sifting a cupful of kidney beans for soup. I began by saying, "Poor Benny. It looks like he's got too much time on his hands. He says he's going crazy with boredom."

Mama replied, "I keep sending him on errands to get him out of the house." She frowned. "What else is there for him to do?"

I said casually, "I heard that Yeshivas Ohr Torah is going to reopen in Heide. Wouldn't that be a good thing for Benny to do — study Torah?"

Mama looked up sharply. "Isn't that far away?"

"Only twenty-three minutes by train."

Her head sank for a moment. "That's right. I must have forgotten." She was quiet for a few minutes. "You know, I think that might be just the right place for our Benny," she said finally. "In fact, I'll send him for an interview as soon as the place opens up."

I nodded, satisfied with the outcome of the conversation. Still, I couldn't help wondering when I would be able to successfully plead my own case.

Two days later, I tried again.

It was late afternoon, and I found Mama sitting in the family room going through old photographs in a picture album. She seemed to be in a tranquil mood; a small smile was on her face, and her eyes softened as she looked at the photos from long ago. Ah, I thought. Now's a good time to speak.

"Mama," I began, "I saw a notice in a shop. They need a girl to work the cash register in a hat store." I paused. In my most persuasive tone of voice, I said, "It would be perfect! I'd get out of your hair for a few hours each day and bring a paycheck home, too."

"What did you say?" Mama looked up, squinting slightly. "Did you ask about taking a job outside the house?"

I nodded, my stomach tightening. This was not going to be easy.

"Naomi, I'm surprised at you." Slowly, she closed the photograph album. "That's no place for you to be, working in a shop."

"Others do it. What about Cousin Frieda? She works as a stenographer in an office. She makes a great salary, too! Why can't I?"

My mother pressed her lips together. "Your cousin Frieda is in her forties, a mature woman. As you know, she never married. That job is her whole life." Mama shook her head. "I will not let you go out and work for strangers. And that's that!"

"Mama, you're not being fair," I cried. "Everyone has something to do except me. I'm eighteen, for goodness' sake."

She stood, facing me. Her eyes locked with mine as she said firmly, "The answer is still no!"

Much as I feared opposing Mama, I wasn't ready yet to give up the fight. I stretched out a hand beseechingly. "But Mama..."

Suddenly the doorbell rang. My arm dropped. I turned away and went to answer the door.

I unlocked the front door — and my heart stopped. There, before me, stood my sister Evelyn, her husband, Daniel, and their daughters, Rachel and Lili. We stared at each other, unbelieving.

I shouted, "Everyone, come quick! They're here!" I rushed forward and threw myself into Evelyn's arms, hugging her as if I would never let go. One by one, they threw their arms around my neck and kissed me profusely. The girls giggled and dashed into the house ahead of their parents. My brothers came bounding downstairs. There were hugs and smiles and laughter all around.

Mama appeared, the album tucked under her arm. "What —" Her mouth dropped in astonishment. "Evelyn! Daniel!" Her throat caught. She wiped away a tear and ushered them into the family room.

After the commotion had passed, we quickly got to work throwing together a meal of sorts. They were starving! Minutes later we were all sitting around the table enjoying a repast of leftover vegetable soup, potatoes, carrots, and hard-boiled eggs.

As I watched everyone eat and pass each other food, spicing their conversation with jokes and general comments, I savored to the fullest this blissful, unexpected family reunion. For the time being, I would put aside my fight for a job and something to do. Looking around at all the smiling faces, I only wished I knew of a way to make our present happiness last.

THE BLESSING

The next day, we all assembled in the family room. Mama's face seemed to have acquired an added glow. I could sense how happy she was to have her daughter and family back home, especially her two granddaughters, Rachel and Lili.

Rachel was dark-haired like her mother, with luminous black eyes and rosy cheeks. While the adults talked among themselves, she pored over a book. She was exceptionally studious. Lili was blond and had pale blue eyes, resembling her father. With her fair complexion, there was something delicate and angelic about the younger girl.

As a young child, I had always looked up to my sister Evelyn, who was ten years older. I could come to her with any problem. She took me on walks and didn't discard me when she met up with friends of her own along the way. I truly felt her warmth and love. Later, she married Daniel, a Gerrer Chassid and a Talmudic scholar. He suffered from tuberculosis and frequently went to a sanitarium for treatment. I had always been intrigued by the fact that Evelyn, so robust herself, had chosen such a frail man. I believe she deeply respected his brilliant mind and unswerving devotion to Torah.

Evelyn sat in one of the armchairs, sipping tea and giving an animated account of her family's flight from Belgium. The train they had boarded took them across the French frontier, and they had anticipated a family reunion at Uncle Henri's place in Paris.

"Imagine," Evelyn said, resting her cup of tea on a nearby table. "The train pulled into a station in the north of France, which turned out to be the last stop. We soon found that the invading armies were to the south of us, advancing on Paris. There was a mob scene at the train station. Obviously we could go no further."

Mama clucked her tongue. "How disappointed you must have been."

Evelyn nodded. She went on, "We met acquaintances from Antwerp. They told us that some civilians managed to get on board English boats and were taken across the Channel. The idea appealed to us, and we decided to give it a try."

"But you were not anywhere near the coast," I observed.

"Exactly. So we had a bit of distance to go. Eventually we reached St. Pol-Sur-Mer and found lodging. But after two days, all inhabitants were ordered to evacuate this seaside resort, which lay at the doorstep of Dunkirk."

Leon leaned forward in his seat. "Did you have any idea that Dunkirk was targeted for an attack by the *Luftwaffe,*" he said, "and that you narrowly escaped an inferno when the Battle of Dunkirk erupted?"

Daniel spoke up. "No reason was given for the evacuation. Everybody was forced to move inland. Only afterwards did we hear of the massive British escape at sea."

Evelyn picked up the thread of the story again. "We had to turn back. We decided that, with the children and all, we'd be best off back home. It was a long trek. How we managed to come back to Antwerp could fill a good-sized book."

Mama, Leon, Benny, and I listened raptly to their tale.

"I thank the Lord for your safe return," Mama declared in a husky voice. "I'm utterly grateful that we, at least, are back together again."

Benny threw in, "The four of us could tell you and Daniel a thing or two about the Dunkirk campaign. We were in Coxyde, in the perimeter of the combat zone! Mama's right," he added. "We should thank God that we're all here today."

Benny's interview with Rabbi Freigut, head of the yeshivah in Heide, took place a few days later. Benny returned from the meeting awestruck. "I spent nearly an hour alone with a saint, a *tzaddik*. Reb Freigut is a man of God. His face shines. I'm not kidding. From the expression in his eyes, I felt he could see deep within me." Benny spoke in a hushed voice, a faraway look in his eyes. He continued, "There's this thing about his voice. It does something to me inside. I can't explain it." He touched his chest. "I still feel the flame burning in here."

I listened in amazement to Benny's account. I could hardly believe this was the same mischievous brother who liked to play pranks on me! I had never known him to be mesmerized by anything spiritual. But now Benny revealed an inner spark that I'd never expected to find in him. I wondered if it would last.

Benny returned to Heide as soon as the yeshivah reopened. His letters proved that Reb Freigut, with his tremendous knowledge and understanding, continued to inspire our Benny. My brother studied diligently. The letters he sent home were filled with Torah insights and admiration for the *rosh yeshivah.*

I read his letters with mixed emotions. On the one hand, I was truly proud of him and his commitment to Torah study. It was certainly a turnabout I hadn't expected. On the other hand, I felt envious. He had discovered what truly mattered to him and was now set on his life path, it seemed. When would that happen to me? Did I have to wait until I married to find my direction in life? Wasn't there anything I could do right now?

Some time elapsed, and we received word that nights in the country were getting cool. Benny needed additional bedding. I stuffed two woolen blankets and a pillow into a suitcase. Mama carefully wrapped up a nice package of food that he might be lacking in yeshivah — cheese and other items.

Meanwhile, Leon made preparations to deliver everything to Heide. I said, "I think I'll accompany you on the trip."

Leon looked at me. "Why? There's no reason for you to come along, Naomi. What's the point?"

"Well," I said hesitantly, "I've heard so much about Reb Freigut. You intend to discuss Benny's progress with him, don't you? So maybe I'll get a chance to meet him, too, and be inspired."

Leon shook his head. "He's not that kind of a rabbi," he explained. "He's not a Chassidic rebbe to whom people come for a blessing. He's no mystic or expert in Kabbalah."

I rolled my eyes. "Oh, Leon, I know that. I know he's no wonder rabbi, and I'm not in search of any miracles." I paused and looked down at my hands, faintly embarrassed. "It's just that I've heard there's something saintly about this man. I can't tell you why, but I'm eager to get near him, if only for one minute." I raised my head and looked at my brother. "It would mean so much to me."

Leon was silent. Finally he said, "Mama wouldn't like it, you know."

I felt a sinking sensation in the pit of my stomach. He was right.

Just then, Mama passed by carrying a small platter of cut fruit. She held out the plate, and I bit into a cold slice of apple. "Thanks, Mama, it's delicious!" Then, before Leon could say a word, I quickly told her of my wish to see Reb Aaron Freigut.

My mother listened thoughtfully. "Poor Naomi," she said in a soothing voice. "You're so terribly bored at home. I understand why you're eager for a chance to travel around a bit."

I shook my head. "No, that's not it, Mama. At least, not entirely." I drew in a deep breath. "It's Rabbi Freigut. It's him I want to see."

Mama's eyes clouded for a moment. "I don't understand. In my time, young girls did not go off visiting rabbis in yeshivah. Who did such a thing? Certainly not I or any of my friends."

I bit down on my lip. How could I explain what I didn't fully understand myself? It seemed the right thing to do, and I did not want to deny myself this special opportunity. "I feel it would benefit me in many ways and give me the encouragement I need," I said quietly.

Suddenly Mama smiled. She said, "If you feel a strong need to see this rabbi, by all means you should go."

My eyes snapped open in surprise. "Really, Mama? You'll let me go?" I threw my arms around her. "Thank you! Thank you so much!" From the corner of my eye, I saw Leon. There was a scowl on his face. Well, I was along with him for the ride, whether he liked it or not.

The following morning, Leon and I boarded the train. We sat in a third-class carriage, facing each other on wooden benches. Leon pulled out a tractate of the Mishnah and immediately began to pore over it. At the Kappelen stop two people got on and crammed into our compartment: a man with a briefcase and a heavyset woman dragging two tote bags with live poultry inside. I caught a glimpse of feathers and the legs of a chicken tied together with a string. The four of us exchanged no words. Leon seemed to be deliberately ignoring me. I wished he would get over whatever annoyance he felt so I could fully enjoy the train ride and the passing scenery.

The stillness in our carriage amplified the sound of the rolling wheels below: *rat-a-tat, rat-taat-tat, rat-a-tat, rat-taat-tat.* The steady rhythm had a soothing effect. I leaned my head back and closed my eyes.

"Hey, Naomi, wake up! We're in Heide." Leon's voice had a hollow ring to it, as if it came from far away. I heard a train's whistle.

I opened my eyes and suppressed a yawn. "I wasn't sleeping, was I?" Then I sat up straight, blinking. "We're here!"

As we descended from the train, Leon grumbled, "I'm the only one who's going to the yeshivah with a girl tagging along after me."

I stiffened and said coolly, "I'm sorry my presence annoys you so much."

At this, Leon lowered his eyes guiltily. "Oh, I'm sorry, Naomi. Guess I've been giving you a hard time for no reason." He scratched his chin and gave me a grin. "Forgiven?"

I paused a moment, then nodded. I could never stay angry at Leon for too long.

The two of us trudged down the cobblestone road. Leon lugged the suitcase, while I carried Mama's food package. Dogs barked at us as we passed a few small, weather-beaten houses. We took a shortcut through the woods, where I inhaled deeply of the pine fragrance my mother had talked about.

Finally we arrived at the yeshivah, a complex of three villas, with a reduced attendance of only twenty-one boys. After waiting a few minutes, we were ushered into a spacious, book-filled room with a large desk at the center. A man in a simple, black frock coat beckoned us to sit down. This had to be Rabbi Freigut. He wore glasses and had a small black beard tinged with silver.

Leon and Rabbi Freigut began discussing Benny's progress. "Your brother Benjamin has been applying himself and is one of my top students." He spoke in a rich, deep voice. "With continued diligence, he could go far."

Leon nodded. "We'd like him to go on with his studies as long as possible."

"And what about your own studies, young man?" The two began to analyze certain passages in the Talmud in great detail. I tried to follow their gist but was soon lost in a maze of undecipherable words. I gazed wistfully out the window behind Rabbi Freigut at some pine trees in the distance.

Truthfully, I was disappointed. I had expected a different kind of person entirely, someone whose presence would inspire me to a deeper level of faith. Perhaps Leon had been right. Maybe I had been seeking a mystic rebbe after all. Rabbi Freigut seemed so ordinary, certainly not saint-like. I didn't understand what had caused such a tumult in Benny's heart.

The sound of Reb Freigut's voice startled me. "So you're Benjamin's sister Naomi. Are you happy with the reports you've been getting from him?"

I nodded vigorously. "Very."

"Tell me," he said gently. "What was it that brought you to the yeshivah? Is there something you'd like to discuss?"

I glanced up at him. He was looking intently at me, his gray-green eyes boring into mine. My breath caught. In that one look, I saw everything: a deep and abiding love for his students and a concern for me that was unlike anything I had ever experienced. It was the look of a loving father — no, more than a father. I glanced down, shaken to my core. When I could look down at him again, I was able to detect that special radiance Benny had mentioned.

I stammered, "It's unclear to me what my role should be. How does someone in my circumstances best fulfill herself?"

Reb Freigut removed his glasses and rubbed his eyes. He said, "These are difficult times for young women of marriageable age, dark and confusing times. It's easy to fall into sadness. You must do whatever you can to avoid that."

"But how?"

"Sadness comes from not feeling useful," he replied. "You should try to engage in some form of *chesed* — a volunteer activity, work that helps others. Also, it's good to keep up your interests and hobbies. Do you have any that you enjoy?"

"I like to play the piano, but since the war I've stopped." I hesitated. "I didn't know if it was appropriate."

Reb Freigut shook his head emphatically. "You should continue playing if it gives you pleasure. Also, taking up a new interest or hobby will lift your spirits considerably."

I listened carefully to everything he said. I was struck by his penetrating insight. Not once had I mentioned that I was feeling depressed or low. But his advice was right on target. He had sensed the sadness I was battling.

"Thank you," I said softly.

Then he added, "May you meet your *zivug,* the mate predestined for you, at the good and proper time."

I gulped. The last thing on my mind was marriage. I felt far from ready for such a step. But, I comforted myself, the rabbi had said, "at the proper time." All in all, it was the perfect blessing for me.

On the train ride home, Leon was more lively and talkative, especially since we had the compartment to ourselves. He pointed out the window. "Look! I think the site intended for the new yeshivah building is coming up."

"Really?" I put my fingers against the glass and peered out but could detect nothing. I clearly remembered the ground breaking and the laying of the cornerstone. There must have been two thousand people at the ceremony. It was a moment filled with bright anticipation for Antwerp's religious Jews. On that day, the promise of a future generation of Torah scholars had appeared to be as good as sealed.

The train moved further along, and soon I saw the tract of land that had generated such high hopes. It was a disheartening sight. Construction workers had finished digging up the building's foundation. The excavation was now a mere depression overgrown with an abundance of weeds. We detected a large stone, partly sunken, lying forlornly in one corner.

As the train rolled along, a picture of that cornerstone kept flashing through my mind. It evoked images of the exuberant gathering I had witnessed — the rousing speeches, the performance by the boys' choir, and, most of all, the joyous dancing when the band began to play. They'd danced and danced for hours.

Leon stood next to me at the window, his face the embodiment of gloom. "We're looking at the end of a dream," he said bitterly.

TRANSITIONS

It was late afternoon. I heard the bell ringing and ran to open the door. A middle-aged couple stood facing me. The woman was heavyset, with dark blond hair and mannish oxford shoes. The man was pot-bellied and broad-shouldered, with lots of laugh lines around the eyes. They look disheveled, I thought.

Before I had a chance to ask who they were or what they wanted, the man explained, "We are Jewish refugees. We're from Rotterdam and are looking for a furnished room." He spoke in Dutch. As unkempt as they looked, there was something cheerful about the pair. I wanted to help them. Although in Belgium Jews still lived under normal conditions, I'd heard reports that Jews in Holland were already being singled out for Nazi persecution.

Suddenly Mama was standing behind me. She cleared her throat. "We don't really rent out rooms," she said, looking doubtfully at the couple.

The man lowered his eyes. Removing his hat, he said, "I thought we'd take a chance. See, we're illegal and can't register in a hotel. We're desperately in need of a place to stay, at least overnight. Somebody told me that maybe you would help us."

No one spoke for a while. I sensed their anxiety and my mother's reluctance. I took her aside. "They seem like decent people to me," I said in a low voice. "They're probably just worn out and rumpled from their travels. Let them come inside and talk. Then we can decide if it's appropriate for us."

Mama nodded, then stepped forward and invited them into the family room. Their names were Willie and Bertha Haas.

I went to the kitchen and put up the kettle for tea. While the water boiled, I arranged a tray of biscuits. Thanks to Leon's clandestine business, our pantry was now better stocked. Mama had overruled Leon's objection to our using any of his black-market supplies for ourselves, and we all ate better as a result. When I brought the cups of tea and the tray into the family room, I guessed at once that Mama had agreed to let the refugees stay, at least for the night. The Haases now seemed relaxed. They smiled and thanked me for the refreshments.

Bertha was telling my mother about the restaurant they had been operating in their hometown. "It wasn't a large or fancy place," she said, "but my cooking, if I dare say so myself, earned us a reputation. The Orthodox elite dined with us. Not just from Rotterdam but also from other cities."

"That's the absolute truth," Willie exclaimed with pride.

When Bertha spoke, her face became animated. Her eyes shone, and I no longer saw her as a dowdy, overweight woman.

Willie was also charming, with his easy laugh and comfortable manner.

After awhile, Mama excused herself and signaled for me to follow her. At the foot of the staircase, she said quietly, "Do you think we're making the right decision, taking them in?"

I said firmly, "Yes, especially since they have nowhere else to go."

Mama replied, "That means more work for you. We have to get a room ready and put fresh linen on the beds."

I recalled Rabbi Freigut's words. Already I was being given a chance to perform a bit of *chesed*. I said, "That's all right with me. We can give them the room on the second floor. And there's a fresh bundle of laundry that was delivered this morning." Then I went upstairs to air out the room and make the beds.

Little did we know that Willie and Bertha would be the first of many boarders to come and go.

The Haases quickly became regular members of our household. Willie tried his hand at marketing and soon proved quite efficient at it. He was a charmer, and people took to him easily. He walked about the Jewish quarter and flashed a smile at anyone he thought might be a Jew. Depending on their response, he would either pass on his way or start a conversation. He soon learned the loosely guarded secret that, in the courtyard of an ancient structure in the Lentenstraat, chickens were being ritually slaughtered. Thanks to Willie Haas, there would be no shortage of fresh kosher chickens in our household!

As for Bertha, we were not able to keep her out of the

kitchen for long. She introduced us to a Dutch specialty, the *stampot.* Carrots and other vegetables were mashed with potatoes to a consistency somewhat firmer than a purée. Laced with chicken fat and drippings and seasoned with herbs, the *stampot* was served in bowls. After I sampled this novel dish, I exclaimed, "Mmmm, it's not only scrumptious, but filling, too."

"That's the idea," Bertha replied. "On the whole, Hollanders are economical, and you'll never get the yield from simple potatoes that a *stampot* gives you. That's why it's going to be on your menu at least twice a week."

"I, for one, wouldn't mind if it were four times a week," I said. "How come your food never tastes greasy? You use chicken fat in just about everything, but there's never a fatty after-taste."

Bertha laughed heartily. "You don't expect me to give away my professional secrets, do you?" She paused, then added in a soft voice, "Come and watch me work more closely. I won't chase you out of the kitchen." Again she laughed, and the laughter proved contagious. Mama and I couldn't help laughing along with her.

As a former restaurateur, Bertha was in the habit of preparing large quantities of food. We began having hungry people join us for dinner. On weekdays, one or two refugees usually ate with us. The following week, Leon and Benny brought home three young men after shul Friday night.

One of the young men Leon had invited kept returning more and more often. Fritz was in his early twenties and had arrived from Hanover before the war. He was clean-shaven and very tall. German Jews were generally much taller than the

Jews in Antwerp. He had obtained the white identity card that granted temporary residence to aliens and within months had become a skilled diamond cutter.

One day, he approached Mama and said, "I wonder if I could rent a room and move in here? I've been staying at a friend's house, but now I have to move out."

Mama was hesitant. I noticed again Mama's instinct for caution. The whole idea of taking in boarders was a new one to her. She seemed to need a bit of prodding from her children. Leon suggested, "Let's give him the little room with the single bed. Nobody's using it anyway."

A few moments passed, and then Mama gave her consent.

Before I knew it, Fritz was reciting his prayers with Leon and Benny every morning, sitting in the family room listening to the radio, writing letters, reading. He liked to talk about diamonds and the diamond trade.

"Prices have gone up," he declared with a confident air. "Especially diamonds for industrial use. The demand for gemstones has driven the cost of polished goods way up, too. There's money to be made."

I said, "Maybe that's why the Germans wanted the Antwerp Jews to return — to revive the diamond trade." I confided my hope that the Nazis were really not after the Jews in Western Europe, who, after all, were small in number and did not pose the same threat as the Eastern European Jews. This was what the Germans had been telling us, and I desperately wanted to believe them.

Fritz, however, wasn't interested in discussing politics, only diamonds.

After my talk with Rabbi Freigut, I had resumed my piano

lessons with Julia, a former classmate and gifted teacher. Fritz asked if he could sit in the salon when I played.

"Look, Fritz," I said frankly. "I've got to practice these exercises over and over. It's the most boring thing to listen to. Besides, I'll be very nervous having someone in the room with me."

But Fritz was not to be discouraged. The next day, he offered me a lipstick in a fancy case. He said, "It's the latest from Paris — *le rouge baiser.* Let me show you how it works." The top was a silvery dome, and when he turned the glittery black case, the dome split open to let the red stick appear.

I was fascinated by the contraption and would have loved to own it. But I told him, "I'm sorry, I can't accept it."

"Why not?" he said, clearly hurt. "I would give it to my sister, but she's still in Germany. Please, I want you to have it."

He made it sound so fraternal. He kept insisting. In the end I took the *rouge baiser* from Fritz. But when he offered me a wristwatch a week or so later, I categorically refused.

At that point, I took my mother aside. I mentioned that I was annoyed with the attentions I was receiving from Fritz.

Mama smiled and said, "I was about to tell you. He spoke to me yesterday asking for my approval to court you. He said he'd like to marry you."

"Oh, heavens, no!" I uttered with a gasp. "What did you answer him?"

"That I had to ask you first, and that now was a bad time to begin a serious relationship," Mama replied.

I let out a sigh of relief. Thank goodness for my mother's good sense. I said, "I'm glad he spoke to you and not to me. He's a nice enough fellow, but I'm not interested. I'm certainly not ready to think of marriage — with anyone!"

Mama seemed relieved to hear my response. She relayed my rejection in the gentlest possible manner. Within a week, Fritz moved out.

In general, I enjoyed our boarders very much. They added spice and dash to our daily lives. At times, though, I noticed that Willie and Bertha seemed depressed, especially after receiving letters from Holland. Willie told us in confidence that Bertha's sister, Elsa, had lost her bakery shop. According to the new decrees, Jews were no longer allowed to own businesses. Later, Elsa's husband was taken with other Jews to a forced-labor camp. I listened to this news in shock. So the reports I'd been hearing of the treatment of Holland's Jews were true.

It was hard for me to imagine that level of persecution in the midst of our day-to-day existence in Antwerp. Although different from the life we had known before the war, our existence remained bearable. My heart went out to the Haases.

A few days later, my friend Helene paid me a visit. I'd been unaware that her family had arrived back in Antwerp from Vichy, France. We laughed and cried, hugging one another. We had gone to public school together. There was no Jewish girls' school in Belgium, and, naturally, being two of the few religious students in the class, we had formed a close tie with each other. Helene was physically delicate, but her character was strong. We had always provided each other with companionship and support, and now I was thrilled to find her back in Antwerp.

In my bedroom, Helene removed some drawings from a portfolio and showed me exquisite copies of picture postcards that she had duplicated. I admired the artistry of her work.

"Guess what?" she said enthusiastically. "I've inquired about free courses at the *Academie des Beaux Arts*. I'm going to enroll, and I'd like you to come with me."

"Oh, Helene," I said. "I don't have your ability. I can't even draw a straight line."

"Give yourself a chance," she argued persuasively. "They've got excellent teachers. You may have talent that needs to be brought out."

I found the idea of being a student at Antwerp's famed art school very tempting. But would Mama let me go?

To my utter shock, she agreed with hardly any fuss at all. As I dressed for my first day of school, I reflected on what had brought about her changed attitude. Perhaps the influx of boarders had increased Mama's trust in my character judgment. I believed she appreciated my levelheaded manner and the way I dealt with the various people who had come our way. Also, I had a feeling that the marriage proposal from Fritz had jolted my mother's perception of me a bit. Her youngest daughter might not be such a child after all.

Art classes met every morning. On our arrival in the classroom, each of us sat down by an easel. The sculptured head of a Roman emperor stood on a raised shelf in front of the class. I had to render the head's likeness from the perspective that I saw it — at a three-quarter angle. Everyone worked with a charcoal stick on a drafting sheet.

While I struggled, I couldn't help noticing how confident and easily the fellow next to me progressed. Joe, a non-Jew from Schooten, was no doubt the youngest and most gifted in the class. I also sneaked admiring looks at Helene's work, which made me deplore my own lack of dexterity. Yet I liked the milieu I was in and wanted fervently to belong. I sighed and tried doggedly to do a passable job.

One day, as Helene and I approached the academy, a small gray Opel pulled up at the entrance. A tall, thin man with a goatee stepped out of the vehicle. He was flanked by two German officers in uniform. The trio entered the building and marched straight to the administration office.

"Did you see that guy? D'you know who he is?" asked a voice behind us.

Helene and I turned around. It was Joe, our classmate.

"He's none other than Raymond Delbeau," Joe told us. We stared blankly at him. Joe explained, "Professor Delbeau used to teach here. The man's a genius. But he got kicked out. Stirred up too much trouble with his crazy ideas, it seems."

I was rather intrigued. "What's wrong with him?"

"He's a nonconformist. Walks around with bare feet at the peak of winter. A free spirit. He's tried to come back many times to teach here, but they wouldn't have him. But if he's in with the Nazis, they may be forced to take him back."

As we walked into our classroom, I remarked to Helene, "I hope he doesn't end up being my teacher."

The following morning, when Helene and I entered the lobby of the academy, we walked into a noisy crowd. Students were asked not to go to their classes. Those who had an inkling of what was happening argued vehemently with each other. After a time, the director called for attention. A hush fell over the assembly as the students listened to the announcement:

"Due to unexpected developments, we have no choice but to rearrange the attendance in some classes in order to fill an additional room. Some of you in classes 1A and 1B will now transfer to 1C. Professor Delbeau will be your instructor."

A roar of protest greeted this information. I heard my classmates whispering, "The Nazis got him in. That's what happened!"

As soon as the clamor abated, the director continued. "We will proceed by calling your names in alphabetical order."

I listened tensely to the roll call. I didn't want to be in this Nazi collaborator's class. But with a sinking sensation, I learned that I had, indeed, been transferred to Professor Delbeau's room. Disheartened, I went to collect my easel and other belongings. Aside from being Jewish, I was a poor artist. What kind of treatment could I expect from this man?

After a few days, the initial grumbling of the students in 1C subsided. They realized in no time that Professor Delbeau had exceptional teaching skills. My fears of falling into disgrace and being harassed by him turned out to be unfounded. In fact, he encouraged my efforts. He often proclaimed, "Anyone who has learned to write can learn to draw." Once he repeated that statement to me personally. Then he ended by saying dryly, "Of course, that doesn't mean the drawing will be pretty to look at."

Classes met Mondays through Saturdays. I never attended school on Shabbos, of course. As a result, I came to class one Monday and found my easel moved. I no longer saw the Roman head in its proper perspective. Professor Delbeau noticed the look of consternation on my face.

In an angry voice, he called out, "Who moved this young woman's stand?" There was silence in the classroom. He thundered, "If I ever catch anyone doing such a thing in the future..." He let the sentence trail. Then he came over, sat down by my easel, and started correcting my work.

"Why were you absent on Saturday?" he asked in a friendly tone. "Do you have to help your mother clean the house?"

I froze. Seconds passed while thoughts flashed through my mind: What should I tell him? He didn't know I was a Jew. Should I lie?

I blurted out, "I observe the Sabbath. I'm not allowed to work. I'm Jewish." I sat rigidly in place, awaiting his reaction. To my relief, Professor Delbeau didn't move a muscle in his face. Nor did he treat me differently in any way afterwards.

Weeks went by. More and more often, students began to linger after class to listen to Professor Delbeau expound on a variety of subjects. Sometimes I stayed behind to listen to him as well. Once I heard him say, "I saw a three-legged table dance down a short flight of stairs. Right here in this building. Such is the power of man's will activated through hypnotism! By the way, did any of you know the easiest subject to hypnotize is a chicken?" He was definitely odd but fascinating.

On another occasion, the students were discussing the Nazi's sweep of conquests, which appeared to be unstoppable. Professor Delbeau declared, "No matter what nationality you are — no matter who or what you are — *be* it, one hundred percent! Whether you're Russian or German or whatever else. Be it in full measure and be proud of it!"

I wondered how this advice fit in with Professor Delbeau's concept of Nazi philosophy. I was certain no such ideas were being advocated in *Mein Kampf*. Raymond Delbeau was a strange bird!

When I brought my drawings home to Evelyn, Mama, and

Leon, their benevolent smiles should have told me I was merely dreaming. My drawings were mediocre at best. Yet I refused to recognize the signs of their negative opinions. I persisted in my efforts, fantasizing that one day I would surprise everybody with my artistic achievement. Besides, this new interest had certainly lifted my spirits. I looked forward to each day. And that was the most important thing of all.

One afternoon, there was a commotion in the hall outside our classroom. I heard angry voices that grew louder and louder. At last, the strident shriek of a whistle cut the air, and the disturbance gradually subsided.

It didn't take me long to discover that my former classmate, Joe, had provoked a pro-Nazi student by loudly cursing and expressing his contempt for the Third Reich and its *Führer*, Adolf Hitler. The altercation came to blows, from which both young men emerged with bloody faces.

Helene filled me in. "That Joe fought like a tiger. He really gave it to the other guy."

"But after they broke it up, the two of them made peace, didn't they?"

"Not exactly," Helene said. "The other fellow, well, he'd gotten the worst of it. So he went to the phone and reported Joe to the Gestapo. Five minutes later, two SS men were here."

I gasped. "Oh no! What a terrible thing to do!"

Helene nodded. "If it weren't for Raymond Delbeau, they would've taken him away."

My mouth dropped open. "You mean, Professor Delbeau interceded for Joe?"

Another classmate spoke up. "Exactly! Delbeau's got pull with the Nazis all right. And he saved that hothead this time around. Hopefully he won't be so stupid next time."

This incident only served to lessen my fear of Professor Delbeau — and to increase my bewilderment. Who was he, really?

One afternoon, Evelyn dropped by with Rachel and Lili and gave us a few copies of the latest edition of the *Verordnungsblatt* — a free supplement in Belgium's *Staat Gazette*. I took one copy upstairs and read it in my bedroom. I was disturbed to find a detailed definition of who was to be considered a Jew, published in Flemish, French, and German.

In order to be "race-pure," there had to be no Jewish blood in one's lineage, going back to the fourth generation. I shook my head. Unfortunately, I was used to certain negative depictions of Jews in Belgium, starting from before the war, in pro-German magazines. I had seen caricatures of Jews with exaggerated features, making them appear sinister and conniving. Once I had read a description of a certain Jew as "naked and reeking with garlic, ready to flee the country."

I read on in the *Verordnungsblatt*:

"Every Jew from age fifteen and up is to be inscribed into the Jewish register. All Jewish business firms will be recorded and their assets, foreign as well as domestic, declared. Furthermore, Jewish restaurants, cafés, and hotels must henceforth display signs, stating in three languages that they are Jewish enterprises. Failure to comply with these ordinances will result in immediate arrest."

I stared in shock at the words on the page. Was this possible? Laws like this in my beloved country — in Belgium?

I ran downstairs to Mama and Leon. They, too, were poring over the paper. We kept reading over and over again the decrees that would deprive professionals and jobholders of their livelihoods. Jews were to be dismissed from employment in public offices and the civil service. They were being barred from practicing their professions as lawyers and teachers in schools and universities. No longer could they work as executives, directors, and editors for the press or radio. Furthermore, Jewish students were no longer permitted to attend state schools.

Evelyn said in a bitter tone, "How do you like the way they're appeasing us with assurances that religious congregations are not affected?"

Leon snorted, "We'll see how long that lasts."

It was a somber day for all of Belgium's Jews. We had been lulled into thinking it would be different in our country. So this was the first breath of German venom.

Monday morning I made my way to the art academy. Would I still be allowed to attend classes there? Would I be arrested for having dared to show up? I felt frightened and also angry. What an indignity, to suddenly have to go to my own art school with a bowed head, like some criminal. During recess, I approached Professor Delbeau. I mentioned the ordinance regarding Jewish students.

He looked straight at me and said in a firm voice, "You'll keep coming to my class until you're told to do otherwise!"

"I will do that," I replied, encouraged by his words and yet somewhat mystified by the conviction in his tone.

Many thoughts crossed my mind. It was a fact that Raymond Delbeau fraternized with the enemy. Time and again, I was told he was a libertine who had, before the Germans marched in, been dismissed and barred from teaching at the academy. His drunken bouts and his brawling had disqualified him as a faculty member of the Academy of Fine Arts. Yet I, as his student, had yet to see him behave improperly in the classroom. There his behavior was dignified, and he was in full control. In fact, he was an extraordinary instructor! But what were his true colors? Where did his sympathies really lie? Would I ever come to know the real Professor Delbeau?

Two days later, Benny startled us by appearing unexpectedly at the house. We were in the midst of eating supper when he arrived loaded down with a large suitcase and a hamper stuffed with bedding. We all rushed over, delighted to see him yet mystified. Perhaps the study schedule at the yeshivah in Heide had been too rigorous for Benny, after all.

Mama made him sit down and eat something. Then she asked, "What made you come home so suddenly?"

He opened his mouth to explain. I let out a cry and pointed. On Benny's neck was a bandage. "What happened to you?"

Benny looked glum. "Things in Heide got bad — real bad." He ate a spoonful of Bertha's *stampot* and continued, "Reb Freigut feared for our safety and decided to close the yeshivah before anybody got seriously hurt."

I kept staring at Benny. "Looks like somebody already did get hurt. That dressing on your neck could stand a change. The last thing you need is an infection." I went to get the bottle of hydrogen peroxyde, some sterile cotton, gauze pads, and adhesive tape.

Meanwhile, Mama washed her hands and removed the bandage. She looked faintly ill as she stared at his neck. "Tell me," she said anxiously, "how did you get this awful wound?"

Benny grimaced as Mama removed the bandage. Part of it stuck to the jagged cut. Then his gaze shifted from me to my mother and back. He hesitated. "Got hit by a rock," he said finally. "There was a rabble outside the yeshivah. I stepped into the front yard and asked them to leave the premises. One of the gang hurled a rock at me." He gingerly touched his neck. "But it's healing very nicely. I'm lucky. That rock could've struck my face or my eyes, God forbid."

"*Gottenyu*!" Mama's hands flew to her cheeks. "Who were these terrible people?"

Benny shrugged. "Must have been Rexists or members of another *Flamiganten* party. You know, Flemish Nazi sympathizers."

I handed Mama the gauze pads, and she applied one to the cut. Benny was matter-of-fact about the incident, while all I could feel was bewilderment and distress. "I don't understand," I said. "Had there been trouble before this? Or was it a sudden thing, out of the blue?"

Benny sighed. "The mistreatment was gradual, just like Pharaoh's behavior toward the Jews in Egypt. First there were just a few guys who'd mumble insults — you know, anti-Semitic slurs — whenever they met one of us. As they grew in number they got bolder, and the gang became a menace to our lives. They put life-threatening messages in our mailboxes and —"

"Couldn't you get police protection?" I interrupted.

"Oh, Naomi, you are naive," he sighed with a slight smile. "Reb Freigut called them and was told the police force had their hands tied dealing with collaborators of the Nazi regime."

"What happened then?" I asked, fighting the melancholy that was taking hold of me.

Benny bit his lip. "If you'd see our yeshivah now — a shambles. By the time we left, every window had been smashed. The walls had black swastikas all over them. Threats to the Jews were painted in red. I'm sure our tormentors have ransacked it by now. Carried away whatever was worth taking."

Tears filled my eyes. The yeshivah destroyed! The place in a shambles! I prayed that the boys had been able to rescue the Torah scrolls before those hoodlums had inflicted their damage. What an ending for an institution filled with such promise.

We sank back into silence as we finished our supper, each of us retreating into our own thoughts. My illusions of Belgium's Jews immunity to this kind of treatment were slowly being chipped away. This was what our beloved homeland had come to: neighbors who had been friendly and civil to us had, in a matter of months, turned into virulent enemies.

I thought of Professor Delbeau and wondered if his kindness only extended to Jewish students in his school, while those outside his circle were the enemy. If he had seen the gang harming Benny, would he have stepped in and interceded on his behalf? Where did he draw the line? I guessed I would never know.

Again Rabbi Freigut's words came back to me. These were challenging times. It seemed that distinguishing between evil and good was more complicated than I'd realized.

THE REMEDY AND THE PLAGUE

We had finished eating dinner, though everyone was still sitting around the table. I had noticed all through the meal that our boarder, Willie, seemed absorbed in thought, hardly saying a word. Bertha didn't look her cheerful self, either.

"Is something wrong?" Mama looked anxiously from one to the other.

Willie replied, in a low, morose voice, "We've become too comfortable here. It is dangerous. We shouldn't forget we're illegal."

"What's stopping you from leaving?" Benny asked practically.

"If we could, we'd leave tomorrow. But I have to see when the guide can take us," Willie answered. "We need someone who will take us all the way — not just smuggle us across the border into France."

Bertha added, "We'd be lost traveling by ourselves through occupied France. Willie and I don't speak one word of French."

"Just remember," my mother told them, "you have a home here with us as long as you like." She had become quite close to Bertha, and I knew she would miss the couple if they left.

Bertha smiled at Mama and squeezed her hand.

Slowly, everybody left the table. Just then, the doorbell rang and continued clanging vigorously. I rushed to open the door. With my mouth wide open and eyes nearly double their size, I stood staring at the grinning faces of Michael and Sabine. For a moment, I thought my eyes were deceiving me. Then I heard Michael's voice. "Why, Naomi, you look so startled. Didn't you get our last letter? We wrote we were coming."

I managed to shake my head and recovered sufficiently to say, "No. No such letter arrived." Then I began to shout, and the loudness of my own voice astonished me. "Mama! Leon! Benny! It's Michael and Sabine! They're really here!"

The unexpected arrival of my oldest brother and his wife was met with unprecedented joy. I proudly introduced them to the Haases. They were a stunning young couple, despite being thinner than ever before. Their faces showed no sign of travel weariness, though they'd been on the road for several days.

Michael expressed how happy they were to be back home. They'd returned to their apartment and found it intact. Sabine told us, "We've never appreciated our lovely home as much as we do now, after living in the slums of Marseilles." They had been staying in Free France for the past few months.

To everyone's surprise, Willie Haas asked, "What were the accommodations like in Marseilles?"

"Old, dilapidated buildings, some infested with rats," Michael said. "The furnishings in our room, primitive. A joke!"

Sabine said, "Tell them about the lack of running water and the bedbugs."

Michael went on, "At night we'd wake up and go hunting for the bedbugs that tormented us. I'd seen them before in Paris, but you wouldn't believe the size of the breed in Marseilles."

"I still shudder when I remember those nights," Sabine added. "The toilets were out in the hall — nothing more than a hole in the floor."

Bertha emerged from the kitchen with tea and two red apples. On separate plates, she had sectioned each apple into eighths. Attached at the bottom only, the fruit fell open like petals of a flower in bloom. The corners of Sabine's mouth turned upward. She said, "You sure know how to make food look attractive!" She took a slice of apple.

Meanwhile, Willie was talking to Michael. "Tell me," he said, "how was the attitude of Marseilles's citizens toward the refugees? Were they friendly?"

Michael shook his head. "Not at all. I found the people horrible. We'd go for a walk on the Cannebiere, and we'd hear remarks like, 'Why don't you go back to where you came from?' Or, worse yet, anti-Semitic slurs."

Sabine took a sip of the tea that Bertha had placed before her. "Can you blame us for wanting to come home?" she asked. My mother's welcoming face spoke for all of us: we were thrilled at their return.

When it was time for Michael and Sabine to leave, I accompanied them outside and watched them walk down the street, reflecting on what a splendid match they were. Michael's hazel eyes sparkled with wit and spirit. He had an aristocratic bearing that none of his brothers possessed. I remember the times they had teasingly called him "The Count."

Sabine's face glowed with her joy at being home. It sure was good to see them both again and have them nearby. Even so, I couldn't help thinking that Michael and Sabine had made a mistake when they abandoned the safety of Free France to cross into Nazi-occupied territory. They had voluntarily entered the arena where the lions lay napping. How could we feel secure here, knowing that in nearby Holland persecution of Jews was already an undeniable reality? Willing myself to repress these thoughts, I returned to the house.

The following afternoon, I was passing through the family room, when I found Willie and Bertha in the midst of a heated argument. Although their voices weren't raised, they gesticulated vehemently and spoke sharply to each other. I drew back, wanting to give them privacy. Willie stopped me and said, "Please, Naomi, you've got good sense. I'd like you to hear this."

Embarrassed, I protested, "I don't want to get between a husband and wife. I refuse to take sides."

Yet Willie insisted that I stay. "The time has come for us to move on," he declared. "To wait is useless and dangerous. I, too, was disturbed by the report your brother and sister-in-law gave of Free France and the conditions the refugees found there. Just the same, we must move on and take our chances."

Bertha spoke in an agitated voice. "First of all, I'd have to leave my sister Elsa behind in Holland. Secondly, smuggling ourselves is risky. Even with the best guide, not everybody makes it. And if, with God's help, we get there, how will we manage? We don't speak French!"

Willie responded, "I told Bertha that with luck we may be able to buy passports with visas for Argentina or Venezuela like others did. Staying here is no solution. We risk being picked up any day. Besides, Bertha's sister herself urged us to go."

I listened to them, trying to remain impartial. I understood Bertha's desire to stay put. The fear of the unknown was enough to paralyze anyone. Would I have felt differently in her case? Still, Willie's plan made more sense to me.

I said cautiously, "If you stay and get arrested, God forbid, how would that help your sister?"

Bertha sighed heavily, and her eyes became moist. Finally she said, "Who knows, perhaps the two of you are right. To keep running may be the only solution for us after all."

She slowly sank onto a chair. Her hands, those magical hands of hers, lay in her lap like two limp rags. I watched the tears gather in her eyes. "Please, God," I prayed silently, "help them make the right decision, and guide them to safety."

One day, Leon went to the country — or, rather, close to the Dutch border — to establish a new connection with a farmer. He negotiated the delivery of black-market potatoes and other produce, as well as butter and cheese from Holland. The resourceful new supplier got around quite a bit with his horse and carriage and could even provide contraband cigarettes. Once the deal was made, the farmer transported the illegal goods to the basement of a house he owned in the city. Leon had access to this basement on the Turnhoutse Baan, a commercial avenue in a densely populated, lower-class neighborhood.

The new contact was in addition to Piet, who faithfully supplied Leon with oats, chicory, eggs, and other commodities. Piet was by now a familiar figure at the house. He aroused no suspicion when he arrived, like any visitor, on his bicycle, a hamper tied to the back.

The storage arrangement with the new contact worked to perfection. Leon doubled the volume of his transactions within the next few weeks. He didn't brag or talk about it. Only to Mama did he mention, "Business is booming."

In fact, he had enlisted Benny's services once again — that is, when Benny wasn't away at one of his study groups. Benny had arranged a learning schedule with the boys from Rabbi Freigut's yeshivah who were in the area. As for me, I no longer resented the time my brothers spent together on the black-market trade. I had some of my own interests now: piano-playing, my friend Helene, helping out with the boarders, art classes, learning new dishes from Bertha. All in all, my spirits were up.

One afternoon, when Benny was away, Leon let me accompany him on his way to the basement storeroom. As we walked toward the address, Leon noticed a gathering in the distance. His forehead wrinkled slightly. "Something's up in front of my place," he said. He turned to me. "You're not yet a familiar face around this neighborhood. Why don't you go ahead and investigate for me?"

I walked up a few blocks to the storefront, poked around a

bit, and lingered casually among the crowd of people, gathering information. What I saw and heard filled me with panic. As soon as I could make an exit without arousing attention, I rushed back to Leon.

"Quick, let's get out of here!" I urged.

As we walked away, I kept looking behind me to make sure we weren't being followed. Leon prodded me. "*Nu,* let's have it already. What's going on there?"

I said in a low voice, "They've raided your store. All the goods were taken away and put in a van. It's a special police detail. They're clamping down on black marketeers."

"Somebody snitched. How else could they know about me?" His black eyes blazed in a flare of anger.

"They had a list of names and boasted they'd already arrested some people." I looked behind me again. "I heard an officer say, 'We've caught the others. We'll get this one, too!' "

Instinctively, Leon accelerated his pace. He muttered, "What should I do? Where should I go? I need some time to think."

I said anxiously, "I hate to say it, but you'd better not go straight home. Go to Evelyn instead. If they've got your name on a list, they're sure to know where you live. You can't go home! They'll be sure to find you."

Leon nodded. "You're right, Naomi."

Mama and Benny were home when I returned. I was apprehensive about breaking the news to Mama. I quickly explained the situation, and told how Leon went to hide out at Evelyn's until he decided what to do.

Mama's face whitened.

Benny exclaimed, "Thank God, he wasn't caught! Whew, that was close!"

After my mother's initial fright, I was surprised to see her quickly calm down. She said, "This situation can't last forever." She quoted an old saying: "The stew never gets eaten when it's on the fire. It always cools off." Benny and I looked at each other. How could she make light of what was happening? Didn't she fear that the police — or, worse yet, the Gestapo — would come at any minute to look for Leon?

Meanwhile, Piet, the other black-market contact, arrived at our house. The ruddy-faced man with the watery blue eyes considered himself a friend of the family. He'd mentioned more than once how much he respected and liked Mama and her children. Still, in these times, who knew whom we could trust? The situation seemed to change from day to day.

"Where's Leon?" he asked. "He's supposed to meet me around this time."

I looked from Mama to Benny, and both seemed at a loss for an answer. "He went to Wilryk," I offered, "to see Mynheer Van Caeneghem, the principal of Leon's old school. They badly need food supplies."

Piet thoughtfully scratched his jaw. "I see. Wilryk's a bit far. Did he leave a long time ago?"

My mind raced to think up an excuse. It wasn't easy, this business of fabrication. "He must've figured he'd be back in time for you. Probably got delayed. He could walk in any minute now."

Piet nodded. He seemed satisfied with the explanation.

Mama accepted the provisions Piet had brought along: a few dozen fresh eggs, two kilos each of rice and dried green peas, and two jars of jam. He'd also brought a small basket of Brussels sprouts and, for the first time, some red beets. After Mama settled the account with him, Piet seemed in no hurry to leave.

He cleared his throat a few times. "I meant to tell you, I'll be lying low for a while," he said. "Things are a bit tough right now. They're going strong after the black-market traffickers. They even arrested some already."

"What happens to those they catch?" I asked as casually as I could.

"Well, they lose the goods, of course. Then they get fined and thrown in jail." Piet paused for a long moment and then continued, "But if they're Jewish, it's a different story altogether."

We all stiffened. Three pairs of eyes stared intently at the man, urging him on. Piet hesitated, then explained, "The Jews are handed over to the Gestapo. They shut them up in Breendonk — an old fortress that's been changed into a camp. Prisoners there undergo all kinds of torture you would not imagine. It's a living hell on earth! Not many come back from that place alive!"

Swallowing hard, I looked at Mama. Her face seemed composed, but when I glanced at her hands, I saw they were gripping the edge of the table and her knuckles were white.

As Piet turned to leave, he said to my mother, "Madame, you ought to tell your boy Leon to ease up for now. He must be extra careful!"

I accompanied Piet down the hall, not saying a word. I watched him lower his bicycle down the three steps of our stoop. He jumped onto the saddle, waved his hand, and took off. I felt a bit ashamed at having lied to this simple, kindly man.

As I passed through our salon, Mama was sitting very still in one of the armchairs. I wanted to approach her but, as usual, felt awkward and at a loss for words. If only I could have thrown my arms around her and murmured something comforting in her ear. But the stoic set of her jaw stopped me. Meanwhile, Benny took off for Evelyn's to bring Leon his prayer book, tefillin, and pajamas. He also intended to deliver Piet's dire warning.

When Benny returned a bit later from my sister's house, Mama was still sitting in her chair. "Leon's escaping to Free France," Benny announced. "He's leaving tomorrow morning."

Mama let out a cry. She covered her eyes. When she removed her hands, the face she showed us was serene. "He will need food for the journey," she said quietly and rose from her chair.

She went to the kitchen and briskly started preparing cheese sandwiches. She put hard-boiled eggs, cans of sardines and tuna, and a number of chocolate bars into a rucksack. I packed a few articles of clothing and the most basic necessities he'd be needing for the trek. As I folded all the items, trying to maximize the space in the rucksack, I suddenly understood why my mother always threw herself into a flurry of activity whenever a disturbing event threatened to take place. Busy hands didn't leave one too much time to brood.

Later that evening, Mama, Benny, and I arrived at Evelyn's just as they were clearing the table after dinner. My brother-in-law Daniel was reading a story to the girls. Rachel and Lili greeted us with warm embraces. We all exchanged pleasantries. Leon was reciting Birkas HaMazon, the Grace after Meals. It struck me how undisturbed everybody appeared. But that was our family. We always knew how to exert self-control in the most trying circumstances.

Mama handed Leon a large sum of money, along with a copy of his birth certificate. "You've earned most of this yourself, and now you'll need every cent."

"If all goes well, I should be with Uncle Henri in Nice in just a few days."

"May God be with you always! Give my love to my brother and his wife and daughter. I know he'll help you. And tell him I wish he'd write more often."

The next morning, when the time came to part from Leon, my mother was steady and poised as usual. It was hard to comprehend her attitude. Her son was about to flee the country. Who knew what would happen to him and whether he would succeed in his escape? Still, no tremor of emotion shook her face.

A terrible loneliness overwhelmed me. I had become accustomed to relying on my big brother and his take-charge manner. What would our house be like without Leon? I would miss the special religious atmosphere with which he infused our home in so many little ways. How odd it was that when two brothers returned — Michael and Benny — another was set to leave. God had prepared the remedy before the plague: we would not be completely alone.

I took courage from my mother's calm demeanor. Leon would succeed. I felt confident that he would reach the south of France and find refuge.

When Leon boarded the train, I glanced again at Mama. No sound came from her, but her eyes filled with tears that ran freely down her cheeks. My heart contracted as I felt my mother's pain. For a moment, her façade had crumbled.

AND THEN THERE WERE TWO

Two days later, Willie came out onto the patio where Mama and I were resting. With restrained excitement he said, "Bertha and I are joining a couple and their twenty-year-old daughter. They've made arrangements with Alex, a smuggler who has just returned from his third trip to the Free French zone. He will guide the five of us as far as Lyon, France."

Mama was startled. "How soon will you be leaving?"

"Departure is scheduled for tomorrow, early afternoon. We'll travel with hand luggage only and must leave our suitcase here. There's no other way." Bertha, who had followed Willie, stood to the side, looking glum. She did not say a word.

I was also silent. Like my mother, I had grown unusually fond of Willie and Bertha and felt desolate about their leaving.

The next day, in a melancholy mood, Mama, Benny, and

I watched the Haases walk off to their rendezvous with the smuggler. There were hugs, and a few tears got wiped away. "We'll let you know if we make it to safety," Willie promised, sounding confident. Our fervent wishes that Alex succeed in leading them to freedom in Vichy, France, went with them.

Shortly afterwards, Benny told Mama, "With our boarders leaving, we're getting low on funds. Now that Leon's gone, I should take over the black-market business."

My mother's eyes blazed. "No, you won't! If it was too dangerous for Leon, it's certainly too dangerous for you." She squared her shoulders. "We'll manage fine. Piet told me he will continue to make his deliveries to us. You'll see. God will provide for our family. You have no need to worry."

She really didn't seem concerned. In fact, later that day, Mama decided that she could even afford to buy me a new coat. To my surprise, she proposed to take me to Madame Cammaerts, a highly respected dressmaker whose work was considered *haute couture.* Madame Cammaerts had fashioned the black coat my mother wore. She had also worked on Evelyn and Claire's trousseaux. Up to now, the neighborhood seamstress, a gray-haired, taciturn little lady, had been deemed good enough for my coats and jackets.

Evelyn accompanied Mama and me to Madame Cammaerts. In her waiting room, Madame handed us *La Mode Parisienne* and *L'Officiel.* We leafed through both magazines until we found a coat the three of us liked and whose style seemed right for me. Then we had to decide on the material. We wound up choosing the finest wool cloth in an exquisite steel blue. Its texture was a kind of basket weave, and it was the most expensive of the fabrics shown. Yet Mama agreed to pay the full black-market price for it. In an outburst of delight and gratitude, I hugged and kissed her spontaneously. Mama said hurriedly, "Well, you are a *kallah maidel*. You are of marriageable age, you know!"

I did know. I was already eighteen; other girls my age were getting engaged. But thoughts of marriage were not uppermost in my mind.

I continued to attend art school with Helene and greatly enjoyed the time spent in that atmosphere of culture. When I stood before the easel and tried to capture the correct angle or perspective of the subject before me, all the problems of the world seemed to recede to a faraway place. It was an oasis of calm in a world of ever-increasing tension.

Two weeks went by. We received word that Leon had made it to Free France. All of us breathed a profound sigh of relief.

One day, Benny came home early from a Torah lecture. He was visibly agitated and headed straight for the kitchen to find Mama. I heard him say in a controlled voice:

"I think I've got to follow Leon. Two of my yeshivah friends were taken away for slave labor in the Borinage." His voice rose. "They're forced to work in the coal mines. Three others have received notices!" Benny took a deep breath, then went on. "I know these fellows. They're friends of mine! Tomorrow they are being deported to a labor camp, and it doesn't even say where!"

Mama stiffened. She had stopped breathing, it seemed. Benny declared, "I'm not waiting till they ship me to some labor camp in Germany or who knows where. I'm packing right away."

My mother stood, frozen, not uttering a word. Benny seemed oblivious to the pain he was causing her. He said, "Shoes! I need good, sturdy shoes!" At the bottom of a corner kitchen cabinet, miscellaneous footwear was kept for the entire family. Benny crouched and began looking through the mass of leather shoes and rubber rain boots. He eventually extracted a pair of thick-soled black oxfords. "These should do it."

In a trembling voice, I said, "Make sure they're the right size for you."

Mama shook her shoulders, as if rousing herself from a bad dream. She recovered sufficiently to let her sense of practicality take over. "Come, Naomi," she said slowly. "Let's go upstairs and help Benny pack."

The following day, Mama and I walked Benny to the station in Berchem, where he boarded the train to Brussels. These goodbyes were becoming dismally familiar.

This time he did not embark at the central railroad station. Uniformed German guards were posted at the entrance to the tracks, where they stopped and questioned travelers at random. It was too risky. The Berchem railway station was merely a stop at the outskirts, on the Antwerp-Brussels line. The train halted there for just two minutes. We stood huddled unhappily at this outdoors station on a cold winter's day, along with a few other bundled-up travelers. Mama was unusually forlorn as she hugged her son goodbye. Benny was her baby, after all.

For days after Benny's departure, my mother immersed herself in chores around the house. While she had always enjoyed cooking and a bit of sewing, she'd never been all that involved with the physical labors of housekeeping. Now her supervision of and assistance to Yvonne — the latest of a string of cleaning women — bordered on frenzy. She helped turn over mattresses and make beds. Short of scrubbing floors herself, she scrutinized every corner. Each piece of laundry passed through her hands before reaching the ironing table. My mother wrote letters to Uncle Henri in Nice, to Claire in Montagnac, to Nathan and Eugene in New York, and to Charles in Morocco.

Michael and Sabine increased their visits to us, he taking time off from his diamond-cleaving. Evelyn dropped by almost every day with Rachel and Lili. In the past, my mother had openly enjoyed the company of her granddaughters. Their vivacity and laughter used to brighten her face and invariably perked her up when she was downhearted. But nowadays, Mama seemed a different person. Though she attended to her household, there was a listless look in her eyes that even Rachel and Lili were powerless to dispel.

One day, a food parcel arrived in the mail accompanied by a letter from Charles. Postmark: Portugal. I eagerly read it aloud to the family:

Dearest Mama, sisters, and brothers,

I came from Casablanca to Lisbon, to sail from this Portuguese seaport to the United States. Nathan and Eugene sent me my ship ticket, and I'm scheduled to leave in two days aboard the liner Vasco da Gama.

Dear Mama, though I should be elated at the thought of joining my brothers in New York, I am sad because I'm leaving you and the others in Antwerp.

I've made arrangements with a grocer in Lisbon. He will mail you a package twice a month, and I'm sure the food will be of help to you.

I'll write again as soon as I land in America and hope to hear from you in return. Please, Mama, take good care of yourself. I miss you a lot. I pray to God that you will all be safe and stay well!

Your loving son, Charles.

After Mama finished reading the letter, she stood still, holding it in her hand. The look in her eyes told me how profoundly she mourned Charles's departure and that of all her sons. Benny's flight had undoubtedly served to aggravate her sorrow. Now she was crying deep down inside, determined to keep her pain to herself.

"Let's open the package and see what's in it," I said with forced cheer.

We unpacked the tea, coffee, sugar, and cocoa — a windfall. Our eyes grew big when we discovered the fruit preserves, dried figs, dates, and unshelled almonds. Such delicacies were an unfathomable luxury in occupied Antwerp.

Here was God's providential hand! Our source of income had been diminished by Leon's departure, but once more our merciful Father in Heaven had provided, just as Mama had said He would.

My mother roused herself from her daze. She exclaimed, "Just look at this. That's my Charles for you! He'll never forget us. Nor will any of my other boys. No mother ever had finer sons than I have. I thank God Almighty for them."

I nodded in agreement. Inside, though, I was hurt. What about her daughters? What about *me*? Didn't I afford her any comfort or joy?

Meanwhile, I was adjusting slowly to the void that followed Leon and Benny's departure. The experiences we had lived through together had created an indelible bond between my brothers and me. Their leaving split us asunder and made me feel bereft. Gone was the sense of protectiveness I had derived from Leon's strength of character. How I missed seeing him and Benny in the morning, their tefillin strapped to their foreheads as they prayed in the family room. And I had loved listening to the singsong of Benny's sweet voice whenever he studied Gemara. My brothers' presence had added interest and keen enjoyment, as well as religious fervor, to my life. Belatedly I realized I had taken their genuine and reassuring companionship for granted.

The silence and emptiness of the house made me weep repeatedly. Now I actually wished I could hang up their jackets and pick up after them, tasks I had thoroughly disliked before.

Then, one day, a letter arrived from the Academy of Fine Arts. I stared at the elegant logo on the envelope, dreading to read its contents. Finally, I ripped open the envelope. It read: "You have been dismissed from attending classes at the Academy of Fine Arts until further notice." That was all. I had been expelled.

It didn't exactly come as a surprise. I'd known it was bound to happen sooner or later. Just the same, I was not prepared for the disheartening effect it had on me. Not only would I miss the classes, but, truthfully, I was a little concerned to be alone with Mama all day. She was retreating further and further into depression.

I called on Helene to commiserate on our dismissal. I thought I would find her morale low. Instead, she was full of plans. "I'm not going to let them get me down!" she declared. "I'm going to find a way to make money!" She had entered a workshop where she would learn the trade of a corsetiere.

"Good for you," I congratulated her. "You've always been good with your hands." I wished her every success.

Within weeks, Helene had acquired the skills of cutting, fitting, and assembling corsets. Her mother and sister were the first to wear her custom-made works. After that, it didn't take her long to attract clients from among family, friends, and acquaintances. She converted her salon into a work space. A Singer sewing machine took up one corner of the room. A square table was covered with bolts of white and beige cotton twill, stays and laces, and hooks and eyes in all sizes.

"You sure have established yourself quickly," I said when I came by to visit. "I'd always visualized you standing before an easel, dressed in a smock, holding a palette in one hand."

A wistful expression flitted across Helene's face. She smiled faintly, but her mouth was set as she replied, "At one time that was my dream, too. But now I'm earning good money and helping to support the family. You see, my father hasn't been doing much business lately." She pulled up a chair for me and sat down at the sewing machine. I watched as she stepped on the treadle. The needle stitched seams and tucks with great speed while Helene's fingers adeptly guided the fabric.

"Seems like you've got loads of customers," I said with admiration. "Not only are you skillful, but I'll bet you're as shrewd as an old businesswoman!"

Helene answered, "It's true I had to learn fast, but I had a lucky break, something I never expected." Her voice dropped low, and I leaned closer.

"More people than you imagine are preparing to leave the country. They can't ship their possessions or take luggage with them. They convert their assets into diamonds or foreign currencies. Then they think up ways to hide these on their person." Helene lifted the corset and gestured at the pocket-shaped lining. "I'm busy up to my ears!"

"I think that's great!"

"Thanks, Naomi. And what are you doing with yourself these days?"

"Frankly, nothing much," I admitted. "I'd like to find a job and earn some money, too."

"There's a dressmaker I know who's looking for help. Let me give you her name and address."

I took down the information. The dressmaker worked out of her apartment, and she lived on a side street not far from our house. This was the answer!

I rushed home excitedly. In the family room, Mama was sitting quietly, looking at photographs, a sign I had come to recognize. Her depression had intensified. Ignoring it, I plunged ahead. "Mama, ever since they dismissed me at the art school, I've been itching for something to do. And guess what? I have a job lead — as an assistant to a dressmaker!"

My mother slowly raised her head. She looked at me as if she hardly recognized me. Dully, she said, "There's plenty of work for you to do here at home."

I gaped at her. What with a cleaning girl and no boarders

there was very little work to do at all. "What do you mean?" I stammered.

"Just today, Yvonne told me she could no longer work for us. `It's for personal reasons,' she said. But that's what all domestics tell their Jewish employers lately when they quit their jobs." I nodded slowly as Mama finished, "I'm not even going to look for someone else." She fell silent. Then she straightened her back, jutted out her chin, and, in a voice reminiscent of her old determination, said, "Don't worry, we'll manage. Just the two of us. You'll see. We'll outlive this war, and Hitler, too!"

My heart went out to Mama, and I held back the tears that welled up in my eyes. Then, as much as I pitied my mother, I was overcome with a greater pity for myself. I stood for a minute biting my lower lip, then I turned on my heels and ran into the salon where I plunked down on the piano bench. Before long, my fingers, as if of their own volition, began playing "Il Lago di Como." Written in B-minor, it had a doleful sound and was the most sentimental piece in my musical repertoire. The tears ran down my cheeks as I played.

The emptiness of the upstairs rooms added to the gloom that pervaded the house. It was important that we take in boarders. Not only would it be good for our morale, but now we needed the income. And Mama did not seem much inclined to let me work.

She decided to rent out the front bedroom, which the boys had shared, as well as the single room on the first floor. I wrote in block letters, "Rooms to let," then placed the sign in the window of our salon.

No one answered for the longest time. Finally, Mr. Spira, a

distant relative from Mama's side and a bachelor close to forty, looked us up. He chose the *mansarde* — a single bedroom used by the sleep-in help we used to have.

Mr. Spira was of medium height and slight of build. His complexion was sallow, and he wore his dark brown hair not parted but swept backwards. I wondered how he kept it so sleek, capping his skull as if it were a molded substance. By contrast, his well-groomed mustache seemed very much a living thing. It peaked under his nose and spread down and out to both corners of his mouth. When Mr. Spira spoke to Mama, I watched the growth on his upper lip become animated.

Our long-lost cousin kept to himself. He was so quiet that I suspected him of walking on tiptoe. He spoke occasionally to Mama but avoided me. If I ran into him on the stairs or in the hall, his reply to my polite greeting was barely audible.

Since the task of chambermaid now fell to me, I had a chance to see the amazing collection of books he had amassed. Certain books were printed in German, others in Flemish, and some even in the Cyrillic alphabet. But most of them were in French. Works by such novelists as Victor Hugo, Gustave Flaubert, and Émile Zola were flanked by those of Goethe and Heinrich Heine.

A stack of French magazines attracted my attention. I leafed through the yellowed pages describing cultural events that had taken place in Paris decades ago. I read that a young pianist named Vladimir Horowitz, in concert at the Salle Pleyel, had been considered a rising star. I was fascinated with a picture of Sarah Bernhardt, the "Divine Sarah," in the title role of *La Dame aux Camelias*. Various art exhibits were in progress, readings by celebrated poets were announced, and much more.

I realized that with the discovery of this unusual library, I had intruded upon the private domain of our overly timid cousin. No longer would I wonder at the seclusion he chose when he retired to the *mansarde* the moment he came home from work. On the days Mr. Spira wasn't cutting diamonds, he hardly budged out of his room.

It was incredible. World War II was raging. The European continent was on fire! But Mr. Spira resided on a different planet, where he lived only through those bloody wars that were recorded in world literature. I felt a surge of envy for our cousin, for his ability to so totally remove himself and escape reality by plunging mind and soul into the realm of the written word. Oh, why couldn't I do the same?

My own escape was the piano. Most afternoons, I spent time at the keyboard. I'd always loved classical music, so much so that at times it elevated me to a state of euphoria. As I concentrated on notes and finger technique, I shut out all other thoughts and luxuriated in the sound of our fine-toned Beckstein. After weeks of diligent practice, I had mastered Mozart's "Rondo alla Turca". Yet, try as I might, I could in no way rival the abandon with which Mr. Spira succeeded in transporting himself into his outer sphere. He was light-years removed from the present-day ugliness and any real awareness of danger that was closing in on us. My envy of our newly found cousin only increased.

One evening I stopped Mr. Spira upstairs, on the way to his room. "What do you say to the terrible news? Yesterday's riots in the Jewish quarter?"

Encountering a blank look, I went on. "After they'd gone to see the Nazi propaganda movie, *The Eternal Jew*, gangs of Flemish hoodlums went on a rampage. They smashed store windows, looted, and set dozens of Jewish shops on fire. Whenever they caught an owner who protested, they beat him bloody."

Mr. Spira shook his head. "I've heard nothing of any such occurrence. I know nothing!"

Still shaken by the news, I gaped at him. "How could you not have heard and not know!" I blurted. "People in the streets haven't stopped talking about it."

"I have avoided going near the Lange Kievit Straat and the surrounding Jewish section for quite some time," he replied with a shrug.

I had wanted to hear Mr. Spira's cultured opinion on what he thought of this outrage. He would surely have an insight to offer, I had thought. Now I raised my voice and cried, "Those ruffians howled like savages while terrifying our people. Before taking off, they hooted, 'This is only the beginning! Next you'll see all your filthy synagogues going up in flames, too!' "

Mr. Spira responded impatiently, "I already told you, I have no idea what went on there." He raised a hand as though to ward off any further news. "I want to hear no more! I must attend to other matters." With that, he turned on his heels and entered his room. His door shut with a thudding finality.

I stared uncomprehendingly at the door. This concerned his fellow Jews. Could my cousin be so removed from reality that he'd become unfeeling to the fate of his own people? I tried to give him the benefit of the doubt. Perhaps his soul was so sensitive, he could bear to hear or know of the outside world only through the filtering lens of literature.

To read about some war when it was safely some fifty or a hundred years in the past, would cause little or no distress. There, while reading *Les Miserables*, he might cry freely and feel his character's pain. But real life was simply too harsh to bear.

That's when it occurred to me that our cousin's solution to the terrible situation of the war was no solution at all. I no longer envied him or wished to emulate his ways. As much as I wished to anesthetize myself from pain, I also wanted to be part of the world. I wanted to marry one day and have children. I wanted to be part of the Jewish community. To work and pray and laugh — and cry, too, if that's what life entailed. I felt pity for my cousin in his self-imposed isolation and determined never to be like that.

Nor was Mama's retreat into depression and numbness a solution. I would have to be strong so as not to fall into the pit of despair.

I did not think it would be easy.

A WAR OF NERVES

A new atmosphere prevailed in the house, and I was completely bewildered by it.

Mama's depression had shifted. Now she was constantly impatient and irritable. And I was the last one able to brighten her mood.

I had been sharing my mother's bedroom with her for the past six months. While she never confided much in me, late at night I usually found her in a more open and receptive mood. Nowadays, however, she simply recited the Shema and went immediately to sleep, hardly bidding me a "good night."

Suddenly I could no longer do anything right in her eyes. Mama remained grim and scarcely spoke to me, except to point out some mistake I had made with the housework.

"Naomi," she would say in a testy voice, "there's dirt behind the armoire. Don't you even know how to sweep a floor properly?"

She'd walk into the salon, run her fingers along the furniture, and complain of all the dust I had allowed to accumulate. "If you'd stop making noise on that piano and concentrate on the housework instead, maybe it would look decent in here!"

Listening to her harsh words, I hardly recognized my own mother. While she had never been very demonstrative or openly affectionate, I had always counted on her gentle strength and caring. Could it be that Mama's nerves were being frayed by continuous worry and she was lashing out at me? I gave up playing the piano and did my best to improve my domestic performance. But although I humored Mama's demands, she continued to criticize my every action. Sometimes I could not help myself and answered back resentfully. Then I would feel guilty and be filled with a new resolve to try and please her.

How dark the future looked for Mama and myself! Instead of giving one another much-needed support, our relationship had suddenly taken a wrong turn. Day by day, it continued to deteriorate.

The mornings I now spent doing housework. In the afternoon, I would go marketing. Lately I'd begun walking farther downtown and staying out longer. I wanted to avoid Mama's edginess as much as I could.

One day, when Evelyn came to visit, she showed me a pink blouse she had bought. "I got it at Lizette, on the Place de Meir," she explained. "There's a sale on them — a special purchase, they said. Prices are low, and you don't need ration coupons."

"I love it. And you got such a good buy," I said, admiring the garment.

"They had a lot of them. Why don't you go and buy one for Mama and yourself?"

"You know what? I think I'll do just that!" I answered spontaneously.

Before long, I was on my way to Lizette, a well-known ladies shop. As I approached the Applemanstraat, I heard the thumping of boots and the sound of singing voices coming closer. By the time I had reached the street, all traffic was halted to allow a platoon of German soldiers to march by. Trapped among other pedestrians, I was forced to stand and watch the helmeted warriors in their *Feldgrau* strutting onward.

With a sinking heart, I listened to their songs of past triumphs and future glory. No power on earth seemed capable of arresting their ceaseless conquests. Suddenly, a surge of anger welled up from deep within me at the forces of evil — mighty and victorious — that were spreading their poison over most of Europe.

The parade was over and traffic was moving again, but I stood frozen. After some minutes, I pulled myself together and proceeded mechanically toward Lizette.

The line of women waiting to shop there extended well around the block, and my first impulse was to walk away. Then I noticed that the line was moving swiftly. It wasn't long before I was inside the shop. It turned out that they sold only one garment per customer. I bought the same blouse that Evelyn had shown me. I would give it to Mama. Maybe this would cheer her up.

Back home, I unwrapped the package. "Here, Mama, this is for you."

"No thank you." Mama pressed her lips tightly together.

"Please take it," I insisted. "I want you to have it."

"But I don't want it!" she exclaimed. "Now come here. I need a hand. Help me wheel my bed into Leon and Benny's room."

I gave her a puzzled look. "Why?"

"From now on I'm sleeping in their room."

"But Mama." I stared at her, biting my lip. "Our room is so much nicer, where we are together."

"So now you'll have my room all to yourself — the nicest bedroom in the house. And I'll have my privacy." There was a bitter edge to her voice.

Tears filled my eyes. Never had Mama spoken so gruffly to me before. "Why are you so angry with me? Please, tell me. What have I done?" I stopped myself, not wanting to say another word, and tried to hold back the sobs I felt rising in my throat.

She stood and stared at me for a long moment. I saw a struggle in her face, as if she were searching for the right words to express herself. Finally she shook her head. She turned and walked out of the salon, where I remained for some time, feeling thoroughly miserable.

I tried to retrace all my actions of the past month. Had I made a thoughtless comment? Was I being too self-absorbed, neglecting her needs? Had my own depression, which had sprung up since I'd been dismissed from the academy, affected her in some way? I had no clue. How I wished she'd find it in her heart to explain! I hoped and prayed that she would bounce back and be her own self again. Surely, after having passed through this difficult phase, the two of us should get along and be a comfort to each other. But perhaps it was not meant to be.

The house was terribly silent. I considered playing the piano but did not want to irritate my mother's nerves further. I decided to pick up my knitting needles. I unraveled one of my own sweaters and reused the yarn to make a cardigan for my niece Rachel. I loved to knit, and it made the hours pass. When I grew tired of knitting and glanced at my watch, I saw it was only five o'clock. The long evening loomed ahead of me.

I went upstairs to the bedroom, which now seemed alien to me, with Mama's bed gone and some of her things missing. For a while I stood by one of the three windows and gazed at the deserted street below. Then I changed into a robe and began rolling my hair up in curlers. I told myself, Naomi, tomorrow you look for a job. You must do something outside this house. I prayed for Mama's consent.

I lay down on the bed with a book I had borrowed from Mr. Spira. I became deeply engrossed in the story and kept turning page after page, way into the night.

Suddenly, the clang of the doorbell startled me and thrust me back into reality. It went on and on, louder than I had ever heard it before. For a drowsy moment my gaze focused on the book, which had fallen to the floor; I must have dropped off to sleep in the middle of reading it. Then I leapt out of bed, bolted from the room, and sped down the stairs. On the fourth step from the bottom, I stopped short. I saw my mother standing by the salon door, her face drained of color. Her eyes were wide with fear, the pupils dilated.

In a trembling voice, she said, "If we don't answer, maybe...maybe they'll go away."

"Mama, I'm afraid they know we're here. And there's no place for us to hide!"

After a short pause, we heard the pounding of fists on the door and finally the shouting of men's voices, "*Aufmachen! Sofort aufmachen!* Open up immediately!"

Mama and I stood frozen on the spot. Then, slowly, she went to the door and opened it.

Two Germans in uniforms and heavy boots rudely pushed their way past Mama and thumped along our hallway. They stood facing us: a tall, broad-shouldered soldier and a shorter one with an olive complexion.

The taller soldier bellowed, "Who lives upstairs in the front room?" His steel-blue eyes projected an icy glare. Mama shrank back.

I cried out, "It's me! I sleep upstairs. Nobody but me!"

"Get her identity card at once," the shorter one muttered. There was a mean look in his eye, and I sensed that he might be more dangerous than his larger, overbearing companion.

The taller soldier boomed, "Three windows brightly lit! You illuminated half the street, giving signals to English airplanes so they'd know where to dump their bombs!"

His face had grown purple-red. He stopped for an instant to catch his breath, then resumed his barking. "How dare you break the law? How dare you endanger our lives!"

I realized — too late — that by failing to lower the window jalousies I had ignored the rules of the blackout. But suddenly I wasn't the least bit concerned about the consequences and the punishment I would probably receive. As I stood on the stairway in my pink flannel robe with curlers on my head, my initial fear was obliterated by a surge of hatred for these two intruders. How dare they terrorize my poor mother! Their arrogance infuriated me, and I wasn't going to cower before them. In a show of defiance, I lifted my chin.

Mama stepped forward nervously. "My daughter must have fallen asleep with the lights on before it got dark outside. It was an accident, and I assure you it will never happen again!"

Mama's plea seemed to mollify the tall soldier's anger. But his mate hissed at him, "Get her identity card at once!"

I went and searched through my things until I found my I.D. I handed it to the taller soldier. He glanced at the photo, verified that it was my picture, and handed it back to me. But his companion grabbed it out of my hand. In a hostile tone he commanded, "Tomorrow you will come to the *Kommandantur* to pick it up. Be there at nine o'clock in the morning!" Then they marched off with my identity card.

Now that they were gone, my spurt of defiance disappeared. I began shaking all over. I expected Mama to reprimand me, but when I looked at her she seemed to be in a faraway place, frozen inside her own thoughts.

I said weakly, "We're lucky those two were just infantrymen with the *Wehrmacht*. Had they been SS men or the *Feldpolizei*, they would have taken us with them."

Mama nodded. "Good night," she said tonelessly. And with these words she retired to her new bedroom.

I watched her climb the steps. Again the tears rose to my eyes. Well, what had I expected? Had I believed that she would embrace me, that all her anger would have evaporated, our relationship instantly restored? No, there weren't going to be any such miracles tonight. At least, I comforted myself, she hadn't lashed out at me for my irresponsibility. It was a small consolation.

The next morning, after a night of uneasy slumber, I got dressed and was ready to leave before Mama was up. It was not yet nine o'clock when I arrived at the *Kommandantur*, but in the lobby, a waiting line had already formed.

Two armed guards in military uniforms paced up and down. Their helmets were pulled so low they covered their brows. They asked what my business was with the *Kommandantur*, and I explained that I had come to retrieve my identity card. I was directed to the end of the line. More people arrived and stood behind me, while slowly the row in front diminished.

One of the guards came over to me, smiling. He repeatedly assured me that the wait would soon be over, and before long I'd be walking out with my I.D. in my purse. I listened politely but maintained an aloof distance.

After awhile, I became aware of sidelong glances and heard whispers of disapproval from people on line because of the guard's special attention. They must have thought I was fraternizing with the Nazis. I tried to ignore them as well as the guard.

By now, most of the people ahead of me had been called. There were two more to go before my turn.

Suddenly, Mama appeared and walked over to where I was standing. Her wig was askew, and I could see strands of gray hair on one side of her head. She looked altogether disheveled — Mama, who was always so impeccably groomed. Her voice was agitated as she whispered, "I should not have let you come here. It was a big mistake. I'm sorry, terribly sorry."

"Mama, Mama. You mustn't feel that way." I tried to soothe her. "I have to get my I.D. back. You know one cannot be without it. I'd be arrested."

As we talked, I noticed that the guard who had paid special attention to me was keeping an eye on the two of us. He stared strangely at my mother. Next he conferred with the other guard, all the while watching us.

He approached Mama and me. "Madame, you are not allowed to stay here," he told her.

"She's my mother," I protested. "Can't she wait with me? I will soon be called anyway."

The guard shook his head and made Mama step away from the line. For a while, she remained standing on the side, her eyes fearfully holding mine. Then the guard forced her to leave the building. How pathetic she looked, lingering at the exit, her gaze still on me. My heart was overcome with tenderness. I wanted to run and embrace her. Instead, I watched her slowly walk away.

The sound of a voice nearby jolted me. I turned and faced the guard who had been so friendly before. "Are you a Jew?" he asked.

"Yes, I am Jewish."

In an instant, his face underwent a dramatic change. Gone was his pleasant demeanor. In its place was a snarling caricature of a human being. "Follow me," he barked. He led me to the end of the long line.

"But I was next to be called," I managed to protest.

"No buts. This is where you'll stand," he snarled in return.

There was no point in arguing. A feeling of utter helplessness took hold of me. With each new arrival, the guard placed that person in front of me and made me take a step backwards. I bit my lip and fought back tears.

Hours later, I found myself still standing at the end of the line. I considered leaving. Where I stood, I was only a few feet away from the exit. I could easily sneak out while the guards had their backs turned. But then what? Without an I.D. I'd be in peril of being captured. Besides, the German authorities would eventually come looking for me. I would be putting Mama in danger as well. I decided that running out now would be a foolish move. I had to simply endure the humiliation until I was called.

I kept thinking of my mother. I imagined her, forlorn, all alone in the house, heartsick with worry over me. Today she had revealed once again how profoundly she cared, how much I really meant to her despite the rift in our relationship. This gave me strength.

Finally, no more people arrived. It was late afternoon when I began to move forward. My feet ached, and I was weak from hunger, when a man in military uniform came to take me upstairs to the commander's office.

The office was spacious and richly furnished; the Germans had requisitioned the foremost buildings in the diamond center for their administrative needs. An officer of high rank sat behind a massive, glossy mahogany desk. He appeared to be a man well into his fifties. His forehead seemed extended because of a receding hairline. He looked up and motioned for me to sit down on the chair facing him. Then he scanned my identity card, which the attendant had placed on his desk.

I didn't take my eyes off the officer's face while he read the report on me. He raised his eyebrows, causing his forehead to wrinkle. It stayed wrinkled for a long time. I was filled with apprehension. Oh no, now I'm really in for it, I thought. "Dear

God in Heaven, please don't let my mistake turn into a calamity," I prayed fervently.

Finally the officer said, "Now, young lady, tell me exactly what happened last night."

I was surprised at the cordial tone of his voice. Somewhat more at ease, I explained how I had meant to lower the jalousies on all three windows but had fallen asleep over a book while it was still daylight. I remembered Mama's plea to the soldiers in our house. "It was an accident," I told the officer earnestly. "It won't happen again. I assure you, sir, it will never happen again!"

The officer clicked his tongue as though chiding a child. "*Ja*, I can understand you fell asleep. But this is wartime, and your failure to observe the blackout meant danger, grave danger, for all of us. And we can't have that, can we now?"

I shook my head. He kept looking at me, but there was no trace of anger in his expression. He said, "I will let it go this time. But remember, in case of any further transgression, you will be punished under the law!" With that he handed my I.D. back to me.

"Oh, thank you! Thank you very much! Please believe me, sir, I will never break the law again," I exclaimed. Tears of relief had welled up, and I used a handkerchief to wipe my eyes as I walked out of the building.

Never before had the distance from the Pelikaanstraat to our house seemed so long. I couldn't hurry fast enough to get back home and set Mama's mind at rest. When I got there, I was greeted with outcries of joy from Daniel and Michael, and hugs from Evelyn and my two nieces, as well as Sabine. Then Mama stepped forward. Her face was choked with emotion.

She wiped away a few tears and reached out to hug me. She held me for the longest time within her tight embrace.

My mother said hoarsely, "You were next in line. When you didn't come back, I was sure you were being deported. What else could I think?" Once again, tears wet her face.

Michael said, "We all came to comfort Mama, who was going out of her mind with worry."

"Mama was blaming herself," Evelyn declared. "She kept repeating she shouldn't have let you go to the *Kommandantur.*"

Daniel broke in, "So tell us, Naomi, where were you all this time?" Everyone's eyes turned questioningly to me.

We all sat down in the family room, and I gave the entire account of how the German guards had treated me once they'd found out I was Jewish.

"Then what happened, Aunt Naomi?" Rachel wanted to know. Her beautiful black eyes shone with intense interest.

I told them of the decent treatment I had received at the hands of the older, high-ranking officer. How he had scolded me gently, like a daughter, and then returned my I.D. card. "God must have heard my prayers," I ended simply.

Michael said, "That officer was of the older generation. It's the young ones who are so vicious."

But Sabine shook her head. "He's no *tzaddik,* that commander, or whatever he was. He just made the same mistake as the 'friendly' guard. He couldn't tell — with Naomi's Nordic features — that she's a Jew. Do you think he would've been so nice if he had found out?"

Everyone fell silent as they digested this information. It was probably the truth. After seeing the way that guard's face had radically altered when he learned of my Jewishness, I was now suspicious of any show of kindness. How quickly congeniality could turn into cruelty!

Mama rose from her chair and reappeared with sandwiches, hot tea, and a tin of chocolate wafers, which she'd managed to save by keeping them out of my reach. Our mood lifted, and we began to eat and savor the family get-together.

Daniel, who had been silent until now, said quietly, "The *Führer* has proclaimed, 'We shall wage a war of nerves! We will bring to their knees the accursed enemies of the Nazi regime!' "

His words shattered the air of celebration. Evelyn stared reproachfully at her husband, but she didn't say a word. Nobody stirred.

I felt my throat close tightly as I looked at Daniel. I could clearly read his thoughts: The guards at the *Kommandantur* were merely doing what they considered their duty. I had been singled out as the enemy. When they harassed me, they were obeying their *Führer*'s command to wage a war of nerves against the Jews.

Our little celebration ended on an oppressive note. But later, when everyone had left, Mama asked me to help return her bed to the room where I had slept alone the previous night. My heart leaped at these words. This was what I had longed for. I wanted to throw my arms around her, but again, something stopped me. It was her matter-of-fact manner. "Let's see," she said, a hand on her hip. "How can we accomplish this most efficiently?"

And so, while we wheeled and maneuvered the bed from one room to the other, we talked about mundane affairs, as if the return of the bed signified nothing unusual. I sighed inwardly. This was Mama's way, and I would have to accept it: no words that might clarify and explain; no fervent emotion unless the situation truly warranted it. But she was my mother, and now there was peace between us. It was enough. I would just have to learn to read between the lines a little better.

We got ready for bed. I made doubly sure that the jalousies were all the way down with no peep of light to betray me.

After we were settled for the night and before she recited the Shema, Mama sat up in bed and turned to me. I looked at her lovely face, which seemed older, and I wondered: When had the wrinkles on her forehead become so deeply engraved? She appeared shrunken, frail, and vulnerable.

Mama sighed and drew in a long breath. "I'm so sorry for the way I acted," she said quietly. She stopped, and I sensed that the words she was about to utter were a terrible strain for her. She continued in a slow, pain-filled voice. "First Nathan and Eugene went to America. Then Charles left. When Leon and Benny had to flee, I was scared that soon it would be your turn. I was harsh to you — I don't know why — perhaps to harden myself for the day when you will have to leave me, too..." She closed her eyes, anguished. "Forgive me."

My throat constricted. I reached over and gently stroked her arm. "It's all right," I said. The little night lamp at her bedside cast a glow over my mother's face. In the soft light, she suddenly appeared the mother I longed for, luminous and loving.

THE ADVENTURES OF RICK WALLABY

An advertisement in the daily newspaper caught my attention. It read, "Wanted. Sales representative for Antwerp and environs. Good terms. Write to: Alain Publications, P.O. Box 2886, Brussels."

I wasted no time in sending out a letter offering my services. A week later, Alain Publications answered my application. It was a publishing house whose product was a biweekly magazine, modeled after American comic books and entitled, *The Adventures of Rick Wallaby*. The firm agreed to let me be their exclusive sales agent for Antwerp and the outskirts on a commission basis. I would receive thirty percent of the gross income.

It seemed a fairly good arrangement to me. From what I knew, the Belgian public doted on whatever Hollywood's creators of illusion and fantasy produced — first the black and white motion pictures, followed by talkies, and finally colored movies. They adored Greta Garbo and had adopted Mickey Mouse. Their fascination with stars of the silver screen never flagged. And cowboy films ranked as favorites with moviegoers.

I soon learned that the stories in the periodicals I was to sell emulated the scenarios of American Westerns. Rick, a cowboy of the Western frontier, performed heroic exploits, fighting cattle rustlers and other outlaws. He invariably set out to protect innocent and vulnerable settlers who were about to be victimized. Repeatedly he found himself in precarious situations from which there seemed no escape; yet, each time, Rick succeeded in freeing himself and walked away unscathed. I believed this would be a sure hit with the Belgian public.

Now all I had to do was persuade Mama to let me work.

Luckily, since the incident of my blackout violation and the dreadful experience at the *Kommandantur*, Mama's depression and irritability appeared to have lifted. She wasn't completely her old self, but the negative air that had enveloped her had lessened considerably.

When I approached my mother about working, she seemed neither pleased nor displeased, but simply resigned. "I can't protect you forever," she said with a sigh. "I trust that our merciful Father in Heaven will watch over you."

But when she learned the nature of my work, she grimaced. "It's so" — her hand moved vaguely, trying to find the right word — "flashy and cheap, selling these silly Hollywood stories to unsuspecting innocents. What can I say?"

I had to admit, this Rick Wallaby did sound like a two-dimensional character. It was certainly nothing that would ever enter Mr. Spira's library. And it wasn't exactly a higher calling or anything that could compare to Leon's work as a teacher of Torah.

But my brother Michael supported me. "If people want to satisfy themselves with this stuff, that's their decision. And he's not such a bad guy, that Rick. From what Naomi tells me, he's some kind of a hero. Besides, it gives Naomi a chance to develop a head for sales and business. Maybe she'll like it. Work is work," he stated. Mama threw up her arms in assent.

Armed with a few sample copies, a pen, a notebook, and a well-rehearsed sales pitch, I set out to solicit orders. I began by calling on the stationery stores in our neighborhood.

I started by saying, "A long, bleak winter lies ahead of us. The days will grow shorter, and evenings will be endless and dreary. Since the blackout, the streets are desolate at night. Hardly anybody feels like leaving his house to brave the uninviting darkness."

At this point, I feared the storekeepers would yawn and hint that they wanted to be rid of me. Instead, each and every one of them nodded in agreement and appeared eager to hear more.

Encouraged, I overcame my self-consciousness.

I continued: "What better escape is there from a depressing evening at home than a mental voyage to a faraway land? To be in the company of a fearless American cowboy and share his triumphs over evil? The reader will become so engrossed in Rick Wallaby's adventures that World War II and the German occupation will be forgotten."

My words hit the target. The storekeepers placed their orders. Soon I went calling on every stationery store in the city and its boroughs. To reach Berchem, Wilryk, Zurenborg, and other sections, I traveled on my bicycle. Not once did I walk away from a store empty-handed. Big or small, I booked orders wherever I turned up, singing the praises of Rick Wallaby's adventure magazine.

Stacks of the first copies arrived promptly at our house after I let the publisher know the quantity I needed. The bulk fitted snugly into the refinished fireplace in our dining room. The next morning I began making arrangements for delivery.

Helene's brother, a young teenager, was willing to accompany me on his bicycle. We both had baskets attached to the front and back of our bikes. Working with a city map, we planned the shortest route that would cover all our stops. Even so, we had to make more than one trip. After deliveries were completed, I went to collect the money due.

I paid the boy immediately for his help. Then I checked the amount against the orders. In less than two weeks the second shipment arrived. After I collected full payment for both shipments, I intended to convert this sum into a money order, which I would mail to Brussels.

On the way to the post office it occurred to me that I ought to retain the thirty percent to which I was entitled. I went back home and asked my mother if I should take my commission out of the customers' payments.

"I'm not sure it's the right thing to do," she answered. "How much does your share come to?"

"Well" — I peered down at my note pad — "according to my calculations, I earned 520 francs. Isn't that great? I'm really proud of myself."

Mama beamed at me. She said, "I must admit, I am impressed with the way you've handled this business. Now, about the percentage — why not ask Cousin Frieda? She can advise you better."

I nodded. It was a good idea. Cousin Frieda, an older woman who had never married, was respected in the family for her experience in the business world. An outstanding stenographer, she took dictation in French, German, and Flemish. Her proficiency in English enabled her to handle all correspondence for the Red Star Shipping Company. Her salary was kept a secret from us. It was presumed to be unusually high. She seemed the perfect person from whom to seek guidance.

After I explained my situation, Cousin Frieda thought for a while, then said, "Naomi, I'm surprised you signed no contract with this publishing house. But if you intend to have an ongoing relationship, you must observe what's considered proper conduct in business." She paused. "As I see it, you're thinking of helping yourself out of the company's `cash register,' so to speak. Your publisher may resent this. If I were you, I wouldn't risk doing that."

Her advice made sense to me. I rushed home. That same day I mailed the entire proceeds of the sales to Alain Publications. With the money order, I enclosed a note, asking for prompt return of my commission.

One week went by. Then another. No payment or further shipment of magazines arrived. On the letterhead of the first correspondence I had received, I discovered that an Alain Crosselot headed the publishing firm and lived at 39 Rue de la Toison d'Or in Brussels. I decided to make a trip to Brussels and find out what was going on.

I arrived by train at Brussels's *Gare du Nord,* and a short bus ride took me to the Crosselot address.

I rang the bell. A plump, middle-aged woman answered the door. She wore an apron over a dark dress. This, it turned out, was Alain Crosselot's mother.

Quickly I explained my business with her son. Madame Crosselot clasped her hands together and lamented, "My Alain is gone. He left the country in a hurry. He never once told me what trouble he was in." She sighed heavily and with a half-sob in her voice said, "He's my only one. Who knows if I'll ever see him again?" She shook her head. "I have no idea where he could be right now."

As I listened, I experienced a sinking sensation. "But...but what about his publishing firm?" I sputtered. "I sent them the entire proceeds of my sales. They owe me 520 francs. Please, tell me who I should see about my commission."

The woman pulled a man's handkerchief out of her apron pocket. She dabbed her eyes, blew her nose, and said, "Hmm, there's Monsieur Demaret. You can talk to him. Let me write down his address for you."

"Is it far from here?" I asked as she handed me the slip of paper.

"No more than a five-minute walk," she assured me. "Keep going until you see the sign that reads, `Rue des Capucines.' Number twelve is to the right of it. You can't miss it."

I left Madame Crosselot just as she was about to burst into another torrent over her son's departure.

As I walked toward the address I was given, I told myself that all was not yet lost. Perhaps I would recover the commission from this Monsieur Demaret.

I rang the doorbell. A man in his fifties appeared. He was

short and thin, almost frail. "Can I help you?" he asked courteously.

"I am the sales agent for Alain Publishing," I told him.

As soon as I uttered these words, his entire face brightened. "And I am the author of *The Adventures of Rick Wallaby.*"

"Really!" I exclaimed. Somehow I had never gone so far as to imagine the person who actually composed those tales.

We eyed each other carefully. "I've heard of your wonderful performance as a sales agent! I'm extremely glad to meet you," he said in a tone that rang true.

I stepped into his studio where he lived and did his writing. The place was cluttered beyond belief. The surface of every piece of furniture was covered with magazines, books, and all kinds of printed matter.

The writer sat down behind a huge, messy desk. Monsieur Demaret's speech generated electric energy, and he could be utterly charming. However, when I broached the subject of my unpaid percentage, he shook his head. "I can't help you," he told me. "I myself am in a most unfavorable financial situation."

I was not going to give up so easily. "As their writer, I'm sure the firm paid you advances to keep producing the series," I persisted. "I know that's how it's done."

He smiled a sad smile. "Not by Alain Crosselot," he said ruefully. "He's always been slow to pay anybody. But I liked the rascal, so I never made a fuss. Now I'm stuck with three issues, all written, edited, and ready for the printer."

"You mean you went ahead and prepared three manuscripts, and it's all for nothing?"

He nodded grimly and moaned, "All that work, and I'll

never see one cent for it." He slumped back in his chair behind the desk, looking tired and old.

Both of us remained silent for a seemingly interminable time. In frustration we stared at each other. The air was full of our anger, our defeat.

Suddenly, Monsieur Demaret sat upright. His eyes sparkled. "Say, I've got an idea. You and I together, we'll be a team. It's guaranteed to work!"

His abrupt change of mood startled me. "Did you think of a way we can still collect our money?" I asked with a renewed glimmer of hope.

He made an impatient gesture. "No, something else entirely. You've got to hear this."

I leaned forward in the chair. His enthusiasm was contagious. "Now you've got me curious."

"I'm going to write a new serial. It'll be out of this world! Something so exciting the stores'll never be able to meet the demand. And you — only you — will be their supplier." His arm dramatically swept the room. "Not only for Antwerp but for the entire country."

"Me?" I cried out. I jumped up from my chair and took a step backward. "Oh no! Not me!"

"Why not, young lady? You've got exactly what it takes! Drive! Personality! Intelligence!" His hands waved briskly about as he went on. "You'll be earning a fortune for both of us. Don't you see? Working together we can't fail!"

I replied firmly, "After what just happened to me, I can't take any such chances. I'm really not interested anymore."

His face sagged as he stared bleakly at me. But I could see that he was not yet ready to give up. "Look," he said. "In no time you'll be able to buy a small automobile to get around in. A girl like you is bound to be outrageously successful!"

"Thank you for your vote of confidence, Monsieur Demaret. I am flattered, I truly am. And I know that someone else would grab such an opportunity. I can't do it. I'm terribly sorry, but I really can't."

He escorted me to the door like a forlorn puppy. I felt so bad for him I was tempted to change my mind — but only for the briefest moment. With a wave of my hand, I bade Monsieur Demaret and the entire publishing industry goodbye.

During my train ride back to Antwerp, I reflected on my disappointing day in Brussels. My mother would be devastated when she learned the truth about Alain Publications. How was I going to tell her I'd been made a fool of? I resolved not to dwell on it further. Tomorrow I would find another job, and nobody was going to cheat me out of my pay ever again!

When I arrived back home, I found Mama sitting in the family room with two men. They were in the midst of a serious discussion but stopped talking as soon as I walked in. Mama introduced me. They rose for an instant and greeted me politely.

"I'm renting our mezzanine to these gentlemen," Mama explained. "Monsieur Jaques Tischler is a diamond dealer and his brother, Elie, a goldsmith. They're going to set up a jewelry workshop in our house."

"A workshop?" I raised my eyebrows. That was odd. People usually rented rooms to live in, not for work.

One of the men explained, "We have a shop in the heart of the diamond section, but we've heard news..." Here his voice dropped low. "An auto mechanic who works for the

Germans warned us that there's going to be a raid on the diamond center very soon. The Nazis plan to close off streets and block all entrances so that nobody can escape."

I stared anxiously at Mama. "We must warn Michael!" I exclaimed. "He does his diamond-cleaving at home but meets his bosses at the Diamond Kring or the Club. That's where he picks up and returns the goods."

Mama nodded gravely. "Yes. First thing tomorrow morning we must warn him. God forbid, your brother should be caught in their net."

The two men left. Mama and I sat over the kitchen table, discussing various matters: the possibility of a German raid, how we would warn Michael, and the new boarders. In all the rush of new information, somehow my embarrassing day in Brussels with Alain Publications was eclipsed. And for that I was utterly grateful.

THE TREK TO HET STEEN

The Tischler brothers were installed in their new workshop, and Michael was forewarned about the oncoming raid in the diamond district. Otherwise, nothing much had changed. I was still looking for work.

One week went by. Then another. Michael continued to drop in every afternoon with Sabine, and they kept Mama company in the family room.

One Friday, Michael arrived a few hours before Shabbos started. All the food had already been prepared, and Mama, Michael, and I sat around the dining-room table, chatting. At one point, Michael remarked, "It's just as I suspected. That predicted raid at the diamond center turned out to be nothing more than a false rumor."

Mama put down her cup of tea. "Who says it's not going to happen? I wouldn't be so sure."

"Look, Mama," Michael said in the patient voice he

adopted whenever he was trying to explain something he considered obvious, "each diamond dealer must declare all the goods he owns, so the Nazis have full control. They're imposing a tax on every transaction."

Mama frowned slightly. "What about the nonregistered diamonds? There must be quite a number of those around. Maybe the German authorities got wise to it."

Michael shook his head. "Believe me, they've got too good a thing going. A raid makes absolutely no sense. Besides, if there's going to be a raid, it would've happened by now." He shot her a puzzled glance. "Why are you being so pessimistic?"

"Of course I'm pessimistic," she retorted. "Isn't it good sense not to trust the Nazis?"

I listened to both of them. My brother's reasoning sounded logical to me, although I well understood Mama's desire to protect Michael. He ended the conversation, saying, "There will always be alarmists who spread frightening rumors. Why take them seriously?"

At this point, Mama rose from her chair. She rubbed the side of her head. "If you'll excuse me. I'm going to lie down for a while. I feel a headache coming on."

I watched her go. Poor Mama. When it came to arguing, Michael was just as stubborn as she was. No wonder she had a headache!

After Mama left the room, Michael turned to me. "By the way, Monsieur Shulweiss, one of the men I work for, is looking for office help — someone reliable and trustworthy. The help would handle the diamond merchandise and do some billing, too."

"That sounds easy enough," I said eagerly. "Do you think

I could get the job?"

"I'll arrange an interview for you," Michael promised.

I beamed, excited at the prospect of working once again.

The following Monday I was on my way to meet Michael and Monsieur Shulweiss at the Diamond Dealers Club. As I walked toward the Pelikaanstraat, I reviewed my brother's instructions. I was to arrive at the lobby precisely at eleven o'clock. Since only members were allowed into the "inner sanctum" of the club — which was permanently off-limits to women — I would have to ask the guard in the glass booth to page Michael and his boss.

I approached the diamond center's boundary. At that instant, a military truck drove up and planted itself in the middle of the street. German soldiers wearing helmets and carrying submachine guns spilled out of the vehicle. Civilian traffic came to an immediate standstill, and a detachment of the *Feldpolizei* roared up on motorcycles.

I hurried out of the way, crossed the street, and stood gaping from a safe distance. Straining my eyes, I saw that within the roped-off confines, armed guards were taking positions at the entrance to each building. Even side doors in back alleys were guarded. Trapped in their halls and offices, no diamond dealer could possibly elude the Gestapo's clutches.

I stood glued to the spot as the realization struck me like a blow: Oh no! Michael is in there!

My throat tightened, and I could hardly breathe. I began to feel faint and was forced to lean against a wall, eyes closed. No, it couldn't be. Michael was too smart. He would have escaped before it was too late. But the longer I thought about it, the more I had to admit, painfully, that he had been caught in the Nazi net. Now I had to figure out what to do about it.

One after another, people who'd been headed for the diamond district made a discreet turnabout and disappeared. I began plodding home. The entire way I was tormented by the prospect of having to break the news to my mother. How I dreaded seeing the anguish on her face!

I found Mama and the Tischler brothers gathered in the hallway. They were listening with grim faces to one of their customers, who had arrived minutes earlier. The man related how he had missed getting caught in the raid by no more than a hairsbreadth. With a nervous laugh he kept repeating, "Was I lucky today! Was I lucky today!"

Meanwhile, Mama had no inkling that Michael had been with Monsieur Shulweiss at the Diamond Dealers Club when the Nazis closed in. As long as she expressed no anxiety about his whereabouts, I refrained from telling her the unfortunate truth. Repeatedly I blinked back tears of distress as my brother's image appeared before my eyes. Somehow I managed to wear a façade of nonchalance in front of my mother.

When the men had departed, the silence downstairs amplified the ticking of the wall clock in the family room. I said out loud, "I must get busy, or this afternoon will never end."

"Keeping busy never was a problem for me," Mama remarked. She had brought down her navy skirt. After she examined it carefully, she ripped the seams. "I'll still get a good deal of wear from this skirt once it's turned inside out," she announced. The shortage of new fabric had led many who could sew into the thrifty practice of reversing their garments.

The skirt was taken apart, and I helped iron each piece.

After basting the reassembled garment, Mama slipped into it. The fit was perfect. "If you'll stand on the footstool, I'll pin the hem," I said.

In a squatting position, I began to even out the length. Just then, the clanging of the doorbell tore through the quiet house, startling us. "It's past six o'clock," Mama exclaimed. "Who could that be?"

I went to open the front door. For a moment, I stood gaping at Sabine. I had never seen my sister-in-law look any way other than well-groomed and properly dressed. Now she stood on our doorstep with her blouse unevenly buttoned and her hair disheveled, wearing bedroom slippers. Her usually glowing complexion looked pasty, and her eyes were puffy and red.

Before I had the chance to say a word, Sabine threw her arms around my neck and wept bitterly. Between sobs, she stammered, "It's Michael. He got caught in that diamond raid. The Nazis are holding him."

Mama had followed me into the hallway and heard everything. I led both women into the family room. My mother clutched her head and cried, "Michael ignored my warning! And now what I feared most has happened!"

I covered my eyes, suddenly unable to bear Mama's pain. Why, oh, why had we not listened to her judgment, dismissing it as a mother's overprotectiveness? Then I squared my shoulders. This was not the time for self-reproach. I looked unwaveringly into Sabine's swollen eyes. "Have you any idea where they've taken him?"

Sabine stopped weeping. She said, "He's in the city jail with the diamond dealers they caught with illegal, nonregistered goods." Her eyes began flooding again. "I went to the jail. They wouldn't let me see him. I even tried to bribe one of the guards, but it didn't work. Tomorrow Michael will have a hearing." Her shoulders shook as she wept.

"Michael only worked for other people," Mama wailed, wringing her hands. "He didn't own the diamonds he cut. Why did they arrest him?"

I replied sadly, "They must have figured that he was a partner of Monsieur Shulweiss and that he owned a share of the merchandise."

The evening wore on. Sabine consented to stay overnight. We made plans to go to her apartment in the morning so that she could change into something more appropriate. Then she and I would make our way to the jail. Somehow we would plead Michael's case. Meanwhile, Sabine's agitated slumber, her groans and garbled mutterings, kept me awake most of the night.

The next morning, Sabine was eager to leave for the city jail. Despite her protests, I persuaded her to put on a becoming dress and shoes to go with it. I also succeeded in having her apply a bit of makeup.

"In times of crisis it helps to look your best," I told her.

"Maybe so," she answered with a sigh.

When we reached the jail, a crowd was waiting by the closed gate. A Flemish guard called out, "No one is allowed inside. I've got my orders! You folks had better go home!"

A few people moved back; some started to leave. Then I heard Sabine's voice as she ventured forward. "Excuse me." To my surprise, she flashed a dazzling smile at the guard.

He hesitated a moment before saying sternly, "Well, what have you got to say?"

"I was told my husband will have a hearing today. He was arrested in a diamond raid. It's all a mistake! Please tell me where I can find him after the hearing."

The guard replied, "That group was transferred early this morning. None of them are here anymore."

We were both shaken by this information. Yet Sabine still managed a grin and said pleasantly, "Could you just tell me where they've taken this group?"

The guard wrinkled his brow and scratched behind his ear. "Hmmm, well, let's see. Het Steen. That's it! You know, the ancient fortress at the river's edge. We're so overcrowded here that they're making Het Steen into a prison now."

Sabine and I looked at each other. Het Steen was a medieval castle, built like a fortress. Its granite walls were two meters thick, and the few small windows hardly let any light in. The gloomy structure actually jutted out over the Scheldt River. We thanked the guard and left.

We boarded the tram that would take us to the port district. With a somber expression, Sabine turned to me and mused, "Just the thought of being locked up in that horrible place makes me shudder. It has displays of torture devices they used in the Middle Ages." I winced and tried to keep my imagination from picturing the worst possible scenario.

"Last stop!" the conductor shouted. "Everybody out!"

We had arrived at the entrance of the wide thoroughfare that led to the waterfront. "We'll have quite a walk from here," Sabine told me. "I wonder why the tram doesn't go any farther."

When we reached the end of the thoroughfare, we saw military barricades. Heavily armed German sentinels stood on guard.

Sabine and I turned right, onto a desolate stretch of road. Not a living creature was in sight. The hulk of Het Steen loomed in the distance, and we marched toward it.

In the ominous silence, our footsteps resounded. On approaching a bend in the road, we heard a click as someone cocked a firearm. My mouth fell open when out of nowhere a man's voice thundered, "Who goes there? Halt or I'll shoot!"

Sabine and I froze.

A German sentry stepped out of his booth. With his rifle ready, he came slowly toward us. "What are you doing here on restricted territory?" he yelled.

"We...uh...we didn't know. Honest, we didn't," I stammered.

"Hah, excuses! That doesn't help in wartime. Trespassing in a military zone is a crime! You'll be punished accordingly." Angrily he slung the rifle over his shoulder and snapped at us, "You're coming with me."

The sentry walked up to two soldiers in uniform stationed on the road. They saluted each other with outstretched arms, shouting, "*Heil Hitler*!" I heard the sentry relate in a muffled tone that he believed he'd caught two Flemish female spies. Then he clicked his heels and stepped back. The two other soldiers ordered us to follow them.

I was gripped with nausea, and my stomach churned. Sabine walked numbly beside me, as if she were beyond feeling anything at this point.

Soldiers in fatigues milled about trucks that doubled as sleeping quarters. One tall, blond man was shaving, his mirror poised on the front fender. He hummed a tune as he plied his razor. At the far end of a tent hung an improvised clothesline.

Towels and army shirts flapped in the mild river breeze. I took in all these details as if I stood watching from faraway. Was this truly happening to us? The whole scene had an air of unreality. I realized I must be in a state of shock.

Presently Sabine and I were led into a cottage. An officer sitting behind a desk was dictating to his male secretary while we waited. Finally the officer turned to our escort. "Who are these women?" he asked. "Where did you pick them up?"

One soldier replied, "Lieutenant, sir, they were approaching our military post. The guard stopped them just in time. Ever since the last act of sabotage, our sentries are on the alert when it comes to detecting spies."

The officer nodded. "So. Let's find out what they have to say."

Sabine quickly moved close to the desk. Her gaze was steady as she declared, "We're not spies! We're not saboteurs! My sister-in-law and I had no idea we were trespassing in a military zone."

"We didn't see a single sign that prohibited walking down the road we took," I added with conviction.

"The port of Antwerp was proclaimed off-limits to all civilians. It's your responsibility to know the law and obey it!" the lieutenant snapped. Then he fell silent. The two soldiers who had escorted us had stationed themselves on either side of the entrance door. Meanwhile, the officer picked up a letter opener from his desk and leaned back in his chair. His eyes wandered to and fro, scrutinizing Sabine's face and then mine, all the while tapping his palm with the blade of the letter opener.

The atmosphere in the room grew more oppressive with

each moment of prolonged silence. By now, I was a mass of raw fear. I struggled to conceal my inner trepidation, but at one point, I had to grab the edge of the desk to control my trembling. Unknowingly, stupidly, we had walked straight into the lion's den. We were in the hands of the Gestapo!

The officer said, "Well, I'm waiting for an explanation."

Without hesitation, Sabine responded, "I can speak for both of us, sir. We deeply regret breaking the law!" She took a short breath, then continued: "We were going to Het Steen. My husband is imprisoned there. He was arrested by mistake. Today he's having a hearing. And he'll definitely be cleared! My sister-in-law and I came to take him home."

The officer arched a brow. "Are you so certain your husband will be found innocent? Maybe so. However, no civilian is allowed anywhere near Het Steen without a permit from Gestapo headquarters. I will have to arrest the two of you."

"Couldn't you excuse us, just this once?" Sabine pleaded with tears in her eyes.

He tapped the letter opener against the desk and looked at us closely once more.

I sensed the officer had not yet decided how to deal with us. Was there a kind heart beating beneath his rigidly disciplined exterior?

I appealed to him, "Please, oh, please! Give us a break this time. We'll never violate the law again. I can promise you that!"

He didn't answer for quite awhile. Suddenly the Lieutenant rose from his chair and beckoned one of the two soldiers to approach the desk. "Karl, you will take these ladies in my car," he ordered, "and drive them to the thoroughfare. Let them off at the last stop of the tram."

My shoulders sagged with relief. "Master in Heaven, thank you," I whispered, mopping my face with my sleeve.

Karl saluted dutifully and brought us over to a gray Opel. We got into the back seat. He drove the car without uttering one word, his face set in a harsh expression. When we reached our destination, he opened the door for us and hissed, "Get out! You're two lucky dames. If it were up to me, you'd never get off so easy. Looks like the lieutenant is getting soft or something."

With that, he put the car in high gear and blasted off.

The tram was slow in coming. We sat down on a bench while we waited. The spirit and verve that Sabine had displayed when she faced the officer had vanished. She slumped beside me on the bench. "Oh, Naomi," she moaned, "will I ever see Michael again?" Once more she began to cry.

I put my arm around my sister-in-law's shoulders and tried to calm her. But what could I say? True, the officer had released us from possible arrest. Yet we were no nearer our goal than when we had first started out.

Michael, dear Michael. My thoughts reverted to my childhood. Whenever I had suffered from one of my throat infections, Michael, more than anyone, had lingered at my bedside. We would play checkers or dominoes, and he never failed to cheer me up. When Papa died, he, being the eldest son, was the one who made Kiddush, who sold the *chametz* for Pesach, who organized the building of the Sukkah. For me, he was a father and favorite brother wrapped up in one. Was I now going to lose him?

As we turned the corner of our street, I found myself slowing down to delay giving Mama our disappointing news. But how long would we succeed in hiding the truth from her?

As we entered the house, the Tischler brothers emerged from the family room talking animatedly. They stopped at the foot of the stairs to greet Sabine and me with a vibrant "Hello!" They did not utter an additional word, but we were struck by their cheerful expressions.

Without consciously knowing why, the gloom ebbed from our faces. The next instant, intuition prevailed, and we both sensed what had taken place. As clearly as if we had seen him with our own eyes, we knew Michael was home! I let out a scream, and Sabine sprinted toward the family room with me at her heels.

Michael stood with his back to the mirror over our fireplace. We rushed toward him so excitedly he nearly lost his balance. He laughed and exclaimed, "Boy, that's some welcome I'm getting!"

Mama looked absolutely radiant. She kept repeating, "Thank God for this day!"

Sabine lifted her face, and in the mirror I saw her eyes brimming over with tears. She laughed and cried together. I stood and watched, beaming, because I knew this time Sabine was shedding tears of happiness.

Quickly Mama and I assembled a gala meal. To make the repast as festive as possible, we dug into our canned-food reserves. Evelyn and Daniel came over with the girls and brought a pot of fresh vegetable soup. For dessert, the last can of Hawaiian pineapple slices was dished out, which we all thoroughly enjoyed.

While we sat around the table, we heard a blow-by-blow account of Michael's release. During the hearing at the jail, Monsieur Shulweiss had testified that my brother only worked for him and didn't own a single diamond. It so happened that the Flemish office clerk, employed by the Germans, knew and respected Monsieur Shulweiss. His wife had worked many years as the Shulweiss' laundress. The clerk whispered some specific information to the Germans in command, and, without further ado, Michael was set free.

My brother reflected, "I had the strongest feeling that God was right there with me, shielding me through the entire ordeal."

I pondered this while slicing the last bit of pineapple on my plate. If Michael was being watched over by his guardian angel, I thought, couldn't it be that the rest of us were also invulnerable? That all of us rated Divine protection and were destined to live out the war?

But a moment later, another thought crossed my mind. How long could our present euphoria last? The Gestapo had Michael's address now. They knew he worked on precious stones. On any given day, they could invade his apartment and rob him of the diamonds — or much worse.

Later that night I found two small maps and hung them on a wall in my bedroom: maps of France and the United States. I placed a pin in Montagnac, a remote village in southern France. I prayed, "Dear Father in Heaven, I beseech you, let no harm come to my sister Claire and her husband, Julius, and their three children. Let them continue to be safe there. Amen!"

Two more pins on the French map indicated that two of

my brothers were adrift in Nice. I prayed, "Merciful Father in Heaven, please shield Leon and Benny from every possible danger under the Vichy regime. Let them stay safely in Nice until the end of the war, so they can return home to us when it's all over. Amen!"

I added a fourth pin to the map of the United States, in the city of New York. Even though Nathan and Charles, as well as Eugene and his wife, Sally, were well beyond the Nazi's grasp, I prayed, "Dear Father in Heaven, please guide and protect them. They're newcomers in America, this strange land across the ocean. Please, let all four stay healthy and well, so we can all be reunited as soon as this war is over. Amen!"

As I recited these prayers, my gaze on the pinheads, one by one the images of my siblings took shape in my mind. They no longer seemed so far away. This comforted me. And now Michael had returned to us. I went to sleep shortly after, and in my dreams we were all reunited, on one continent, in one country, a family restored.

THE SHIDDUCH

I had another job lead. Evelyn arranged an interview with friends of hers, Eric and Sarah Sprung, who ran a business — something to do with a patented, secret formula for dentists. It sounded obscure and a little mysterious to me.

A few days later, I rang their doorbell on the Henri Conscience Straat and the landlady, a Madame Rabstein, let me in. She looked fortyish, with short auburn hair that was smartly styled. With an amiable smile, she directed me to her tenant's suite.

I found Eric in the room that served as his laboratory. He stood behind the table wearing a white coat and was in the midst of adding ingredients to a mixture in a large bowl.

"Hello, Naomi," he greeted me, looking up momentarily. "You're right on time. Watch me finish this batch. Soon we'll be able to start filling the *flacons*."

I moved closer to the table. Eric proceeded to weigh a

precise amount of white powder on a scale and added it to the bowl. Then he poured boiling water into the mixture and let it cool. Finally he blended everything, stirring continuously until it became a smooth paste.

"This looks like soft putty. But putty is odorless, while this paste has a strong, antiseptic smell," I remarked, bringing my handkerchief up to my nose.

Eric replied, "Everybody reacts that way at first. Before you know it you'll get used to the odor." He inhaled deeply. "This stuff works! A weaker product could never be so effective in the treatment of tooth decay."

I smiled to myself. He certainly was passionate about his work.

He taught me how to fill the navy-blue *flacon*s up to their necks, using a tool that looked like a butter knife. Glass stoppers sealed the paste inside. Afterwards, we put on labels marked "Dentracine" and carefully aligned the *flacon*s in a box for shipment.

When it was time to leave, I noticed that the odor of Dentracine no longer bothered me. I also realized, to my delight, that I had a bona fide job, with a real salary — 150 francs per week — which Eric paid me in advance.

So began my stint as a working girl. I finally had a job, and it was wonderful. It was good to feel useful. I liked being greeted by the cheerful Madame Rabstein every morning. I liked the physical aspect of the work, the stirring and mixing and packing. And I liked the company of the newlywed couple, Eric and Sarah. By nighttime I was usually tired and had no trouble falling asleep. Even Mama couldn't help commenting that my new career as a laboratory assistant suited me well.

During the midday break, I either went home or got together with Helene, who worked close by. We would treat ourselves to a chocolate drink at La Coupe Glace, an ice-cream parlor in the vicinity. As time went on, our talk became increasingly personal. One afternoon, Helene told me that she'd been introduced to a young man whom her parents regarded as a marital prospect. They favored the match and were encouraging her. Helene was seriously considering the young man. Then she said, "You and I are ready for marriage, you know."

I shrugged. "Actually, I'm not in the least ready for marriage. Besides, everything is so unstable now, what with the war and all." I waved a hand dismissively. "As far as I'm concerned, this is no time for long-term commitments."

"But Naomi," she argued, "you can't tell me that you don't have feelings. Don't you want a family of your own?"

I looked at her. "I seem to have such feelings well under control," I replied. "For me, getting married will have to wait."

And that was the end of our conversation.

Ironically, just a short time later, I found myself beginning to understand what my friend had meant when she talked about being interested in marriage.

Elie, the younger of the Tischler brothers, was a skilled goldsmith, and his brother, Jacques, a successful diamond dealer. Mama had rented them our mezzanine for daytime use. Together, the brothers operated a jewelry workshop in our house.

There was always a sparkle in Elie's eye and a witty remark on his lips. One afternoon, he appeared in our salon, holding a few sheets of music. I had resumed playing the piano, and sometimes, after work, I'd come home and practice for a while.

"Could I join you?" he asked. "I know some musical pieces that require four hands. It would be nice if we could play something together."

Suddenly Mama appeared in the doorway, a frown on her face.

"Naomi," she said sharply, "I need you in the kitchen."

I was about to protest, but the look on my mother's face stopped me. Reluctantly, I got up and excused myself.

When we were in the kitchen, the door safely closed behind us, Mama turned to me. "I don't think it's proper for you to be talking to that young man."

"All he wanted was to play some music."

"I forbid it!"

"But why?" I stared at her. "What harm could there be?" I stopped for a moment, then added, "You didn't seem to mind when Fritz paid attention to me. How is this different?"

Mama's forehead wrinkled slightly. Then she said, "Fritz was direct. He wanted to court you for the purpose of marriage, and he spoke to me first. His intentions were honorable, and he seemed a fine, religious young man. But this fellow's only bent on flirtation. Besides, he doesn't strike me as particularly religious."

I turned away. "Well, there's no point in talking further," I said coldly. "You certainly have everything figured out." With that, I stalked angrily to my bedroom and shut the door loudly behind me. Life was so unfair! How could Mama judge Elie so harshly without even knowing him?

The following day, I decided to do a little research of my

own into our boarder. I dropped in on my sister-in-law Sabine, and it turned out she was good friends with someone who knew him well. In a matter of minutes, I had the scoop.

Elie Tischler was born and raised in Cracow, Poland, in a traditional Jewish home, where he received a thorough religious upbringing. But Elie took a different path from his family. He became an ardent Zionist, and religious observance didn't play any part in his idea of a Jewish homeland. He also had a passionate interest in the Yiddish language and was a lover of the Yiddish theater. After he moved with his brother to Belgium, he renounced religious practices entirely. Not only that, but he had begun to acquire a reputation as someone who could not settle down — a man who loved romance but not marriage. Elie was in his early thirties.

When Sabine finished her report, she surveyed me with penetrating eyes. "You wouldn't be interested in this Elie Tischler, would you?"

"Oh no," I said, quickly gathering my things. "I was just curious."

I walked home from Michael and Sabine's apartment, mulling over what I'd learned in amazement. So Mama had been right: he wasn't religious, and he was a flirt to boot. I began to realize how naive I was when it came to these matters. I now regretted my cold words to Mama and managed to stammer an apology when I returned home. My mother simply nodded. I wondered where she had come by her reservoir of knowledge and insight about such things. I would never know. Even if I had the nerve to ask her, she would not confide in me.

This episode must have stirred Mama's thoughts in some

way, because later that week, after we had eaten our noontime meal, she said, "I'm expecting Reb Getzel the *shadchan* this evening. I've sent him away twice but he doesn't give up."

She never had trouble dismissing him before. "Oh, Mama," I groaned, "we've been through this so many times. I'm not interested in getting married. It's the wrong time."

Mama folded her arms. "Then tell me, please. How do I get rid of Reb Getzel? He has one line: `War or no war, a young girl must get married. There are no Jewish convents!' He has a long list of prospects."

"I'm sorry, Mama," I declared firmly. "I don't intend to meet any of them."

That evening, when the bell rang, I went to open the front door. A man stood on our doorstep wearing a black hat and a caftan. His beard was white and long, and his dark eyes were framed by shaggy, red-brown eyebrows. He gave the impression of being an old man, yet his posture was straight as a rod. He carried an umbrella, though it wasn't a rainy day. Then I remembered: an umbrella was the traditional matchmaker's stock in trade.

"I'm Reb Getzel," he announced, stepping into our hall. He scrutinized me from head to toe. He had a mischievous glint in his eye, and it occurred to me that his white beard made him look older than his age. "You're the daughter, eh? I'm here to see your mother on private business."

I led him into the family room. He greeted Mama, then sat down on a chair, cupped both hands over the handle of the umbrella, and rested his chin on his hands, not saying a word. Mama and I glanced at each other. Then Reb Getzel made a quick motion with his hand. Ah, so that was it. He wanted me out of the room. I gladly complied.

Later on, after the matchmaker had left, Mama cornered me upstairs while I was brushing my hair. "Just listen to this description," she said enthusiastically. "The young man, Bernard, comes from a fine family. A religious man, I was assured. He's bright and talented. At twenty-eight, he's already made a name for himself in the diamond trade." She looked beseechingly at me. "So please, my child, go out with him this one time. That doesn't obligate you to marry him, you know. Do it for your mother's sake."

I stopped brushing my hair and listened to the description. It sounded fairly appropriate. Mama had good sense about such matters. Perhaps my interest in Elie had shown that I wasn't so set against the idea of marriage after all. Maybe this is what had motivated Mama to invite the *shadchan* over.

"All right," I consented. "I'll meet him just to please you."

My mother's face lit up. With her eyes lowered conspiratorially, she said, in a near whisper, "I'll tell you something in the strictest confidence." All this *shidduch* business gave Mama new life. Her entire demeanor suddenly seemed girlish and excited. "Some time ago," she continued, "Sabine mentioned that her younger sister wanted to go out with this young man, Bernard, but he wasn't at all interested. Yet Reb Getzel told me that when your name was mentioned he was most eager. He said he can't wait to meet you!"

I was flattered, to say the least. It actually made me look forward to the meeting. But I put on a show of reluctance for Mama. "Okay, okay, I'll show up for the date. I promised you I would, didn't I?"

Sunday afternoon I got ready. I looked at myself in the

mirror in my princess-style gray silk with *bois-de-rose* flowers. "Too *balebatish,*" I mumbled. Next I tried on my navy two-piece with its pleated skirt, white collar, and cuffs. "Aha! Much more flattering," I said out loud. I would wear my coat on top. Then I reached for my high-heeled shoes and dressy purse.

I couldn't help being nervous. Would he like me, this Bernard? Would it be uncomfortable spending a few hours with someone I didn't even know? I began mentally preparing questions to ask him if the conversation lagged. Helene had told me that on one of her dates, she and the young man suddenly had nothing to say to each other. After a few minutes, he turned to her and asked, "Do you play a musical instrument?" It seemed so stilted, Helene almost burst out laughing. I vowed not to ask him that question even if things got really dull.

Bernard arrived ten minutes early for our three o'clock appointment. I heard him talking below with Mama while I applied the last touches of makeup. Then I came down the stairs into the salon.

He stood when I entered. "I'm very pleased to meet you," he said. Mama, sensing my awkwardness, rushed forward and said eagerly, "Naomi, Bernard was in the same class with your brother Eugene."

"Oh, really?" I studied him more closely. He was of medium height and looked quite presentable in his finely tailored suit. His bearing conveyed the self-assurance that some people attain through success. "What a coincidence," I remarked.

"Yes, and I also know Michael through the diamond

trade," he volunteered.

He took his leave of Mama in a charming manner. It struck me how pale his face was. His complexion lacked color. Then I berated myself for being so critical. I must keep an open mind.

We left the house and walked toward Borgerhout's borough hall. The streets were rather isolated. Soon we reached the Turnhoutse Baan, a well-populated avenue where Jews were seldom seen.

Finally, we entered a café in Deurne, a place where we could count on not meeting friends or acquaintances. Aside from a bar with a few stools, there were half a dozen booths with upholstered banquettes and faux marble tables. I smiled at Bernard, appreciating his thoughtfulness in choosing a place that was somewhat secluded. He hung up my coat with a gallant flourish. Aha, I thought. Elie Tischler was not the only charmer in the world! I began to perk up. Perhaps I would enjoy myself after all.

"What would you like to drink?" the waitress inquired. Her voice jolted me back to reality.

"How about some light beer," Bernard said. "De Kroon?"

"I don't usually have beer," I said. "But why not this once?" I grimaced slightly. "Anything beats that brew they call coffee."

For himself, Bernard ordered a Stout, the strong, dark beer favored by men. He smiled when the waitress brought two frothing steins to the table. These would afford us nearly two hours of privacy.

"So you know Eugene, and Michael, too," I said.

"Actually, I know most of your six brothers," he admitted.

It came to light that Bernard was also a fan of the Beerschot

— a local soccer team. He laughed, remembering what fanatic fans my brothers had been.

"Oh yes," I responded. "Whenever they couldn't watch the Beerschot play on a Sunday, it was a tragedy for them."

We spoke of this and that. After some time, he turned to me. "What do you do with yourself all day long?" he asked.

"I am a laboratory assistant," I said proudly. I began to tell him of my day's activities. As I spoke, however, I noticed that his eyes wandered, focusing first on the bartender and then on the nearest pictures hanging on the wall. At one point, I saw his nostrils flare — a sure sign of a gentleman's yawn. I fell silent, embarrassed. My work was exciting to me, but it was probably dull to others.

"Please continue," he said.

"I'm boring you," I answered quietly.

"No, I'm fascinated," he assured me. He slumped slightly in his seat, smothering a yawn.

"What is your work like?" I asked, turning the tables. "How did you manage to make a name for yourself so quickly?"

Bernard brightened. He sat up straight. Soon I heard a blow-by-blow account of how he had begun his diamond business from virtually nothing. He told the story well, with amusing detail. I listened raptly for the first fifteen minutes. As he continued talking without pause, I began shifting uncomfortably in my seat. When would this anecdote end?

Finally, Bernard leaned back, a contented expression on his face. "I have plans to leave the country," he confided. "There's a good chance of getting a visa to a country in South America. But first I want to find myself a wife." He paused, and then looked at me directly, adding, "Which I believe I'm going to find right here — in Antwerp!"

"That's nice," I said blandly.

On our walk back, Bernard talked animatedly. I listened, speaking very little. At my doorstep, he asked if he could see me again. For a moment, I hesitated. Then I said I was willing.

"Let's meet on Thursday, at the entrance to the borough hall. How's two o'clock?"

"That would be difficult," I told him. "I work at that time."

He looked puzzled. "You work?" Then he gave his head a little shake. "Oh, that's right. Something in a dentist's office." He nodded. "Then how about five-thirty, same place?"

"Sounds okay with me," I answered. I felt a certain weariness that I had never quite experienced before. Then I thanked him and said goodbye.

As soon as I walked into the salon, Mama bombarded me with questions. "How did it go? Where did he take you? Did you enjoy his company? He seems a nice enough young man."

Her violet eyes had a bright sheen to them. I hated to disappoint her. "He was pleasant," I ventured cautiously.

"So, *nu*," she said, tapping her foot, "do you think you'll be seeing him again?"

"Mama, he's so pale!" I blurted.

"I was also wondering about that," she said reflectively. Then she covered her mouth, as though sorry she had spoken.

Ah, so she had noticed, too. If I had liked him, I thought, I wouldn't have paid as much attention to this tiny flaw. But more to the point, if I was truly ready for marriage, perhaps I would not have judged him so harshly for monopolizing the conversation. My head began to ache.

"I don't want to see him again," I declared.

Mama frowned. "All because of a pallid complexion? That's ridiculous!"

I shook my head tiredly. "I just don't enjoy his company." It was difficult to articulate exactly what it was that didn't appeal to me, why I felt so lackluster and cheerless after our date.

Luckily, Mama made it easy for me. She patted my shoulder. "Well, that's another story. If he's not for you, you certainly don't have to go out again."

I breathed a sigh of relief. Then my eyes widened in dismay. I told Mama that I had already accepted a date with him.

"Why didn't you refuse in a nice way when he asked?" she reproached me.

I dropped my eyes. "I couldn't. I guess I was a coward. Please explain things and ask Reb Getzel to tell Bernard it's off."

Two days later, Mama reported that the matchmaker was furious and refused to relay the message. "He said that at this point it's an insult to the man. He urged you to keep the date since you had already accepted." She sighed and added, "He kept repeating what a stupid mistake you'd be making."

I looked aghast at Mama. I had discussed the situation with Helene, and she told me Bernard hadn't acted properly by asking me out directly. His behavior, she felt, had left me with no other course of action. In fact, Helene said most girls in my position would have done the same thing. No, I would not be cornered into seeing Bernard again. "You can tell Reb Getzel that as far as I'm concerned, the case is closed!"

Before the week was over, the *shadchan* visited our house again. He entered the salon, umbrella in hand, and eyed me sternly. "Against my better judgment, I informed Monsieur Bernard that you were unable to keep the date."

Next to me, Mama sighed with relief and thanked Reb Getzel. He accepted the glass of tea Mama offered him. "And now," he said, "let me tell you about this other young man. Believe me, this is an even more suitable match. I'll explain why."

While the matchmaker went on with his description, I listened with a sinking sensation. I waited until there was a pause and then plunged in, "Reb Getzel, I don't believe I'm interested in meeting anyone right now. This date was, well, a kind of experiment to see if I was ready. I don't think I am."

The matchmaker stared at me, bewildered. "What kind of talk is this? Not interested in meeting anyone? An experiment'? What is this fancy talk?"

I suddenly felt foolish. I lowered my eyes.

Mama said, "Please! Please, Reb Getzel. My daughter is really not ready. We must wait awhile."

"Wait?" Reb Getzel cried. His reddish-brown eyebrows shot up. "Wait till she gets old, maybe? That's very unwise. Everyone knows, men are like wine, but women are like milk; they do not get more desirable with age. And remember, there are no Jewish convents!"

By now I was getting angry. So I was milk already getting sour? I was going to spoil with age? I compared my sisters' appearance now to the way they had looked at twenty. Each of them seemed more beautiful, more vibrant. In fact, it was their husbands who looked the worse for wear, balding and aged. Julius had put on ten pounds, and Daniel's consumptive illness was wearing away at him. I bit my tongue so I would not argue with the *shadchan.* My mother was handling the situation well on her own.

She was saying appeasingly, "Naomi is still very young. I'm sure a short wait won't hurt her chances. Let's give her a bit more time."

At that, Reb Getzel arose from his chair. Utter indignation at Mama's suggestion was written all over his face. He pointed a long finger at me. "You're making a very big mistake, young lady." He marched out the door.

He had forgotten his umbrella, and I followed him. As he was buttoning his caftan, he muttered, "Just like my daughter was." He shook his head sadly. "Foolish and stubborn."

I held out his umbrella and said softly, "Your daughter also doesn't want to date just now?"

He frowned. "For years she kept telling me, 'Tatte, I have to be ready.' What foolishness! You meet a young man, I told her, and suddenly you're ready!"

"And how is your daughter today?" I persisted.

Reb Getzel looked abashed. "She's happily married," he admitted in a low voice, "and has three beautiful children." He put a hand over his heart. "Oh, but what aggravation she gave me, that one!"

At that, he tucked his umbrella under his arm with offended dignity and left. The door shut. I stood in the hallway, looking at Mama. Her eyes were big and solemn and shiny. I pressed my lips together. And then, suddenly, we were bent over, giggling helplessly like schoolgirls.

TRUE COLORS

Back at the laboratory, we were running out of *flacons* and awaiting a new shipment. Eric had placed the order a number of weeks before, but we'd heard nothing. Rather concerned, he went to the main post office and put through a phone call to the glass factory. The connection was bad, and he was told to write to the shipping department. A letter mailed twelve days ago remained unanswered.

Eric grumbled. "I'd like to know what's going on there. Up to now, deliveries never took more than one or two weeks."

"Is the factory far from here?" I asked.

"It's in Momignies, a small town near the French border," Eric's wife, Sarah, told me. "Quite a trip from Antwerp."

"Is it possible to leave and come back the same day?"

"Come to think of it, that is possible." Eric's face brightened. In no time, he'd unfolded a detailed map of Belgium on the table. He pointed with his index finger. "Look,

Naomi, here you have it — the town where the glass factory is located. It's in the Ardennes, the southernmost part of the Hainaut province." He turned excitedly to me. "Would you be willing to undertake the trip?"

I had studied that area in geography lessons at school, and I knew the ride there would be lovely. But before I could answer, Sarah burst out, "That's way too far for a young girl to travel alone."

The farthest I had ever traveled by myself was my round trip to Brussels. In the northern provinces the land was perenially flat, and I had always longed to see the hills and lush scenery of the Ardennes.

"I wouldn't mind making the trip," I said, and then added, "That is, if my mother approves."

Not surprisingly, my mother objected to my traveling such a distance by myself in German-occupied Belgium. But I was able to impress upon her how important this assignment was to Eric's business. "And I solemnly promise to be alert and extremely careful from beginning to end," I finished.

She answered, "I wish you wouldn't go. But if your help is so badly needed, I'll have to trust you and pray that God will watch over you every moment of this journey."

After that, Mama even helped me work out the itinerary so I'd be able to return the same day. Ever practical, she said, "You must take enough sandwiches along in case you get stranded and have to stay overnight."

"If that happens, there's no need to worry," I assured her. "Believe me, I can take care of myself."

Early Monday morning, I boarded the train and was on my way. A young woman and her child joined me in the second-class compartment. The two of them made an odd contrast: the daughter was fair-skinned with a headful of blond curls; the mother, olive-complexioned, with dark eyes, thick black brows, and black hair. Decidedly Semitic.

Soon after, a woman in her thirties sat down facing me. She wore a stylish dress, high-heeled shoes, and silk stockings. A gray felt hat with an ostrich plume completed her outfit. I couldn't help noticing the newspaper she carried — *De Flag,* a publication of the Flemish Nazi faction.

Other passengers joined our compartment. The scenery outside was more interesting now that we had passed Brussels and were approaching the Ardennes. There were winding brooks and rivulets and waterfalls descending from craggy cliffs. I stared enraptured at the green, rolling hills and terraced forests. I had never viewed such natural splendor. It filled me with awe and a sense of peace.

There was a blessing for seeing the ocean, I knew, one for witnessing lightning and thunder, and another for seeing a rainbow. Surely there had to be one for lovely scenery, but I didn't know of any.

The little blond girl at the window stood on tiptoe as she watched the fleeing landscape. "Mama, look! I see cows! I see horsies!" she cried excitedly.

"Yes, darling, that's right," the mother said, smiling.

"Oh, look! A mama duck with baby ducks!" The child squealed with delight, pointing at a pond.

Grins appeared on the faces of the passengers. The little girl was truly adorable. But I noted that the woman in the gray hat kept pursing her lips, staring fixedly at the mother and child. She made me nervous.

A woman sitting next to me exclaimed, "Look at that little girl! She's the cutest thing I've ever seen."

The gray-hatted woman sat up suddenly. Her eyes were blue and ice-cold. She said harshly, "So what? They're Jews — subhumans and parasites! For our own protection, even the tiniest bedbugs must be exterminated!"

I jerked in my seat. A chill went through me at her words. The other passengers clucked their tongues disapprovingly, but the woman continued loudly, "The Jews are the worst enemies of our fatherland! We've tolerated them far too long!" She pointed at the mother and child, who were staring fearfully at her, cringing in their seats. "We must rid ourselves of this scourge!" Her ostrich feather quivered from the impact of her outburst.

I felt sickened. By now, the child was sobbing quietly in the arms of her mother, who gently stroked her hair. Suddenly I was no longer afraid that those in the compartment might suspect that I, too, was Jewish. I cried out, "Lies! You're repeating nothing but the trumped-up, vicious lies you've been fed! It's people like you who poison it for everyone!"

The woman stared at me blankly. She seemed taken aback by my outburst. Just then, the train slowed to a stop. The woman stood up with her newspaper tucked under her arm. She hissed, "The time is coming when every true Fleming shall wake up and worship the *Führer. Heil Hitler!*"

Then she was gone. Long after she had left and the collective muttering in the train had abated I trembled and had trouble swallowing. My tongue seemed paralyzed. Had that been *me* shouting back at the woman? Quiet little Naomi? I wondered at my fearlessness.

My head was pounding. I leaned back and tried to blot the scene from my mind. When the train approached Chimay, I realized we were in chateau country. From the window, I glimpsed grandiose castles dating from centuries past. Their towers and turrets rose majestically from manicured lawns. But the scene no longer filled me with pleasure. It reminded me of my pro-Nazi fellow citizens. It was small comfort that most of the passengers had disapproved of that one Nazi sympathizer. Perhaps the woman was right: soon every Fleming would be worshipping at the altar of Hitler.

At last I switched trains at Chimay and caught the old rickety local for Momignies. The wooden, third-class benches were certainly not built with the travelers' comforts in mind. Although it was only a short ride, the rocking and jolting left me frazzled.

When I arrived at the glass factory, the foreman brought me into the administrative office. I introduced myself to Monsieur Clement, head of the shipping department, and handed him Eric's letter. He opened the envelope, leaned back in his leather chair, and read the contents. His brow wrinkled.

"Ah, you must understand," he said, "we no longer have access to all the raw materials the way we once did. We cannot produce the blue glass for your *flacon*s anymore." His eyes clouded. "I sincerely regret that we're unable to fill your order."

Was that the problem? The color of the glass? I said, "Couldn't you make the *flacon*s in a different color? Brown, for instance?"

Monsieur Clement sat up straight. His face brightened. "Brown, did you say? Now there's an idea." He drummed his fingers on the desk. "Well! If you're willing to settle for dark-brown glass, then we could still do business."

"Dark-brown *flacons* will do just fine," I said without hesitation.

"Very good, mademoiselle," he replied energetically. "In that case, you can expect our shipment in a few days."

With my mission accomplished, I headed back for the train station. It seemed clear that I would make it back to Antwerp by nightfall. I smiled to think how quickly and simply the *flacon* problem had been resolved. Eric and Sarah would be proud. My headache was gone, and now my stomach was growling. I took some food out of my bag and ate with gusto. For dessert, I munched on an apple that Mama had furtively added, along with a pear. The fruit was an unexpected treat.

Exactly on schedule, the locomotive tore into the station. With screeching brakes, the train was brought to a halt; but the hissing of the steam engine and the belching of the smokestack continued until the local puffed out of Momignies. At Charleroi, I switched to the express for Brussels and settled down on a window seat. Everything was going perfectly according to schedule. I was glad when nobody sat opposite me. I reclined in my seat and quickly dozed off.

The voice over the loudspeaker woke me. I sat up with a start, blinking. Outside it was pitch dark. "Ladies and gentlemen," the voice blared. "We will soon arrive in Brussels. The train will stop for three minutes at the *Gare du Midi*, then continue to Antwerp's *Gare Centrale*." The announcer paused briefly. "Attention! Attention! Because of the curfew, Jews on this train are forbidden to travel past Brussels at this hour!"

I rubbed my eyes and groaned. I had forgotten about the

curfew, and so had Mama. This unexpected development shocked me and filled me with apprehension. As soon as the train stopped at the *Gare du Midi* I prepared to get off, unsure of where to go. A middle-aged, conservatively dressed man smiled at me and remarked, "Ah, you're Jewish, too."

It seemed I had little in common with the man, but I felt that special camaraderie of a Jew meeting up with a fellow Jew in the midst of one's travels.

"Yes, I am," I replied. "I live in Antwerp."

"You're getting off? I suppose that's the safest thing to do. But where are you going to spend the night in Brussels?"

I shrugged. "I'll get a room in a hotel, hopefully nearby."

The man lowered his voice. "Just be careful. The hotels around here aren't exactly respectable."

It wouldn't bother me if the hotel wasn't elegant, as long as it was clean and one could sit somewhere and drink a cup of coffee. Those weeks that I had been on the road with Mama, Leon, and Benny, sleeping in barns and ramshackle rooms, had lessened my standard of luxury by quite a bit. I looked at the man. "What about you? Where will you be staying?" I asked.

"I'll take my chances. I'm staying on the train," he said, his voice still lowered. As I made my way past him, he repeated, "You be careful! A girl alone at night — especially around here. *Bonne chance!"*

I felt like saying, "Sir, perhaps you should worry more about yourself. Riding past curfew! You could easily get caught, you know!"

As I walked along the dimly lit streets, I seemed to remember hushed rumors about big-city station districts where certain hotels housed unsavory characters. Decent people shunned these areas like the plague. Was I getting too sure of myself, thinking I could handle every situation? Perhaps that Jewish man was not just being unduly protective. I wondered...

Le Rossignol was a small hotel on Brussels's Place de la Gare. It seemed more up-to-date and cleaner than the taverns on the side streets. I walked in and approached a waiter who was serving beer to three German soldiers.

"You'll have to see the *patronne*, Madame Sidonie, about a room," he said, pointing. "That's her over there, standing near the bar."

Madame Sidonie was a rather broad-shouldered woman in her forties, her hair dyed a reddish-blond. Her manner was friendly and efficient. "I have a vacancy one flight up," she told me when I explained that I needed lodging for the night. "It's a nice room. You'll just have to wait down here while the chambermaid changes the linens."

After I signed the register and paid my bill in advance, I stood looking around, at a loss about where to sit down. Besides Madame Sidonie, a waitress, and two young women with their dates for the evening, I was the only female in the busy restaurant.

Madame Sidonie walked over and said, "Come with me."

I followed her to a small table near a window. She invited me to sit down, then moved the café curtains aside so that I had a good view of the square. Soon I noticed that people walking by outside had an even better view of me.

The ersatz coffee I had ordered was served. I had thought of washing my hands and eating one of Mama's sandwiches at the table, but I changed my mind. Passersby kept eyeing me, and I became anxious to get out of the showcase and eat my sandwich in the privacy of my room.

Before I could finish the coffee, a *Wehrmacht* soldier approached my table. He clicked his heels together, saluted in military fashion, and said in fluent French, "Mademoiselle, would you care to join me for dinner?" He smiled — a smile that was more frightening than the gun worn at his hip.

My hand trembled so much that I had to put my coffee cup down. For an endless moment, I sat motionless, staring. With great effort, I managed to stammer, "Uh...I...my coffee. I must finish it first..."

"In that case, I expect you in five minutes," he replied. He pointed at his wristwatch. "Five minutes from now. In the vestibule, mademoiselle. *A bientot!*"

I sat, trembling in my seat, though all I really wanted was to get up, flee the restaurant, and never, ever see that man or the hotel again. But the man's words so benumbed my brain, I could not think clearly. His words struck me with the impact of an order that one could not possibly disobey. Tears sprang into my eyes. I was gripped with a sense of panic and felt totally powerless. Of all possible situations, this was one I had not foreseen.

Suddenly Madame Sidonie stood in front of me. With her face close to mine she whispered, "You don't have to go with that *Kraut!*"

I looked at her through my tears. "How can I escape? He's waiting for me in the vestibule near the stairs. What should I do?" I moaned helplessly.

"Come, I'll take you to your room. It's ready. We'll use the back stairway. Let's go!"

As if in a dream, I followed Madame Sidonie through a back entrance to the second floor of the hotel. She unlocked the door and switched the light on in my room.

I locked the door, as if to shut out the image of the soldier. My head whirled, and my breath came in short gasps. Madame Sidonie sat down beside me and put a hand on my shaking shoulders. "Don't worry, he cannot get you now."

Shuddering, I sat up on the edge of the bed. With the back of my hand, I wiped away the tears. "Thank you, madame," I said weakly. "You've been so kind to me, and I'm deeply grateful. I can't explain why I became so intimidated, so completely helpless, confronting that German officer. Usually I know how to take care of myself just fine." I bit down on my lip. "And now I acted like a frightened goose."

"You mustn't blame yourself," she said soothingly. "You were exhausted and weak from a long trip. Those bullies make it their job to prey on unsuspecting innocents like yourself." She stood up and headed for the door. With her hand on the doorknob, she turned to me and said: "This much I can tell you, my girl. In the beginning, the invaders behaved like gentlemen toward the population. But now they're showing their true colors. From my ringside seat, I've watched them become more brazen and cruel by the day. And if you ask me, things will get much worse before they'll ever get better!"

I double-locked the door after Madame Sidonie left. Too tired to get organized for the night, I kicked off my shoes and stretched out on the bed to rest for a short while.

The pale rays of the climbing sun invaded my hotel room at dawn and woke me. It took me a few moments to remember where I was. Then I realized that the heavy window curtains had not been drawn, that I had fallen asleep and slept through the night on top of the blankets, fully dressed.

A few hours later, safely on board a train to Antwerp, I reviewed the events of the past twenty-four hours. On the ride to Momignies, I had seen firsthand how the Flemish were capable of acting toward Jews. Insidious anti-Semitism was gradually becoming part of the national outlook. On the way back, I had come face to face with the arrogance and outrage every civilian — both Jew and non-Jew — had to suffer at the hands of the Nazi invaders, that self-appointed "master race." My half-hour of success at Momignies hardly seemed to justify the ordeal of the trip! I was terribly shaken by those ugly encounters.

The thirty-minute ride from Brussels to Antwerp seemed to last an eternity. By the time I saw Mama, at ten in the morning, I'd composed myself so that she wouldn't detect any of the tumult I had undergone. What good was there in unnecessarily agitating her? However, I couldn't help holding my mother a bit longer than I usually did. "I missed you," I said in a muffled voice, my face buried in her slender shoulder.

At one-thirty that afternoon, I was once again ringing the doorbell at the house on the Henri Conscience Straat. Madame Rabstein let me in, as always, with a smile. Sarah and Eric were just finishing their lunch. They rose enthusiastically to greet me. How good it felt to be in this familiar setting, surrounded by people I could trust. I explained to both of them why the *flacon* shipment had been delayed and how I'd arranged with the head of the shipping department to substitute brown ones.

"The order should be arriving in a few days," I concluded.

"Well done!" Eric exclaimed, nodding approvingly. He turned to Sarah and said triumphantly, "I told you she could do it! You were betting she was too young to go out there alone, that she wasn't capable enough."

Sarah covered her eyes in mock shame. "I admit defeat," she said, then smiled apologetically to me. "You see, I think of you as Evelyn's tag-along baby sister. Remember how she used to take you with her on our walks?"

I nodded, grinning. "How could I ever forget?" Evelyn, my eldest sister, had always adopted a protective attitude toward me, the baby sister. More than anyone else, she took me along with her when she went somewhere. I suppose that was how her friends had perceived me — a little girl in need of protection.

Sarah continued, "I didn't realize how much you'd grown up since then. You've become a person in your own right."

I laughed off Sarah's earlier misjudgment of me and said, "Oh, well, I'll forgive you this time." Inside, however, I was churning with strong and conflicting emotions. I felt as if I had finally arrived, recognized for my worth by a peer of Evelyn's. It was truly a wonderful moment, one that confirmed my strength and individuality.

At the same time, I was still shaken with self-doubt. This trip, if anything, had pointed out my limitations. I had been overly confident and had dismissed my fellow Jewish passenger's sound advice regarding the respectability of the hotels. I was not as self-sufficient as I'd thought. I still had some growing up to do. That much was certain.

ENTANGLEMENTS

A week later, the shipment of brown *flacons* arrived. As soon as the remaining Dentracine was bottled, it was sent to Eric's agent in Brussels.

"I'm going to prepare one more batch," Eric announced. "Naomi, you'll be responsible for bottling it after Sarah and I are gone."

I looked up in surprise. "Are you leaving?"

"It's time for us to set out for Portugal," Eric explained. "We must arrange our passage to Buenos Aires from Lisbon before our visas expire."

I had known all along that my job with Eric would not be permanent. Even so, I was upset to hear that the end was so near. I was losing a job I thoroughly enjoyed; but even more painful was the sense of abandonment I felt as people I liked kept departing and leaving me behind.

I had learned from Evelyn that Sarah and Eric had been

married in The Hague, Holland, shortly after the armistice. They came to Antwerp in transit to South America. At their request, Evelyn had rented a temporary apartment for them from Madame Rabstein. As planned, Eric had manufactured a supply of Dentracine here, which his agent in Brussels would distribute in due time.

"Next week, God willing, we'll be on our way," Eric continued. "And you, Naomi, will be in charge of winding up our business here. For as long as that takes, you'll continue to receive your present salary."

I stared at him incredulously. "Do you think I can handle this whole business by myself?"

"Absolutely!" Eric cheerfully replied. "This afternoon, you'll meet my accountant. He'll stand by to help should any problem arise. And he will pay your weekly salary."

I felt relieved. Between the agent in Brussels and the accountant, the responsibility would not fall on my shoulders alone.

Before his departure, Eric advised me to do the bottling and packaging in the improvised lab. "You'll find everything you need there," he said. "And the rent for the suite is paid up till the end of February — still more than two weeks off. That should give you ample time to clean up after you're finished."

The day after they left, I rang the bell at the house on the Henri Conscience Straat. Madame Rabstein opened the door. I noticed at once that her pleasant smile was missing.

"What do you want here?" she asked curtly. "My tenants have moved out."

I was bewildered by her change in tone. "Why, Madame Rabstein," I said, looking at her in astonishment, "I'm supposed to finish the job of bottling their product upstairs. Those were my orders from your tenants."

"That's too bad," she said in a sharp voice. "Since those people are gone, you can't come into my house!"

"But the rent is paid up for the entire month! Today is only the fourteenth."

"Let me give it to you straight," she hissed, a hand on each hip. "I don't want you messing with that smelly stuff anymore." Her eyebrows drew together harshly. "The terrible odor has spread through our entire house. Even my children's clothing smells, and their classmates make fun of them. I want all of that stinking goo out of here, do you understand?"

Her rising fury made her face burn. I stared at her, open-mouthed. I couldn't believe that this was the same sweet landlady who'd always let me in with a warm smile.

She raged on, "I'll let you take the whole paraphernalia out of here — if you're quick about it. Otherwise, it will end up in the garbage!"

I found my voice. "Don't throw it out!" I shouted back at her. "I'll come and take it! Soon!"

In my bewilderment, I turned around and started running homeward, without a clue as to where I would bring all the lab equipment and who would help me move it.

Back at our house, Mama listened patiently to my tale of woe. "In my opinion, that Madame Rabstein is a real hypocrite!" I concluded bitterly.

"All right," Mama said, "I understand how you feel, but calling names isn't going to solve your problem." She folded her arms. "First of all, you're going to need a place to put everything." She paused, considering. "I know. Our first-floor back room isn't rented. You could use that room in the meantime."

It was a fabulous idea. Why hadn't it occurred to me? "Could I?" I cried gratefully, throwing my arms around her. Then, without further delay, I got in touch with Helene's younger brother. He rented a pushcart, and the next morning, we transported the contents of Eric's lab to our house.

We returned home by way of the Lange Kievit Straat, which was the heart of Antwerp's Jewish quarter. Since the trouble began, I had avoided going near there for months. Still, I little expected to find the area practically deserted. Most of the stores were abandoned. Compared to the crowds that used to bustle to and fro, there now seemed nothing more than a trickle of people moving along the street.

Well, what else had I expected to find? It made sense that whoever was able to would have fled the Jewish quarter after the riots that took place there last spring. A feeling of despair swelled inside me. Slowly, my neighborhood, my town, my country, were disintegrating into something alien and frightening.

For a while, we walked behind two Jewish men, one of them bearded. All at once, two German soldiers approached from the opposite direction. They stopped short, facing the two pedestrians.

"Remove those hats!" they bellowed.

The frightened men obeyed. The next instant, both soldiers forcefully slapped their faces and strutted off, guffawing. The two Jews stood there, faces stunned and shoulders bent like whipped animals.

I could hardly bear to look at them, to witness the

humiliation of these two grown men — my fellow Jews. Helene's brother and I glanced at each other. He seemed ill. I swallowed hard to resist a fit of nausea. The Nazi's satanic laughter kept ringing in my ears. We hurried down the street with our pushcart. We couldn't get away fast enough!

With the young fellow's help, I was soon settled in the back room, one flight up. When I reported my unexpected move to Eric's accountant, he insisted on paying Mama rent for the room. So my moving turned out to be beneficial on all sides.

True to his methodical self, Eric had left me a list with instructions and guidelines to facilitate my task. Among other things, I was instructed to add a specific amount of magnesia to the Dentracine mixture in the bowl before filling the *flacons*. When I was about to weigh the white powder, I noticed that the scale wasn't working well.

As I started down my half-flight of stairs, I saw Elie Tischler coming out of his jewelry workshop. I had not seen him in ages. Since he only came to our house during working hours, we rarely met. But now we stood face to face on the small mezzanine landing.

"Well, hello," he said in a hearty tone. "What an unexpected pleasure. I was wondering if you still live here."

"My job kept me away from home a great deal," I explained. "But from now on, I'll be working here in the back room."

He grinned. "That's wonderful. We'll be neighbors."

Halfway down the main flight of stairs, I stopped short, turned to him, and said, "You know what? There's a neighborly good deed you can do for me. I'm having trouble with my scale. Maybe you could look at it."

"Gladly," Elie said.

Back in the lab, Elie took one look at the scale and exclaimed, "This thing must be a genuine antique!" He removed the copper pans from both sides and examined the weighing mechanism. "It needs regulating. Let me get my tools," he said, and stepped out of the room.

Elie returned two minutes later and went to work with a screwdriver and wrench. Then he picked up the scale and set it on the mantelpiece, where he kept testing it. His fingers moved nimbly, displaying the touch of a master craftsman. "*Voilà!*" he called. "Aside from the adjustment, it needed a more level surface than your table. Now the weight should be exact."

"You sure are an expert. I was really stuck. Thanks loads! I wish there was a way I could repay you."

We were standing near the mantelpiece. "Perhaps there is," Elie said. "How about a date tomorrow night?"

"I...I can't," I said.

"Please," he pleaded. "I want to get to know you."

Silently, I shook my head.

"Why not?" he persisted.

"My mother doesn't approve of our meeting. She would forbid it."

"And you?" he asked. "What do you want to do?"

My good sense told me: This situation is absurd. There is no future here. I said awkwardly, "For you, this is simply a date. But for me, I have to consider each person I meet in the light of marriage." I paused, looking directly at him. "Our paths are different. Our goals are not the same. I was brought up in the strictest faith, to marry a religious man, to raise children in an atmosphere of Torah. To deny my beliefs would never make me happy."

As I spoke, the words took hold of me, and I became filled with the firmest conviction. This wasn't an easy thing to do, but it was the right thing.

Elie said quietly, "Sometimes differences can be overcome."

I shook my head. "It would never work. I was meant for a different life. This is what my Papa would have wished and what I wish for myself."

With a touch of impatience, Elie said, "What do those things matter when two people care for each other?"

I fell silent, my head lowered. Just then, an old Yiddish saying popped into my head. "A bird and a fish can fall in love," I offered, "but where will they make their home?"

Elie's eyes widened, and then he laughed. "You've got a point there, I must confess. I will respect your wishes. I won't trouble you any further."

I watched him leave the room, glad I'd found the strength to reject him. Life was complex enough without the wrong kind of entanglements!

The third week of February 1942, unusually cold winter weather descended on Antwerp. One day, the doorbell rang, clanging repeatedly, with an urgency that made me run out of my workroom and bolt down the stairs. I found Michael and Sabine standing on the doorstep, shivering in the frigid air. Sabine wore a sweater thrown hastily over an old housecoat. Michael's shirt was partly ripped, and the pockets of his pants were hanging out. Without uttering a word, they rushed past me to the family room.

"What happened to you?" I cried, following them.

Michael plunked down on the sofa, and Sabine began pacing the floor. Just then, Mama entered the room. Seeing her son and his wife in disheveled clothes, obviously shaken and dazed, she gasped.

"You both look as though you've escaped from some nightmarish scene. What kind of ordeal have you been through?"

Sabine's eyes filled with tears. She hid her face from my mother for a moment. "It was terrifying," she said hoarsely. "The Gestapo forced their way into our apartment with drawn handguns. They frisked us, then searched all our closets. They pulled out every drawer and kept barking at us, 'Where did you hide them? You better tell us! Where are the diamonds?' "

Michael sat up slowly on the sofa. "They grabbed the stones from my worktable. But that didn't satisfy those hoodlums. The two of them went through everything in the house. They left the place in a shambles," he groaned.

"I thought they'd never leave," Sabine went on with a barely suppressed sob. "Finally, on their way out, they bellowed, `We'll be back! And next time we're not leaving until we find all your illegal diamonds!' "

The silence in the room grew oppressive. Michael broke the stillness. "Those gangsters will be back. They've got my address. The time may be ripe," he mused aloud, "to escape to the unoccupied French zone like so many have already done."

"What about the decree of February 7th?" I asked. "Jews are forbidden to leave the country. Now it's illegal for Belgian

Jews to cross into occupied France."

"Of course it is," Michael replied. "But I think I know a smuggler I can trust to take us safely across both borders: the Belgian-French one and the demarcation line into Vichy, France. His name is —"

"Just a minute," Mama interrupted. She walked over to the door, opened it, and looked around. "We should remember, even the walls have ears." She returned to her chair. "All right, let's hear it now."

Michael proceeded in a lower tone. "Jules Baron used to be a diamond cleaver like myself. For some time now he's been going back and forth, bringing people to the south of France. I've been told he's an excellent guide — the best there is."

Mama took a deep breath. "This will take careful planning."

Michael agreed. "We should have a family council with Evelyn and Daniel and have Jules Baron sit in on it." As he went into further details, the irony struck me: Michael and Sabine had voluntarily left the Free French zone, only to plot now how to best arrange their return.

As they got up to leave, Mama and I escorted them to the door. A thought suddenly occurred to me in the hallway. "All your money is invested in diamonds. How come the Gestapo didn't find them in your apartment?"

A huge smile appeared on Michael and Sabine's faces. My brother turned gratefully to her. "I thank my wife for that. It was her idea to put our stones on the upper ledge of the door frame. It's only two centimeters wide, but there's room for a fortune in diamonds up there."

"We got away with it today," Sabine remarked soberly.

"Next time we may not be so lucky. Michael is right. It's time to get out of here!"

My sister-in-law's words echoed inside me long after she left. Until recently, talk of escape had been taboo in our family. Whenever things became intolerable, we just held our breaths until the danger passed and conditions eased. Now, suddenly, I saw our situation with a clarity that frightened me. We were sitting ducks on a minefield that could explode at any second. We could no longer take comfort in our nice house, the black-market food, and the life of small pleasures we had constructed for ourselves. It was time to act!

I thought of Willie and Bertha Haas and wondered how they fared. We'd heard of their safe arrival in Vichy, France. Did they manage to buy visas to enter a South American country? Were they able to emigrate? I wished I could find out.

Jules Baron came to our family meeting a few days after the diamond raid. Evelyn and Daniel, Michael and Sabine, and Mama and myself sat around our large dining-room table. Monsieur Baron stood at the head of it, where he spread open a map. He detailed the various border crossings, the guides, or "*passeurs,*" who would take us across, and the methods he used to avoid nightly raids by the Gestapo in occupied France. "We're leaving in another week," he informed us. "You're allowed only one bag each to remain as inconspicuous as possible for the entire trip."

When he mentioned "one bag," I looked at Mama. Her face had blanched, and her hands tightly gripped the table.

"The decision is yours to make," Monsieur Baron stated. "I'm only here to tell you that if you want to flee I've got the safest route any guide could come up with at this time." He rolled up his map. On his way out, he said, "I cannot let you have more than twenty-four hours to reach a decision. I've got a waiting list. Because Michael is my friend, I gave you priority."

After he left, a long silence filled the room.

Michael sat with his head buried in his hands. "Maybe we've been too hasty about this escape plan," he said finally. "Things have become quiet again. I've concluded that the Gestapo won't think it's worthwhile to pay us another visit."

Sabine said soberly, "The danger we'll be facing on this trip is probably far greater than what Jules Baron would have us believe."

Michael nodded. "I agree. Besides, the diamond trade has picked up again. The trouble seems to be over, and there's still money to be made in Antwerp. We can always decide to escape later on."

One by one, I listened to each member of the family retract from the idea of fleeing Belgium.

Daniel coughed heavily, and I saw Evelyn cast her husband a worried look. As of late, his pulmonary tuberculosis had worsened. I expected to hear some words of wisdom from Daniel. To my disappointment, he said, "We'd have to leave everything behind, all that we've worked for our entire lives. What's more, I'm not sure I have the physical stamina to undertake this journey."

Mama exclaimed, "One bag to take with me, he said. Just one bag!" She heaved a deep sigh and moaned, "And how could I possibly abandon this house? It represents everything I cherish!"

Evelyn put an arm around her. "Oh, Mama, if we must

escape to save our lives, then a house should mean nothing. It's just a structure made of bricks and cement."

Inwardly I applauded Evelyn's words. They were the first I'd heard that made any sense to me. But I continued to listen and keep quiet. In the presence of my oldest sister and brother, voicing my opinion was of no use whatsoever. In their eyes, I was still the baby, someone whose ideas could not be taken seriously. It didn't matter how much I might have achieved in the eyes of others.

Mama stiffened in disappointment and pain. "How can you say that about our house — 'a structure of bricks and cement'? This house is full of mementoes and precious memories of my happy life with Papa. When I'm here, I feel his presence in every room." Overcome with emotion, she said in a husky voice, "This is the house where I gave birth to my children, the home that makes me relive all the years of their growing up. Antwerp may never see another family as beautiful as we were!" Mama bit her lower lip as she tried to force back the tears. "Believe me, it would hurt too much to tear myself away from my roots."

Later, after I absorbed what Mama had said, I wondered how she ever had the strength to flee Antwerp when the Germans had begun bombing two years before. Perhaps that's what it would take now — the undeniable fact of explosives and bombs — to uproot her from her beloved home. Apparently, the situation of the Jews was too volatile and ambiguous to inspire any clear-cut action in her and all of our family.

Unlike Michael, I did not feel that the situation would blow over. This quiet interval was simply a Nazi tactic to lull us into a false sense of security. We had to flee. But like Michael and the rest of the family, I was frightened. When Jules Baron had brought out the map and spoken about the various crossings and the nightly raids, it had all seemed too real, too imminent. One week was not enough time to accustom myself to the realities of escape.

Meanwhile, life went on as usual. Eric's accountant came to fetch the last *flacons* of Dentracine. I had bottled the final shipment of the dental compound; the time had arrived to close up the business. Even so, the accountant decided to pay rent for our room through the following month and to include pay for March and April in my paycheck.

"You've done a good job, mademoiselle," he told me. "Eric wanted you to receive a bonus."

I thanked him profusely. The extra money would come in handy; that much was certain. The accountant offered to send someone over who would buy all the equipment I no longer needed, too — the Etna burner, scale, bowls, and leftover *flacons*.

The following day the man came and bought all the paraphernalia. Afterwards, Mama and I worked hard on the back room, converting it back into the bedroom it used to be. We aired out the odor of Dentracine and set the beds in their former places. My mother was soon able to rent the room to a young woman, a Polish Jew, who had come looking for a place to stay.

Suddenly, I was no longer a laboratory assistant and a working girl. I was back to square one.

THE YELLOW STAR

Spring had finally come, and the lilacs were in bloom. Our new tenant, Sofia, a woman in her thirties, asked if she could cut some down from our tree.

I had grown close to our Polish boarder. Because of the curfew, our evenings were long and boring. Sofia often joined Mama and me in the family room at night. I'd serve tea, and sometimes we played checkers, dominoes, or a game of lotto. After Mama went up to bed, Sofia and I would speak for hours about all kinds of matters. It was wonderful having someone I could talk to freely. Since she was not fluent in French or Flemish, we communicated in Yiddish.

Sofia worked at Beth Lechem, the soup kitchen established by EZRA — a Jewish, communal social service that provided help to the poor and disabled. Beth Lechem functioned under the direction of the *Judenrat,* as did the Jewish Association of Midwives, the Hebrew Loan Fund, and the societies of child and nursing care.

"It's my good fortune," Sofia told me cheerfully with her infectious smile. "Besides getting paid, I am guaranteed a proper meal every day."

I admired her good spirits. Despite having to fend for herself in a country where she didn't speak the language, not once had I heard a complaint cross her lips. I, on the other hand, had grown a bit morose lately, with too much time on my hands and too many bad thoughts crowding my mind.

Sofia's request for flowers brought me out of my self-absorption. Together we walked into the garden. I took the ladder from the shed, and, using a sharp kitchen knife, Sofia gathered a large bouquet of the fragrant lavender blossoms.

While I supported the somewhat shaky ladder, I told her how every spring, in years past, at least a half-dozen neighbors used to ring our bell, asking for some of our gorgeous lilacs. They would walk away with big armfuls and warm thanks, delighted with the flowers. I sighed, adding wistfully, "But that was before the war, in a different world, when our neighbors were our friends."

I was in a particularly low mood that day. Michael had come by with a form letter he'd received. The letter, sent to all the *diamantairs,* was typewritten on official military government stationery. It announced the complete closing down of Antwerp's diamond industry by May 31, 1942.

Michael read on: "All remaining diamonds must immediately be sold through the intermediary, Monsieur Walter Frantzig, who will arrange the transactions. Polished diamonds will be sold to Antwerp's Diamond Office at a price determined by that office." He lowered the letter. "You can assume," he said bitterly, "the seller will be paid a mere fraction of what the merchandise is worth."

I understood Michael's bitterness. He had passed up a chance to escape, thinking that everything would blow over and that the diamond trade was booming. It was becoming harder and harder to sustain hope that life would revert back to normal. Still, there was no more talk in our house of escape to the unoccupied French zone. It was as if Jules Baron had never existed.

After I helped Sofia with the flowers, I lazed around in my bedroom reading the *Nieuwe Gazet*, a daily paper with its quota of Nazi propaganda. Now that I was no longer working, I had plenty of time to read. The paper provided the latest update regarding the laws and ordinances against Jews and reinforced the old ordinances forbidding Jews to go to parks, frequent cafés or movie houses, or shop in department stores. Nowadays, I was so well informed that people came to me to ask what was going on. As much as possible I tried to spare Mama, keeping hurtful information from her.

Today's paper proclaimed that any Jew six years of age or older would be forbidden to appear in public without wearing the Star of David. This six-pointed yellow star, with the black *J* in the middle, was to be sewn onto the upper left side of the outer garment and had to be clearly visible.

Trembling, I put down the paper. This decree, it was true, came as no surprise. Nazi delegates had been discussing the matter of initiating the Jewish star for some time but had decided against the idea because the populace was not "ripe" for it. The chief military commander had declared, "The regulation might evoke compassion in the hearts of an otherwise indifferent population."

But now, the ordinance had been passed. Apparently, the Nazi powers had determined that the population's indifference had hardened to the point of utter rigidity. It was this assessment of the Belgian civilians that sent chills through me. As much as anti-Semitism had crept into the country, was it possible that an entire people could have stopped up any crack of compassion and humanity left inside them?

Because of certain delays, the yellow star was not dispensed until June 1, 1942. On that day, the stars were to be picked up at the auditoriums of three designated schools.

The first time Mama and I walked down the street wearing our yellow stars, I felt everyone's eyes on us. The words of the prophet Balaam crossed my mind: "The Hebrew people shall stand alone among the nations," words he had intended as a curse but had been transformed into a blessing. Hadn't Leon told me that *kedushah,* holiness, meant being separate, designated for a higher purpose? I had always experienced this separation as a sign of elevated distinction. But now our being set apart from others felt like a black curse and nothing else.

"Oh, Mama, let's go back home," I implored. "People keep staring."

"No," she replied, her head held high. "We mustn't feel embarrassed to be identified by our religion. We've always been proud of our heritage." Her eyes flashed. "Let those who plan to humiliate us be ashamed!"

No doubt Mama was every bit as self-conscious as I was, but I appreciated her stoic front. As we continued walking, I attempted to hold my handbag so that it covered the star. However, my ruse didn't work, as it was sewn too high. As we returned home, I told myself firmly that I'd just have to come to terms with wearing the Jewish star. I promised myself not to let it upset me anymore.

One afternoon, on my way to visit my friend Helene, I ran into a group of women. They had worked a shift at the De Beukelaer chocolate factory on the Lange Kievit Straat and were coming up our street. All of them stopped, blocking the sidewalk in front of me. When they eyed my star, they started to jeer.

"Hah! Look at her!" a heavyset woman shrieked. "Your time has come! You Jews had it too good. All that's changing, dearie!"

A tall, spindly woman chimed in, "You said it, Emma! We've had to slave all these years at the plant, while those Jews were living in luxury!"

I stood, riveted to the pavement. Biting my lip, I forced back the tears that welled up.

"It's good to see them get theirs," a third, younger woman burst out. "You just wait. Hitler's gonna take good care of you!"

I turned around and darted across the street. Once on the opposite sidewalk, I let the tears stream down my cheeks.

In Helene's home, I plunked down on a chair and spilled the story of this vicious encounter. With a grim expression, my friend said, "If ever we had to be strong, now is the time! And if I were you, Naomi, I wouldn't breathe a word of this to your mother."

For two days I didn't step out of the house. The hate-filled faces of the factory workers kept rising up in my mind's eye, making me cringe. Their malevolent prophecies echoed in my ears. How could I set foot outdoors again? I immersed myself in reading Victor Hugo's *Les Miserables* and became so engrossed in the book that I couldn't stop reading until I reached the end.

Then, one afternoon, Mama came to my room. "We need bread and milk. And we're low on rice and other groceries." She handed me money and some papers. "Here's a list and our ration stamps. Please, Naomi, go to the store."

It was now or never. I couldn't spend the entire summer holed up in my bedroom.

It was a balmy day, and with the first breath of fresh air I felt invigorated. I decided to take a walk before going shopping. Since I had finished *Les Miserables*, it occurred to me that I could use new reading material. I fetched the book and strolled toward the public library on the Rue des Aveugles. This was in the vicinity of the *Academie des Beaux Arts*. It seemed ages since I had been a student there, but actually less than one and a half years had elapsed.

A young man carrying several books came down the steps of the library. He stared at me and I winced. How long would it take for my Jewish star to stop attracting attention? I tried to hurry past him.

"Hey!" he cried out. "Don't you remember me? Let's see... You're Naomi, aren't you?"

I stopped and looked at the young fellow. He did seem familiar, but I was unable to place him. Before I could ask his name, he said, "I'm Rene Janssen. We were together in Raymond Delbeau's class at the academy."

I gave my forehead a light slap. "Oh, of course!" I exclaimed. "Professor Delbeau." Briefly, I wondered what had happened to my art teacher and whether he was still a Nazi sympathizer.

"Sorry for not recognizing you," I apologized to my former classmate. "To tell you the truth, when you kept staring, I figured you were just amused at seeing my star, like everyone else."

Rene shifted his books from one arm to the other. He shook his head. "Not at all, Naomi. I think it's a real shame to make you wear that. Outrageous! I feel bad for you and your people. And if I could help in any way, I gladly would."

His words lifted my spirits. Apparently, not all Belgians were indifferent to our plight. I thanked him.

He glanced down at the book in my hands. "Say, were you going to the library?"

I nodded.

"I don't think you'd better go in there," he told me soberly. "If you give me your card, I'll take out some books for you."

I stared at him, and then his words registered. I must have missed that bit of news in the *Nieuwe Gazet*. Libraries were also off-limits to Jews.

"You could return the book for me," I said finally, "but I guess I won't be taking out any new books for now. Thanks a lot, Rene." I handed him *Les Miserables* with a sigh.

Just before he started up the stairs toward the library, Rene turned to me. "I was wondering if you could help me with something," he said.

"Sure," I replied, pleased and mystified at the same time. It was not a good feeling to always have to depend on others for kindnesses. If there was a favor I could do for Rene, I would be happy to do it. But of what possible service could I be to him now?

He continued, "I'm collecting Nazi paraphernalia. I've got

a swastika armband and other stuff. It'll be historical evidence after the war, you know. Would you have an extra yellow star for my collection?"

My mouth dropped. His request astonished me. "Well, uh, they issued only two stars to each person," I said awkwardly. "I don't really have a spare one right now."

Rene shrugged a shoulder. "Oh, that's all right. Somehow I'll get hold of one before the war is over. It's going to take time, you know, but have no fear — with the Americans on our side, the Third Reich is as good as kaput!" With that, he bounded up the stairs.

I watched him go, smiling somewhat ruefully. He was a well-meaning fellow, but, sympathetic as he was, he had no idea of what we Jews were going through. To have made that odd request was like asking someone who'd been shot and wounded if he could keep the bullet as a souvenir. To him, the star was simply an interesting museum piece. For me it was a stigma, a source of isolation, pain, and possible danger.

I turned down an alleyway, did my shopping, and went back home, hoping that Sofia had already returned from work. She was always animated and knew how to take pleasure in simple things. Sofia also had a flair for fashion and, despite her limited means, always managed to look chic. She would enhance an old dress with a white collar and cuffs or accessorize a drab garment with a striking belt or colorful scarf.

Sometimes, in the evening, she'd go over my wardrobe and give me a few tips on how to spruce up the outfit I was wearing that day. I had gotten into the habit of throwing on any old thing, not caring what I looked like. "What's the point of dressing up?" I'd ask Sofia. In these times, who could be bothered? The only one who saw me was Mama; now that practically every place was off-limits to Jews, there was nowhere to go.

But Sofia was not put off by my attitude. She insisted that dressing nicely wasn't only for others but primarily for oneself — to boost morale. "In these times it's even more important!" she told me.

However, when I returned from the library that evening, I noticed that even Sofia's spirits were flagging. She had just come home from work and seemed unusually tired. We all sat down for a cup of tea around the kitchen table. My mother had set down a plate of *petit beurres* from the last package she'd been hoarding for a long time. "Did you have a hard day at work?" I asked.

Sofia shook her head. "It's just that I hear things." She paused. "Today I learned that the *Judenrat* is preparing a list for the first transport of Jewish men for slave labor. They'll be sent to the Pas de Calais in the north of France to build Hitler's Atlantic wall."

"Are they going to leave wives and children without means of support?" I exclaimed, horrified.

Sofia nodded.

Mama's eyes blazed. "What a disgrace," she cried, "for our own *Judenrat* to select the poor devils to be delivered into the clutches of those Nazi slave drivers."

A black mood spread through the room. We fell silent, sipping our tea without speaking. Inwardly I thanked God that, long ago, Daniel had had the foresight to turn down the "honor" of joining the *Judenrat* when he had been appointed by the board.

The quiet at the table lengthened. There was something I wanted to say to Mama. Already a few months had passed since the family had discussed the possibility of escaping. Since then, every time I tried to broach the topic, Mama would look at me reproachfully, drying up the words in my throat. Perhaps this was the right time to bring up this sore but necessary subject.

Then, on further consideration, I decided against it. My mother would not be budged from her house until she felt the danger was right at her doorstep.

One day, Evelyn dropped in as Mama and I were preparing breakfast in the kitchen. My sister was not an early riser, and I wondered about the unusual morning visit.

"You're just in time for a bite and some steaming-hot ersatz coffee," I said, pulling up a third chair. "Any special reason why you came so early?"

Still standing, Evelyn fidgeted and did not answer. Mama urged her to sit down, asking, "Are Daniel, Rachel, and Lili all right?"

"They're fine," she replied, drawing a deep breath. She looked alternately from Mama to me and back. "A terrible raid took place last night in the Van der Meyden Straat. They dragged people from their beds, hurled them into trucks, and took them away to God only knows where! Daniel hid in a doorway and watched the whole thing."

I swallowed hard. "Why did they pick that street?"

"Many Jews from Rumania live in those apartment complexes," Evelyn explained. "And Daniel learned from someone at the *Judenrat* that Berlin has ordered the deportation of all Rumanian Jews. But last night, without distinction, they took along whoever lived in those houses."

"Oh, dear God!" Mama exclaimed, clutching her head. "We know people who lived there. Martin Bertram, for one. He's Belgian, and his wife is from Switzerland."

"As a matter of fact," Evelyn said soberly, "Daniel saw her fighting like a tiger, kicking and screaming that she was a Swiss national. It took three Germans to subdue her and shove her and the children into the truck."

Appalled, Mama and I gaped at Evelyn. With hands resting in her lap, Mama began to sway slowly from left to right. "They've started deporting Rumanian Jews," she moaned. "Who will be next on Berlin's agenda? What about Belgian Jews?"

Evelyn looked down at her coffee, which had grown cold. "We've ruled out escaping to the south of France. Maybe we ought to consider going into hiding," Evelyn suggested in a desperate attempt to think of a solution. She suddenly leapt from her chair and cried, "I'm heading straight home to talk to Daniel. We've got to find a way out!"

After Evelyn left, I stayed downstairs with Mama. Neither of us intended to leave the house that day. We both remained downhearted as the hours crawled past. Then the doorbell rang, and Helene walked in. She read our faces. "I can tell just by looking at you," she said quietly. "You heard about the raid."

We nodded.

"In my house, everybody's so upset I had to break away for a while," Helene said with a sigh. "The air outdoors has a calming effect. It would do you good, too, to go outside."

"That's not a bad idea," Mama said to me. "Why don't you go for a short walk with Helene? But be especially careful!"

I extended a hand. "Come with us."

But Mama merely shook her head. "I'm better off within these walls. Just let me be."

I wished she had come along, because the summer air did revive me. My friend and I instinctively avoided the Jewish quarter and detoured around it. After walking the length of the Mercatorstraat, we proceeded through the Kuperiusstraat and arrived in Berchem. This was a densely populated section inhabited mainly by the Flemish, lower middle class and not much frequented by Jews. We entered its main street, a commercial thoroughfare featuring closely spaced, diversified shops, such as a shoe store, a dry-goods store, a stationery store, and others. We felt less conspicuous on the crowded sidewalk than on the less busy streets.

"I welcome the change of scenery," I remarked, looking around. "At least here we won't be recognized by any of our neighbors."

"And we're not likely to meet any acquaintances, either," Helene agreed.

Once in awhile we spotted a German in uniform. I remembered Mama's cautionary words but shrugged them off. Hungry for a respite from the fear in our hearts, we pretended to enjoy the window-shopping. It had been so long since we had allowed ourselves to browse and shop and have a good time like regular teenagers — like the teenagers we were. As we gazed at the display in a shoe-store window, Helene observed, "There's no all-leather footwear to be found. The few oxfords they're showing have crepe soles."

I pointed at the window. "Looks like the wedgies with cork soles and the *zoccolis* with wooden ones are the latest fashion."

Suddenly, the persistent tooting of a horn made us turn around. A gray military coupe passed by, leading a column of *Feldpolizei* on motorcycles with sidecars. Helene and I winced at the sight.

After the parade went by we moved on, breathing more easily. We had just walked past a trimming store, when we heard someone calling after us. Looking back, we saw the shopkeeper standing at the entrance, beckoning to us. Helene and I stared at each other apprehensively. Our first impulse was to flee. But as we stood frozen, the woman's voice reached us. It sounded urgent, and she was gesturing expressively with her arms.

Despite our misgivings, we slowly approached the shopkeeper, a blond-haired woman with a florid face. She held the door open. "Don't be afraid. Come in," she urged. After I verified that nobody was lurking within, I entered with Helene. The woman locked the door and stepped behind the counter. Row upon row of boxes nearly reached the ceiling with samples and other trimmings attached to the front of the cartons.

The shopkeeper spoke with astonishing vigor. "I had to get the two of you off the street immediately! You must remove those yellow stars!" She opened a drawer and took out a pair of scissors. "Please, take your coats off."

I stared at her, dumbfounded. "It's the law. We cannot be seen in public without wearing the Jewish star. Any Jew who breaks that law will be in line for harsh punishment!"

"I know all about that Nazi law!" she retorted. The woman

laid down the scissors and planted her elbows on the counter. "Please, girls," she cried out. "Listen to me. Listen with your hearts and mind!

"I was walking on the Keyserlei. All of a sudden, the *Feldpolizei* appeared. Blowing their whistles, they halted all traffic and had that stretch of road cordoned off in no time!"

"You were caught in a raid? Who were they looking for?" Helene asked.

"Not me," she said. "Kids like yourselves, young girls and boys wearing the Jewish star. At gunpoint they were pulled off the sidewalk, made to line up, and finally marched off to the Central Station."

Tears glistened in the woman's eyes. "I lay awake for hours last night thinking of the parents, waiting for their children who never came back."

Helene and I gazed silently at the woman. I wanted to speak, but my throat had closed.

The woman dabbed her eyes with a handkerchief. Then she exhorted us, "Can't you see? The star is condemning you! Without it, you still have a chance to be overlooked. So please, I implore you, let me cut that yellow emblem from your garments before it spells your doom!"

Helene was the first to hand her coat to the woman. I watched her carefully set to work with the scissors. When she finished unfastening the star, I said to her, "Let me have the scissors. I'll do it myself."

After thanking the woman wholeheartedly for having shown us this kindness, Helene and I walked home. Much to our surprise, we had no qualms about parading around without our stars. On the contrary, we felt relieved!

Helene and I parted ways, and I arrived home just in time to see Evelyn, Daniel, and their two young daughters leave the house. Mama told me that Daniel was to accompany her the next day to see Monsieur Van Caeneghem, who lived in Wilryk. The secular principal of the Jewish boys' school had assured Daniel some time ago that he would help our family in any way he could.

"Monsieur Van Caeneghem had the greatest respect for Papa," my mother explained. "All through the years he's been a true friend, and Daniel thinks we can depend on him to find a hiding place for you and me. Still, I'm wondering if that's the right thing to do — to abandon our home."

While she spoke, her eyes wandered vaguely over me. "Where's the star?" she suddenly cried out. "You walked the streets without it! Do you realize what you did?"

She listened in astonishment as I told her about our experience with the shopkeeper at the trimming store. As I spoke, I saw many emotions reflected in her face, until her features finally resolved themselves into one expression: stoic resolution. It was clear that she had arrived at a decision. Hiding was no longer a possibility to be discussed but an absolutely necessity. Danger was no foggy cloud that hovered over other people's homes. At last, this had crystallized into an immediate reality for Mama. Indeed, her next words were, "We must go."

I said in a decisive tone, "Look, Mama. Since you're planning to go into hiding, you risk the life of those who help you if you wear the yellow star. Here, let me take it off your coat, too."

Mama sighed heavily. After a lengthy pause, she said,

"Maybe you're right, Naomi. One way or the other, we're no longer safe."

With small scissors I removed the yellow star, the badge that evoked so many strong feelings in me. It was lying limply on the table, and I idly wondered what to do with it. Perhaps Rene Janssen would get another souvenir for his war collection after all.

I sat there looking at the star for a long time. Finally, I folded it in two and carefully placed it inside my jewelry box, next to a pair of cuff links that had once belonged to Papa.

Right now, that slip of yellow material was a badge of shame and disgrace, but I prayed that one day soon it would be reinstated to its rightful place — a place of honor, beauty, and holiness. Then the Jewish star would shine like a blessing for all to see!

THE OFFER

The wall clock in the family room ticked the seconds away. The timepiece in its oak case was flanked on both sides by a gold-framed oil painting. Since my earliest childhood, I remember Papa standing, every week, on a footstool and stretching in order to wind the clock. If the ticking stopped between windings accidentally, it felt as though a loyal friend had forsaken us. When Papa died, my brothers took over the duty of winding the clock. Ever since Benny went to join Leon and Claire in Vichy, France, it had become my task to keep the timepiece running.

I sat alone in the room with the newspaper spread out on the table in front of me. The ticking of the old clock was amplified by the eerie, unnerving stillness that pervaded the entire house. A week after Mr. Spira's departure, both our other boarders had left. Sofia had taken refuge with a cousin in Liége, the two of them passing themselves off as gentiles. Elie Tischler and his brother had closed their jewelry shop shortly after the liquidation of Antwerp's diamond industry. The last I'd heard, they had gone into hiding with a gentile family until their escape to Southern France could be attempted.

How I missed Sofia! I had become very attached to her and felt the loss of her presence much more keenly than Elie Tischler's departure. Meanwhile, no tenant for either space could be found. Mama and I remained alone in the house, which suddenly seemed far too big and inhospitable for just the two of us.

Everyone was busy with plans. At this moment, Mama was away, arranging a hideaway for us. She had gone to Wilryk with Daniel to visit the Van Caeneghems, non-Jewish friends of Papa's who had long ago promised to help our family in whatever way possible. It was our hope that they would let Mama and me hide out the rest of the war in their home. My mother and Daniel had left over two hours ago, and I waited anxiously for their return.

Everything I had ever known seemed to be in a state of upheaval and change. It unsettled me terribly. But the clock, instead of comforting me with its familiar ticking, merely underscored the emptiness of our familial home.

At last I heard a key in the front door. I ran to greet Mama and Daniel in the hall.

"Was something arranged?" I asked eagerly.

Mama sat down heavily on the first armchair in the salon. "The Van Caeneghems proposed to let me live out the war as part of their household," she said slowly. "They believe I will be safe within their family. They showed me the room that would be my bedroom, and they offered to safeguard our valuable objects."

"You mean the silver, Oriental rugs, and salon tables?"

Mama nodded. "They have a faithful friend with a horse and wagon who could transport the items. If I went, I'd also send along the *Shas* and the other *sefarim* Papa cherished."

It sounded perfect. But Mama seemed strangely agitated. Why were her lips pressed so tightly together? Also, Mama and Daniel seemed to be at odds with each other. My mother's jaw was set in an attitude of utter obstinacy. Then a phrase of hers struck me: "If I went..." I said cautiously, "Isn't it settled then?"

Mama closed her eyes, rubbing her temples in slow circles. She always did that at the onset of a headache. Daniel cleared his throat. "There's a problem," he said. "It seems they've got neighbors they cannot trust — Nazi sympathizers on one side and rabid Rexists on the other. The Van Caeneghems will pretend Mama is their cousin, but because of these neighbors, they're afraid that harboring more than one strange person in their house would be too dangerous."

I was taken aback. I stared at Daniel, then at my mother. "Oh...I see. Only Mama was asked to come."

Mama sat up straight in her chair and cried, "I tell you, I will not leave Naomi to fend for herself. I will not be separated from her!"

Daniel fixed her with a hard, disquieting gaze. "Finding shelter for a girl alone won't be all that difficult. But who knows when such an opportunity will present itself to you again?"

By now, I had recovered from my initial surprise. "Oh, Mama," I responded with passion, "you've got this chance to be safe. That comes first. You must go there! Believe me, I'll find a way to be safe, too. I promise!"

"But how can I leave you?" she wailed, wringing her hands pathetically. "First Charles had to go to war. Later Leon left, then Benny, and now you! I cannot bear another separation, I tell you. I can't!"

"But you have to," Daniel said vigorously. "And Naomi won't be by herself. She'll sleep on the sofa in our living room until we find something better. Doesn't that put your mind at ease?"

"No," Mama said, her voice equally hard. "If Naomi and I cannot be together, the only consolation would be knowing that she is completely safe." She turned to me. "You should escape from Antwerp! You should join your sister Claire in the unoccupied French zone!"

My mother's words jolted me. She had never expressed the idea so forcefully. Her commanding tone made it sound like an irrevocable order. She looked at Daniel. "If you can arrange for Naomi's escape, only then will I accept the Van Caeneghems' offer."

Daniel pressed his palms flat together and rested his chin on the tips of his fingers. "There's someone I know," he said finally. "Andre Farkasz."

"That name sounds Hungarian," I remarked.

"So it is," Daniel said. "When Andre first settled in Antwerp, I was his religious instructor for quite some time. I also made him join our Agudath Israel group. Until the war broke out, he remained an active member."

"You seemed to have had a good influence on him," Mama said.

"Well, yes. Anyhow, now Andre directs guides who've gone back and forth several times to Vichy, France, and really know the ropes. I will ask him."

Dazedly, I listened to my mother and brother-in-law discuss my fate as if I had no say in the matter. Was I a child, then, to be shunted here or there like some kind of object? I opened my mouth, then abruptly shut it. It dawned on me: yes, I was a child. And the thought of leaving Mama, of leaving my family and Antwerp and everything I knew, to venture out on a dangerous escape route filled me with the worst kind of terror.

No matter how much I had gained in self-awareness and maturity over the past two years, I was not ready to forsake my childhood and claim complete independence. I was still young — hardly nineteen! How could they push me out of the nest? I wasn't ready. I needed Mama. And I believed she needed me. I roused myself and cried, "I'm not going anywhere!"

As one, Mama and Daniel gave me a steadfast glare. "But you will," Daniel said in a steely voice.

I looked back at them and lowered my head in seeming acquiescence. It was better that they thought I agreed, especially if it was the only way Mama would accept the Van Caeneghems' offer. It was vital that she be safely settled.

But inwardly I didn't know what I would do. I had to decide something — that much was clear. No one on the street wore the yellow Star of David anymore. Everyone had wised up and was trying to hide his identity. Night raids were happening with increasing frequency. During the day, the Nazi hunt for Jews went on in various, unpredictable ways. Persecution was at its peak.

I decided to discuss the matter with Helene. In any case, I was anxious to see her. We had become accustomed to seeing each other almost daily; but now three days had gone by without a word from my friend. I couldn't wait to talk to her.

I arrived at Helene's house and rang the doorbell repeatedly, but no one answered. As I kept ringing, my apprehension grew.

Finally, Helene's sister, Gerda, opened the door. She looked blankly at me. "Oh, it's you, Naomi. Come in."

"Thank God you're here!" I exclaimed, much relieved. "I was worried. I rang the bell so many times. Didn't you hear?"

Gerda shook her head, then led me into the living room of their ground-floor apartment. Her mother was lying on the couch with a wet towel on her forehead, moaning at intervals. Helene sat on the floor with a basin of cold water at her side. She removed the towel, immersed it in the water, then squeezed it out and replaced it on her mother's face.

On entering the room I said "hello," but neither Helene nor her mother answered. "What's wrong?" I asked awkwardly. "Does your mother have a bad headache? Perhaps I should leave?"

Helene looked up at me with red, swollen eyes. Her hair was uncombed. The front pleat of her tailored skirt hung off-center, and the buttons on her shirtwaist had been thrust into noncorresponding buttonholes. "You're welcome to stay," she said in a flat voice.

I noticed that Gerda's cheeks and nose were rather puffed up. Evidently she, too, had been crying.

"What's going on here?" I asked, seized with apprehension. "What happened?"

Suddenly, Helene's face twisted with pain. She broke out in tears. Between sobs she uttered, "My father and brother are gone. Two nights ago, Nazi animals burst in here and took them away!"

The mother's groans grew louder, while Gerda quietly weeped. I plunked down on a chair, appalled.

"*Oy, oy, oy!* What a catastrophe!" the mother lamented. "What a calamity has befallen us. God Almighty, how can I go on without my husband? Without my only son?"

By and by, Helene began to fill in the details for me. "Gerda was asleep in the attic and the rest of us were preparing for bed when we heard a vehicle brake in front of the house, followed by loud voices. Immediately Mama and I ran to the kitchen. We managed to scramble out of the window onto the small triangle between the houses. We sat till morning on the concrete floor in our nightgowns, with our backs against a blind wall."

"Why didn't the men join you?" I asked.

"There was no time!" Helene cried. "The minute we were outside, those monsters nearly broke down our door. We could hear one Nazi call to another in German, `Here are two of them!' A different voice thundered, `Yes! You are Jews! You're coming with us. Quick! Make it quick!' We heard my father's weak protests. Then the slamming of the door, and silence."

Too stunned to express how intensely I felt for them, I remained motionless, staring at Helene. Finally, I said, "Do you have any idea where they took them? Can't something be done?"

A spasm of pain flitted across Gerda's face. She got up abruptly and left the room. Helene simply stared at me with immensely sad eyes. After awhile she said, "All those who'd been caught in the raid — roughly three hundred people —

were being held in the school at the Groote Hondstraat." She put a hand on a nearby coffee table, as if to steady herself. "Early yesterday morning these poor souls were packed into military trucks and, I'm told, put into trains headed for labor camps in the East — mainly Poland."

I gaped at Helene, unable to conceal my horror at this information. "You mean, men, women, and children alike?"

She nodded. "During the scramble, as the guards shoved and pushed the prisoners to rush them out, my father and Mr. Liebman, a diamond dealer, managed to sneak away and hide in the coal cellar behind a pile of anthracite."

At this point, the mother clutched her head, muttering incoherently. Helene dipped the cloth in water and placed it again on her mother's forehead, murmuring soothing sounds. Then she went on: "After the trucks left, the janitor went down to the cellar and found the two men. He cursed them and ordered them back upstairs. He told them they'd remain in his custody until the next transport arrived."

"How did you find out about this?"

"A young fellow came to Mrs. Liebman with a message from her husband." Helene paused for a moment. With her sodden handkerchief she dabbed her eyes. "The fellow was with the cleanup crew, put to work after the transport left. Mr. Liebman succeeded in sending him to his wife, urging her to come with money and all the diamonds they possessed. He would try to buy his freedom from the janitor."

I sat on the edge of my seat, listening. Some perverse part of me wanted to hear every detail, even while I knew that the ending could not possibly be a happy one. "What happened next?" I asked, unable to contain myself.

"On the way to the Groote Hondstraat, Mrs. Liebman stopped at our house," Helene said. "Her amazing report gave us hope for rescuing my father. I decided to join Mrs. Liebman. Without hesitation, my mother handed me her diamond engagement ring, her precious jewelry, and all the money we had. '*Hatzlachah* — good luck! May God be with you!' my poor mother called after us."

"Oh Helene, what went wrong? Didn't you get to see the janitor?" I asked.

"We got to see him all right," she replied bitterly. "We also saw my dear father and Mr. Liebman, their faces black with coal dust from the cellar. In the janitor's office, we offered him a small fortune in return for setting both men free," Helene continued. "In monetary value, it was probably more than an underpaid school janitor might earn in his entire working life. He could have lived so much better for years to come. But the fiend turned the offer down!"

I got to my feet and began to pace the floor. "Couldn't you persuade him? Couldn't you swear that the secret would never be revealed? That there was no risk?"

Helene cupped her face with both hands and swayed from side to side. The pain she revealed was so intense I had to turn away. "Not only did that Nazi bootlicker refuse the offer, but he broke into a fury and turned ugly and nasty. He bellowed at us, 'If you don't get out of here, I'll hand the two of you to the Gestapo, where you'll be disciplined real good!' "

In the silence that followed, I went over to put my arms around my friend. "What can I say to you?" I whispered. "I wish I knew words that could alleviate your suffering."

"There's really nothing anyone can say," Helene muttered.

When I left them a short time later, Helene was still stooped over her stricken mother, patting her hand, making gentle noises, wiping her face with great tenderness. The sight of my friend comforting her mother in the midst of her own pain moved me tremendously, and I hurried out of their house before they could witness my own tears.

I rushed down the back streets. On approaching our house, I glanced up and saw Mama looking out of the salon window. She was holding the Alençon lace curtains away from her and stood at an angle to have a wider view of the street. The moment she spotted me, she disappeared, and the curtains drifted back into place.

My mother had rushed to open the door for me. As I walked up the front steps, she said, "Thank heavens, you're here! Whatever took you so long? I nearly went out of my mind worrying about you!"

"Oh, Mama, I'm heartsick," I said brokenly. "They've arrested Helene's father and brother. The boy's gone already, and the father is being detained at the school in the Groote Hondstraat. He'll be deported to a labor camp with the next transport."

Mama leaned against the wall, her face white. "Merciful God!" she whispered. "What's going to become of them?"

We looked at each other, neither of us giving voice to the unspoken question: what was to become of all of us? A deep-felt fright assailed me. It had never been more clear to me how vulnerable Mama and I were — how very vulnerable we all were!

"Maybe we should not sleep here tonight," I ventured. "Who knows when the Nazis plan to surprise us, too?"

Mama gave a start. She raised the curtain and peered out. Seeing nothing, she turned back to me, her face noticeably calmer. "We can't just pick up and leave while everything's still here," she said matter-of-factly. "The man with the wagon should be here tomorrow or the day after to move our valuables to the Van Caeneghems' house."

I persisted, "But after what happened to our friends, even one or two days of waiting may be too dangerous! Is it worth risking our safety for material things?"

Mama stared at me strangely. "Don't you understand? I cannot simply abandon what means so much to me," she said, passion in her voice. "Your father's religious books, my own mother's Shabbos candlesticks, our Chanukah menorah, and much more. I must salvage these heirlooms!"

By now tears were flowing from Mama's eyes. I realized there was no use arguing. This was Mama. I could not change her. I said, "If that's the case, let's pack your personal belongings, so the man can take them along, too."

Whatever remained of our luggage was stored in the attic. In order to fetch a suitcase for Mama, I had to brave the ghostly stillness of our upper stories. I mustered my courage and began climbing the stairs. Uninhabited for quite some time, the higher floors gave off an eerie quality that made my skin break out in goose bumps.

But the moment I entered our attic and closed the door behind me, I suddenly felt warm and sheltered, as though enveloped by a protective cloud.

The small window scarcely let any sunlight filter through, yet my eyes quickly became accustomed to the dim surroundings, and I was able to discern every object. There was the wooden highchair with the hole in the seat to accommodate the potty. I vaguely recalled Benny sitting in it. The white, wrought-iron crib had been taken apart, and both sides rested against the wall. Nearby, the old pram, with its oversized hood, tilted forward for lack of front wheels. My gaze fell on the wooden hobbyhorse that had lasted through the growing up of six brothers. One ear, the tail, and most of its mane were missing. Other than that, the horse seemed amazingly well preserved. Here and there I saw ancient cupboards, the coffee table with its fourth leg missing, and a small bag left behind by Willie and Bertha Haas. Would they ever come back to retrieve it? I wondered if they had succeeded in leaving Europe and were safe in South America or, perhaps, Cuba.

Presently I sat down on a steamer trunk.

A wicker hamper stood in one corner. I remembered how the good china was transported in it on the occasion of Michael's bar mitzvah. Since the event was to take place at the end of August, Papa had decided to celebrate it in the country villa in Heide. I delighted in the sweet memory of those days.

I examined the hamper. It would serve for packing all our silver. Perhaps the two sterling centerpieces, used on special occasions to serve fruit to guests, would fit in there, too.

At last I got up to look for the suitcase I'd come to get. I was about to leave the attic, when, on impulse, I lifted the lid of the trunk I'd been sitting on. Inside lay Mama's magnificent gown — the *haute couture* creation that Papa had had shipped from Paris on his return from a successful business trip.

The gown was made of hunter-green peau de soie. A yoke of elaborate beading surrounded the bateau neckline. One foot above the hemline, a wide strip of the same exquisite beading embellished the floor-length skirt. The sleeves were also encircled by a band of identical glitter. The gown was striking, yet perfectly modest and tasteful.

I picked up the cherished garment and hugged it. Tears sprang to my eyes as I remembered how Mama had looked wearing the gown on happy occasions, long ago. "Oh, how regal! A countess! A duchess!" guests would whisper. And I'd gaze at her in awe. To me Mama looked like a queen! All of us children would stare proudly at our mother as Papa stood at her side, beaming. As a child I had longed to be all that she was. To this day, Mama still had a magnetic effect on me. As difficult as our relationship might be at times, it was hard for me to separate from her.

I compared our relationship to Helene's with her mother. To be sure, Helene had plenty of love for her, but she was not as caught up in her mother's life, attitudes, and opinions as I was in mine. Mama's disapproval still made me quake inwardly, as if I were a nine-year-old and not a young woman nearing twenty. The more Mama withheld her open affection from me, the more I craved it from her. At some point I would realize her limitations and then take a few independent steps, but I never seemed able to go far without the thought of Mama fueling me. In an odd way, we were both very attached to one another. I was just beginning to understand these things.

Regretfully, I returned the gown to the trunk. Of course, it would have to stay behind. As I carefully tucked all of its folds and gathers inside, it occurred to me that I hadn't heard Helene's opinion about my escaping to the French unoccupied zone. Somehow, I didn't think she would shed light on the problem. The answer would have to come from within myself.

I climbed down the flights of stairs to my bedroom, carrying the suitcase and the wicker hamper. Along the way, I fancied I heard whispers in the strange, rather eerie atmosphere. It was as though the house grieved and lamented at being abandoned by the people who had lived in it through the years.

A ROOF OVER MY HEAD

I was waiting for Mama in our house. A few days ago, Frans came with his horse and wagon and carted our valuables to the Van Caeneghems' home for safekeeping. That night, Mama moved in with the Van Caeneghems, and I went to sleep on the silk brocade sofa in Evelyn's salon. Before we parted, we made a promise to return to our house each day at a prearranged time. We both still held on to our front-door keys. And so, I stood waiting in our salon, taking in the changed appearance of our home.

My shoulders ached. I did not really enjoy sleeping at Evelyn's. Aside from the sofa, which was short and narrow and made sleeping uncomfortable, I was a bit uneasy around Daniel. He kept dropping subtle and not-so-subtle hints: "When are you going to visit Andre? Your time may be running out"; "What about your promise to your mother?"

And then there was his racking cough. His lungs were

giving out. I'd find him bent over the Talmud, debating a Halachic point in a singsong fashion, with a hand pressed over his heart. It pained me to see my sister's husband so clearly losing his strength. Every time he suffered a bad coughing spell, I'd catch Evelyn wincing.

I spoke to her. "Can't anything be done to help him? Isn't Dr. Dirksen treating him anymore?"

"He is," Evelyn told me. "The good doctor is trying to have him hospitalized. They're waiting for a bed at the Stappaerts Hospital. It's just a matter of time."

Then there was his morale. It was low, terribly low. And it cast a pall over the entire family, even the natural ebullience of my two nieces, Rachel and Lili. Evelyn confided to me the source of Daniel's depression. A good friend of his, Mr. Hilbrein, a member of the *Judenrat*, had recently committed suicide. It seemed the *Judenrat* had been commanded to make up the lists of Jews to be deported. In order to fill the quota, some of those in charge even put down names of relatives. His friend's conscience drove him to take his own life rather than become part of this.

"How horrible!" I cried. "It's come down to where these members of the *Judenrat* are playing God."

"It's not for us to judge their actions. The job was forced on them. But I can tell you one thing," Evelyn said. "No matter how heartbroken Daniel may be because of his friend's suicide, he's extremely grateful that he himself refused the honor of joining the board of the *Judenrat* when they invited him last year."

"I can see why," I said bitterly. I was not as magnanimous toward the *Judenrat* as my sister. These men were saving their own skin by helping the Nazis, albeit unwillingly.

I tried to brush away these thoughts while I waited for Mama. Seeing her had become the high point of my day.

She finally arrived, sneaking into our own house as if she were a thief. We fell upon each other with hugs and kisses. It was our third meeting, and still we could not contain the outpouring of feeling when we saw one another. As we embraced, the thought uppermost in our minds was, this can't last. Still, we were happy to have each other.

We sat down on two torn chairs left behind in the kitchen. Immediately, Mama began urging me to leave the country. "What are you waiting for?" she exclaimed. "Evelyn and Daniel have neighbors who throw insults at them. One neighbor stopped Daniel on the street and said, `When are you joining the Jews that were taken away? I might even help you get there sooner...' "

I gasped. "Oh, Mama! I had no idea sleeping at Evelyn's could mean trouble for the family. I'll have to find some other place."

"Yes," Mama replied, "and that other place should be outside Belgium!"

These words were becoming a sore echo in my ears. First Daniel, now Mama.

My gaze was drawn to the attractive coffee mill still hanging on the kitchen wall. It depicted Delft windmills in blue on white porcelain. I closed my eyes and for a brief moment smelled the aroma of the Brazilian coffee beans we used to grind in it.

I shook myself slightly and returned to the moment.

"Mama," I said, "if you leave with me, I promise to find a

way out of here. Come with me," I implored. "Michael and Sabine won't leave. Evelyn and Daniel still insist on staying. But you, Mama, should escape with me!" I held her hand tightly. "I beg you!"

"We've gone over this so many times. I can't do it," Mama said wearily, withdrawing her hand. "The thought of illegally crossing borders scares me to death. If I panicked, others would get caught, too. Besides, I don't walk long distances very well. I'm too old. It's too late for me."

"Oh, Mama," I said miserably. "Don't talk like that. I'm sure you could do it."

"No, Naomi. I'm staying here!" she asserted flatly. "But you must get away. You no longer have a roof over your head. I urge you to go by yourself. You must join Claire and Leon and Benny in Free France!"

Tears welled up as I stared at her through the blur in my eyes. I felt a lump lodge in my throat. Her refusal had the ring of finality. She would not come with me after all. I was so choked up I could not utter a word.

The clang of the doorbell startled us. Our faces spelled alarm as we looked at one another. The bell continued to ring. "Let's not open up. Maybe they'll go away," I whispered.

"Quick! To the cellar! We must hide!" Mama said hoarsely.

We rushed to the cellar door, then stopped. The first clanging of the doorbell had given way to persistent knocking. "That's odd," I said in a low voice. "The Germans would not knock. They'd bang and break down the door." I paused. "Let me sneak upstairs and look out the window."

From the first-floor window I could see a woman standing on our doorstep. Greatly relieved, I rushed back downstairs to reassure Mama. "It's Madame Mertens!"

Madame Mertens lived diagonally across the street from us. She was a semi-retired dressmaker who practiced her profession for only a few select clients. Some years ago, when Mama needed a new coat, she approached Madame Mertens, who had made her an exceptionally beautiful winter coat. From then on, the two women had enjoyed a casual friendship.

"Don't be afraid of me," the dressmaker said as she walked in and saw Mama's troubled expression. "I'm your friend, and I'd like to help if I can."

"We no longer live here," Mama told her. "I just came to meet my daughter for a little while. Please, come inside the dining room."

"I saw you from my window," Madame Mertens said. "I made sure nobody followed me as I hurried across the street." She absent-mindedly brushed a strand of hair out of her eye. "The other day, I also saw the horse-drawn wagon being loaded with your belongings," she went on. "I assumed you'd be leaving. It's good you went away when you did, because yesterday the Gestapo came looking for you. I was just returning to my house when two Germans asked if I knew you and if you still lived here."

"What did you tell them?" I asked, holding my breath.

"I said that I hadn't seen you for quite some time, that you must have left town," she answered with a mischievous grin.

I glanced briefly at Mama. We had missed our encounter with the Gestapo by a hairsbreadth!

The three of us were standing in the dining room. The adjoining salon no longer had the coffee tables, the small

Oriental rugs, or the large, gold-framed oil painting — a superb nineteenth-century landscape that Papa had picked up at an auction. The void it left on the bare wall filled me with a chill.

But the piano and the crystal chandelier were still intact, as were some other items. The dressmaker's gaze rested on the two oak dining-room buffets on either side of the marble mantelpiece. They nearly reached the ceiling and were adorned with artistic carvings and beveled mirror insets.

"Such splendid furniture!" Madame Mertens exclaimed, clasping her hands together. "Are you simply going to abandon all this and let the Nazis ship it to Germany?"

"What else can we do?" Mama said in a plaintive voice.

Madame Mertens nodded, seemingly deep in thought. After a short pause she said, "I'm willing to buy what you have here for a fair price. I'd pay you in advance and have a mover on the job tomorrow."

My mother's eyes widened in surprise. "What about the authorities?" she asked. "You're a gentile dealing with Jews. Buying anything from us could get you into trouble!"

"My husband is a chief of police," she replied with a smile. "He's way up there in the administration." She lowered her voice and added, "Even though he works along with the occupation government, don't think he shares their Nazi philosophy."

I stared in wonder at this middle-aged neighbor. She was taking a risk, speaking to us in this manner. She continued in a low, confidential voice. "Should you ever need certain personal documents, my husband may be able to help you. Remember that!"

Mama and I were flabbergasted. I couldn't help admiring

the woman's boldness and thanked her profusely for her offer. And that is how our house became emptied of even the little bit of furniture that had remained. At least it would not fall into the hands of the Nazis! We walked away with a fistful of cash.

Since my presence seemed to have alerted Evelyn's neighbors, I decided it was imperative to move as quickly as possible. Two days later, I was sleeping on the sofa in Michael and Sabine's apartment. Their couch was equally uncomfortable. Once or twice, I woke up to find myself sleeping on the floor. But the atmosphere was more upbeat at my brother's home.

Michael and Sabine had a very different relationship from that of Evelyn and Daniel — at least from what I could see. There was much teasing and banter and conversation. They laughed a lot together and argued as well. I could not imagine Evelyn ever raising her voice to contradict Daniel. Their relationship was one of deep respect and consideration. Evelyn greatly admired Daniel's devotion to Torah learning and his keen mind. But there was a lightheartedness I found lacking.

Michael and Sabine didn't have children yet. Perhaps they, too, would become more serious once they started a family. I wondered if it was possible to have the warm friendship of Michael and Sabine, as well as the profound respect that Evelyn accorded Daniel in a marriage.

My stay at Michael and Sabine's was not destined to last. They, too, were making their plans. My brother revealed to me that he'd rented a villa in Brasschaet, a suburb of Antwerp, and they'd be moving into it in less than a week. Nobody in that area knew them, and with their non-Jewish looks, they hoped to be able to conceal the fact that they were Jews in hiding.

By late July of that summer, no one wore the yellow Star of David anymore, so the Nazis were using other methods to track down their prey. They scrutinized faces, looking at ears, noses, the shape of the head. Sometimes the slant of a man's posture or his gait aroused their suspicions. Then, too, the hunters' ears were sharpened to pronunciation. The slightest tinge of a foreign accent would alert them. And in the probe that followed, the victim was branded and the trap sprung. Daily, I witnessed or heard accounts of Jews being abducted off the streets — stories that sent chills down my spine. These were the episodes that had finally triggered Michael into action.

Watching Michael and Sabine huddled together, laying their plans and trying to figure out ways to elude the Nazis, I felt a stinging loneliness. Clearly, they were a pair and were going to face their predicament together. My sisters had their husbands, my brothers, their wives, my mother had her children, Leon and Benny had each other and their yeshivos — a kind of family in itself. And I? I was alone in a way I had never experienced before. Everyone's fate was just about decided, except for mine.

"What about you, Naomi?" My sister-in-law asked one afternoon. She was unloading two bags of groceries, having recently returned from the black market. "Aren't you thinking of going underground, too? With your fair skin and chiseled features, no one would take you for a Jewess."

I was embroidering a tablecloth that belonged to Sabine. I put down the fabric for a moment and sighed. The past few days I'd been more concerned about whether I would have a roof over my head than with any plans for escape. "Oh, I don't know," I said, rather forlorn.

Sabine changed into bedroom slippers and came to sit down with me. "I see you made the beds, cleared the dishes, and mopped the floor while I was gone. There's nothing left for me to do. You're spoiling me!" she said with a grin.

She was trying to cheer me up, and I smiled wanly. Just then, as I plied my needle once more, Mama arrived at the apartment. Michael and Sabine greeted their unexpected visitor with a warm embrace.

I had not seen Mama since the day we'd heard of the Gestapo's visit to our home. What a wonderful surprise to meet her now! Mama and I clung to each other. I seemed unable to let go. Time stood still for the two of us. When I finally released my hold, Mama turned her face away, but I caught her wiping the tears she didn't want me to see.

Mama turned back to me. Forcing back more tears, she said, "That we must be separated when we're still in the same city is just another bitter pill to swallow."

"How are you getting along in that gentile household? How do you spend your time?" I asked as we both sat down. She looked tanned and relaxed, and her wig had never been combed better. Apparently she had invested time washing and setting it herself to make it look as natural as possible. A stiff head of unnatural-looking hair would have aroused suspicion, I suppose, among her neighbors.

"I help out a bit with the housework. Things like setting the table, sweeping the floor, peeling potatoes, and other light tasks," Mama replied. "They also let me putter about the garden. They're growing potatoes, carrots, and some radishes. They tried raising tomatoes, but it was a fiasco. You need a warmer climate than the one in Wilryk for tomatoes."

"I bet you'll end up being an expert on gardening," Michael observed, and we all laughed.

"But a strange thing happens when I'm in the garden of that gentile household," Mama said softly. "While I'm weeding or watering the vegetable patches I'm blissfully at peace with nature. This makes me feel closer to God. I'm spontaneously moved to pray, and..." Mama hesitated, looked up at us, and concluded, "I'm convinced that He hears me!" With a sparkle in her eyes, she added, "It boosts my spirit and gives me such hope!"

Michael shifted awkwardly. He was a bit uncomfortable with expressing spiritual sentiments. He asked, "What about nourishment, Mama? I hope you don't go hungry."

"So far, I'm glad to say I haven't eaten anything that's *treif*. May the Almighty allow this frightful war, this calamity, to end with our family eating only kosher food!"

"Amen!" we all said fervently. Nobody spoke for a time. Everyone seemed lost in thought as we speculated about the unknown future ahead of us.

At last, Mama broke the silence. "Do you remember, Naomi, when Madame Mertens confided that her husband would help us if we ever needed documents?"

"I certainly do. She sounded so sincere, too."

"Well, Madame Mertens meant what she said." Mama opened her handbag and took out two green identity cards. They had blank spaces where individual particulars had to be filled in. A photo of my mother and of myself were attached to the appropriate space on each card. The government seal from the borough of Borgerhout was affixed to both photos, validating the documents.

My eyes widened. "This is absolutely great!" I cried. "Ever since our real I.D.'s had the word *'Jude'* stamped on them, we had to pray no one would ask to see them. This is real gold!"

We gingerly placed the cards on the kitchen table. "Someone has to fill in the blank spaces before these cards are of any use," Michael announced. "Who can think up some good false names and addresses?"

"That's right," said Mama. "Typical Flemish names like 'Janssen' or 'Peeters' or 'Van Dam'."

"I think I'd like 'Vermeulen' as my surname," I said. It was the last name of a girl in my art class whom I'd admired. "But I don't want 'Marie' or 'Jeanne' as a first name. It's too ordinary, too common."

"How does 'Denise' or 'Yvonne' strike you?" Sabine threw in, getting into the spirit.

I rubbed my jaw thoughtfully. "Hmm. Actually, I'd considered 'Madeleine.' But 'Yvonne' would be better. It has a more formal ring to it, as if it might be the name of a lady doctor or even a member of the diplomatic corps. Yes, let it be 'Yvonne Vermeulen'."

"Good morning, Mademoiselle Vermeulen," Michael said in a falsetto voice, bowing slightly and twirling an imaginary mustache. "How are you this lovely morning?"

I giggled. This business of choosing another identity was a little bizarre.

"I think Mama has a nicer handwriting than any of us," Sabine decided. "Would you fill out the information on these identity cards?"

"Of course," Mama replied. "I need a pen and ink. The Montenstraat would make a good address in Borgerhout. Let's say number twenty-four."

Michael brought a pen and bottle of ink to the table. He set it down on a magazine in front of Mama. We stood around and watched as she printed the surname and proceeded to write in the other particulars in script. Nobody breathed a word. After she completed her I.D., she started on mine. There was tension in the stillness as my mother concentrated on her writing.

Suddenly her right hand began to tremble. Before she could lift the pen away, an inkblot appeared on the I.D. card.

"Oh, look what I've done!" Mama gasped. "What do we do now?"

With the corner of a blotter, Michael sucked up the black liquid, but a stain remained. He went to work with an eraser, rubbing gently. Yet he couldn't prevent removing the top layer of the paper along with the spot of ink. Now a white blemish marred the green card.

"No official document ever shows an imperfection. Any inspector who examines this I.D. will know it's false. I've ruined it," Mama moaned.

With his thumbnail Michael smoothed the small, rough surface as much as possible. "Here now, Mama. Write carefully over the white spot. Let's see if the street name will cover it."

"It'll hardly be noticeable," I said reassuringly, though in my heart I was quite anxious. A good identity card was an invaluable asset, especially when traveling. The blotch on my card really worried me.

Mama completed the card with no further accidents. She

stayed on and had dinner with us. Afterwards Michael came up to me privately as I washed the dishes in the kitchen and said, "Be careful of whom you show that I.D. to. A sharp inspector will suspect it's a fraud."

"Mama is terribly upset about it," I said in a low voice. "Well, I'll avoid showing the card altogether unless it becomes absolutely necessary."

"By the way, I think it's high time you kept your promise to Mama," my brother reproved me. "You should contact that person that Daniel mentioned. As you know, we'll soon be moving out of here. How are you going to manage?"

I wiped my hands on a dish towel and turned to face him. "I do intend to leave, but only when I'm ready. Doesn't it make sense to you to set out well prepared for a trip?" I asked, lifting my chin. Of course, I was referring to being internally ready, emotionally prepared.

Michael simply rolled his eyes and wagged a finger at me.

"All right, all right," I said raising my arms in mock defeat. Truthfully, my delay tactics were beginning to tire even myself. The time had come for action, whether I was ready or not. "I agree with you. I'll contact Andre Farkasz very soon — tomorrow even."

Yes, that was my intention. But the next day, before I set out for Andre's, I first had to visit Helene to see how she and her family were getting along. Ever since her father and brother were taken away, she had dedicated herself to giving her mother and sister, Gerda, the vital support they needed.

Beset with a sickening fear, Gerda dared not leave the house or go marketing. Thanks to Helene, their rationed food appeared on the table every day. With grim determination to survive the war, Helene was the planner and the mover for the three of them. And nothing other than Helene's irrepressible spirit could have prevented her fragile mother from sinking into a deep depression.

I found my friend in the midst of packing. My heart sank as I saw her folding pajamas and her all-weather overcoat into the suitcase. Another person going into hiding or escaping? You, too, Helene? I cried inwardly. I told myself that I ought to be relieved she'd found something for herself. But the departure of my closest friend just at this time filled me with desolation.

"Where are you moving to?" I asked her after a few minutes.

"It's only for the nighttime," she told me.

I looked at her, puzzled.

She explained, "During the day, we're still here. But we can't risk another night raid. We've been warned that they're returning to buildings where they didn't catch everybody the first time they burst in."

"So where do you all sleep?"

"My mother and sister spend the night in a rented room. The owners are really nice people. But it's small — not large enough for two, even. And as for me?" A glint appeared in Helene's eyes, and she didn't answer right away. Then she said, "I'm not sure I should divulge my secret night activities to you."

"What are you talking about, Helene? `Secret night activities'! Now you've really got me curious," I exclaimed, utterly mystified.

"Oh, Naomi, I was only teasing." She burst out laughing.

"You'll never believe this: I sleep in the display window of a mattress store!"

"Whaa-t?" My jaw dropped in amazement. "Did I hear right?" I gaped at Helene, and then we both laughed.

"Actually," I said, recovering somewhat, "it's downright ingenious. Who'd think of hiding there but you? No danger of a Nazi raid for you to worry about."

"That's true," Helene said. "I sleep very well behind the hermetically closed window blind, in the exclusive company of beds, mattresses, and mannequins." She folded a cotton robe and put that in the suitcase, too. "My only worry is that I not oversleep in the morning. I must be out of the store before 8:00 A.M."

"Hmm." My brain started ticking. Was this the solution to my problem? Would Helene object, perhaps feel I was encroaching on her territory? "Come to think of it," I said casually, "I don't know how much longer I can sleep in my brother's apartment. They're moving any day now, you know."

"Oh!" Helene looked at me with wonderfully bright eyes. "It would be perfect if you'd join me. I'm sure the storekeeper will have no objection." Helene sat down hard on the suitcase, and together we snapped it shut. "Imagine. You'll have your pick of the finest mattresses" — her arm swept the room — "and I, for one, would welcome having some live company!"

My face lit up. Not only had I found a place to stay, but I would be sharing that space with my best friend. It wasn't family, but it was a close second.

After getting the storekeeper's permission, I quickly returned to Michael's apartment and began packing my belongings. I had to pack very efficiently because we were only allowed to bring a small bag and leave that hidden in the store. I put most of my winter items into a different suitcase, which I dropped off at Evelyn's along with anything for which I didn't have immediate use.

Everyone looked at me incredulously when I told them of my new nighttime residence and wished me every success. In the excitement, even Michael failed to berate me for having delayed once again my meeting with Andre Farkasz.

ANDRE AND MAGDA

The following evening, I joined Helene in the mattress store. Behind the store window, on a raised platform, stood two beds, complete with headboards and mattresses on box springs. They'd been made up with colorful linens and downy blankets to attract customers. Reclining on a chaise longue to one side was a mannequin dressed in a frilly pink robe.

"I must say, the display is rather inviting," I remarked.

"Looks like the second bed was just waiting for you," Helene said. "And let me show you our bathroom facilities in the back: a toilet and a sink with running water!"

We dared only to barely illuminate the shop. Armed with our toothbrushes and toiletries, we carefully sidestepped the stacks of different-sized mattresses as I followed Helene toward the washroom. Fortunately, a single bulb hanging from the ceiling lit up that area.

There was an air of hilarity as we bedded down for the night, my face covered with cold cream and Helene's hair in curlers, as if we were at a slumber party instead of hiding for our lives. Deliberately, we pushed away the frightening thoughts and relished being carefree teenagers, even if it was only an illusion.

"Aaaah!" I let out a luxuriant stretch. "This feels heavenly after all those nights on a sofa. What kind of mattress am I lying on?"

"Well, the label on mine reads, 'Pyramid.' Let me see yours." Helene flopped onto her stomach and reached to read the tag on my mattress. She squinted, then pronounced, " 'Sleeping Beauty.' How appropriate for you."

"No, does it really say that?" I asked. A guilty look crossed Helene's face, and on impulse I reached for the tag myself. It read, "Class Comfort."

"You imp!" I threw a pillow at her.

"Watch it!" Helene cautioned me. "We've got to keep this shop in order, you know."

"I'm sor—" Just then a pillow landed in my face. "All right," I gasped. "You picked the wrong girl to start up with!" And so began a vigorous pillow fight that lasted until a stray pillow almost decapitated the mannequin in her recliner. Laughing and sputtering, Helene and I called a truce.

Finally, we calmed down. Chastened, we recited the Shema, and soon after Helene switched off the light.

The next morning, Helene and I woke up at seven, folded our bedding, brushed our teeth, and washed as best we could in the tiny basin in the back room. We checked for hairs that may have strayed into the basin or any telltale sign that this store had been inhabited by overnight visitors.

Helene located a small utility table. She spread an oversized napkin on it, which she had brought to serve as a tablecloth. Over a breakfast of black bread with jam and shared ersatz coffee from a thermos bottle, we discussed our plans for the day. I confided to her that I would be meeting with Andre Farkasz that morning to see about arranging for a guide to smuggle me into Free France.

"He lives at 127 Mercatorstraat," I explained. "I had to memorize the address. Daniel says it's forbidden to write any of this down. And guess what? He entrusted me with a secret code to make sure they let me in."

Helene was sipping her coffee. Her eyes grew wide as she stared at me.

"Did I say something that surprised you?" I asked.

She set down her cup. "I happen to know Andre and his wife, Magda," Helene said. "She's a corsetiere like myself, and I did a short stretch of apprenticeship under her a couple of years back. I know all about them and the work they do." She looked eagerly at me. "I'd like to come along with you. Is that all right?"

"Sure!" Putting aside the empty thermos, I smiled. "Glad to have the company."

Andre and Magda Farkasz were Jewish and Hungarian citizens. In December of 1941, Hungary declared war on Russia and the United States of America. Because of Hungary's adherence to the Rome-Berlin Axis, Hitler granted that country the status of an ally. Consequently, Hungarian citizens — including Jews — were exempt from Nazi persecution. Andre and Magda were convinced that by virtue of their nationality, the Germans would not touch them in Antwerp.

On the way to the Farkasz' home, Helene briefed me: "Although Magda is a corsetiere who works at home, she's actually a front for Andre. He has saved dozens of Jews by assigning them to smugglers who got them across to Vichy, France. Aside from that, there's no active smuggler he doesn't know. Whenever one of them gets caught, Andre is the first to find out. No need to tell you his dealings are far from kosher in the Nazis' book."

"I'm beginning to understand," I said as we crossed the underpass on the Van de Nest Lei. "From what you just said, should the authorities catch on to Andre's illegal activities, God forbid, those implicated could claim their business was strictly with Magda. After all, some men accompany their women to dressmakers and other such places. Am I right?"

"That's the idea. I only hope Andre isn't fooling himself on account of his Hungarian citizenship. He may have misplaced confidence in his personal safety."

We arrived at the house, a Victorian brownstone with half a dozen steps in front. I pressed the bell using the secret code — three short rings, followed by a long one. I heard feet clambering down a flight of stairs, and a swarthy man of medium height and build opened the door. His movements were quick and energetic, and he instantly conveyed the sense of being a dominating presence in any gathering.

I spoke up immediately. "My brother-in-law, Daniel Klurman, gave me your name and address and advised me to talk to you."

"Aha! My good friend and teacher Daniel," he exclaimed. "He knew me through the Agudath Israel group I belonged to."

"He sent me to you saying I could trust you."

"In that case, young lady, I shall listen and help you with your problem, provided I can," he responded, bowing slightly.

We climbed the stairs to Andre's study upstairs. His wife, Magda, greeted Helene and me warmly. In contrast to her husband's olive skin, black hair, and the darkest eyes I had ever seen, Magda was fair-complexioned. Wisps of blond hair had strayed from under a paisley scarf that covered her head. She was pleasingly plump and projected a soothing, relaxed air. It struck me how different she was from Andre, with his brisk, vigorous movements.

Without a moment's hesitation, Magda invited Helene and me to the dining room downstairs. Seated at the table, I feasted my eyes on the spread of prewar goodies in front of me.

"Look at that bowl of snow-white sugar cubes," I whispered to Helene. "It's been ages since I've seen the likes of it!"

The table was covered with a spotless damask cloth. In the center, a freshly baked cake rested on a raised platter. It looked golden-yellow and moist, and I took a deep breath, inhaling its aroma.

Magda went to the kitchen and returned, carrying a steaming coffeepot. She began filling our cups with the aromatic brew. "Real coffee!" I cried. "What a wonderful change from the stuff we've been drinking."

"Thanks to the black market, we can still serve some of the right things to our visitors," Magda said. Then she added, "I wish it were as easy to get a kosher chicken for Shabbos." She cut me a generous portion of the cake, which I ate with gusto.

Andre donned a yarmulka and returned to take a seat at the head of the table. He smiled at us. "I see my wife is treating you right. But then, she has always been the perfect hostess."

Helene drummed her fingers on the table, impatient with the social amenities. She cleared her throat several times, and then, before I had a chance to speak, blurted, "Naomi's mother wants her to get away. She's been urging her to leave for Vichy, France, for the longest time."

Andre turned to me and did not speak until he made direct eye contact. "I'm sorry to say, not all those who try to escape make it. I receive many reports. More and more Jews are taken off trains or caught on the road by Nazis who've become experts at detecting fugitives."

I frowned. I had hoped for words of encouragement; this report was the last thing I needed to hear. Gathering my courage, I said, "I have a sister near Montpellier. My mother insists that I join her. I have no prospects for a hideout here."

"If you've made up your mind," Andre replied, "then I'd like you to go with Bruno. He's just about the best we've got. But he left for the Free French zone not long ago." He paused, filling his cup with coffee. He sipped while deliberating. "It'll take Bruno more than a week to return. Still, it may pay for you to wait for him. He's by far the best choice."

I gulped. A week! He called that a long wait? To me it seemed as far away as my next breath. I was being thrust into action with far more speed than I had ever dreamed. Still, this seemed to be what the situation called for.

The doorbell interrupted our discussion. It shrilled repeatedly with long, persistent rings.

Andre stiffened, his eyes alarmed. "The people I care to see don't ring that way!" he said tensely.

"It sounds as if it's never going to stop," Magda said,

bewildered. "Maybe I should find out who's ringing?"

"No, wait!" He stopped her, his voice hoarse. "Heaven knows who's at the door. I'm expecting Pierre, my contact from Brussels, but it's too early. He couldn't be here yet. Besides, he always uses our signal."

Magda quickly opened the Singer sewing machine that stood by the hall. Gone was her calm, relaxed air. In a frenzy, she cluttered the machine with fabric and trimmings, creating the impression that she was deeply immersed in her craft.

Helene and I sat frozen. We watched Andre slowly rise from his seat, his black eyes filled with apprehension. "I'm going upstairs to look down from the window and see who it is."

My heartbeat accelerated, and I closed my eyes. I heard the door shut as Andre left the room. Immediately, the doorbell stopped ringing. The next moment we heard three short rings and one long one. In chorus, Helene, Magda, and I breathed an audible sigh of relief. All of us stormed into the hall, where Andre was just about to open the front door.

"It's you, Pierre! It was you all along!" Andre thundered at the young man in the open doorway. "What possessed you to scare the life out of us with your infernal ringing?"

"*Mea culpa*! I am guilty!" Andre's contact from Brussels pounded his chest with his fist. He stepped swiftly into the entrance hall, and the door slammed shut behind him.

"You nearly gave my wife and me heart failure," Andre raged. "I ought to —"

"Please, please, Andre," Pierre pleaded. "What I did was wrong. You have every right to be furious, but I swear it was an accident." With his sleeve, he wiped the sweat off his pale forehead. His expression humble and remorseful, he continued, "Since I arrived early for our appointment, I lingered on your doorstep. I lit a cigarette and by accident leaned against your bell without being aware of it for the longest time."

"You what?" Magda shouted. "I don't believe this."

"As soon as I realized what I had done, I rang our signal. That's the honest truth! You must believe me!" Pierre persisted. With clear blue eyes, he looked imploringly from Andre to Magda and back.

In the silence that followed, Andre and Magda's anger began to cool. With a rueful demeanor, Pierre cocked his head, like some frisky puppy begging for forgiveness after making a nuisance of himself. Pierre was the characteristic Aryan prototype presently glorified by the Nazis, with the blond, blue-eyed good looks one associated with Nordic people.

Andre rolled his eyes and clapped him on the back. Magda offered him coffee. All was forgiven. After consuming a few slices of cake and a cup of coffee, Pierre thanked Magda and rose from his chair, walking jauntily to the door. Before leaving the room to accompany Andre to his study, he turned around and winked mischievously at Helene and me.

"This fellow seems to be full of the devil," I said with a chuckle after the door had shut. "I'm surprised Andre relies on him when it comes to serious business."

"I used to wonder about that, too," Magda admitted. "But in spite of his flippant airs and immaturity, Pierre happens to be capable, honest, and very clever. Andre has repeatedly put him to the test. Each time he's proved himself. That's why we trust him."

"I imagine that, because he's a gentile, Pierre can go places where no Jew would dare to be seen nowadays," Helene remarked.

"Yes, indeed," Magda said. "He's invaluable! Just one example: Because of certain connections he's made, he managed to obtain a *laissez passer* for a Jewish woman and her eight-year-old son. It allowed them to cross the borders legally."

While we waited for Andre to rejoin us, Helene reminded Magda of her apprenticeship to a corsetiere. Soon they were regaling me with stories of long ago. We hardly noticed the time slipping by.

The slamming of the front door when Pierre left startled us. As if in a daze, Andre virtually stumbled into the room and collapsed into an armchair.

"What's wrong?" Magda called out, moving toward her husband. "What calamity did Pierre have to report to you this time? He didn't act the least bit troubled before. What happened?"

Andre was clutching the arms of the chair. His face expressed a mixture of rage, desperation, and inner turmoil. He stared through Magda, not seeing her. Then, looking up, he let out a prolonged groan. "They've arrested Bruno. Dear God, what a loss." He buried his head in his hands. "Bruno was our champion. His record for saving people is unreal. He has no equal!"

"How did it happen? Tell me!" Magda cried, her eyes darting wildly.

"In Lille, well past the border. They took him off a train," Andre answered with a catch in his throat. He sat slumped in the armchair. "Seven people were in his group. To avoid being conspicuous, they'd spread out in several compartments. But every last one was caught! I think the Nazis have developed a sixth sense that helps them ferret out Jews!"

The stillness that followed weighed heavily. We looked soberly at each other. We were all filled with a sense of doom and sorrow. Andre was confirming my worst fears about the whole operation. Perhaps my sister-in-law Sabine had been right when she had said that the risks of escape far outweighed the dangers of staying put. How could I undertake such a journey, knowing the odds against me? And yet, how could I possibly remain?

Minutes went by. Finally I said to Andre, "I can well understand how upset you are. Perhaps I'd better leave now. Maybe you'll let me come back tomorrow." I swallowed hard. "I'll be grateful if you could still help me somehow."

"No, wait, Naomi!" Andre said. He sat up with a jolt. "Don't go." He stood up, his composure fully regained. "Please come upstairs to my study. I have an idea I'd like to discuss with you."

Helene turned to me and said, "Since you're staying on, I'll go join my mother, okay?"

"Go ahead," I replied. I rose and followed Andre into his study.

A massive mahogany desk stood in the center of the room. As soon as we entered, Andre settled himself in the imposing, high-backed chair behind it. He gestured for me to sit down on the chair opposite him. The bookcase was filled exclusively with Hebrew books, which surprised me. Andre, while a religious man, had not struck me as being a scholar.

He placed his hands flat on the desk like a businessman getting down to specifics. "The loss of Bruno comes at an especially bad time," Andre began. "I'm keeping four Jews from the Netherlands hidden in an attic. They were scheduled to leave with Bruno on his next trip. I planned to send you along with this group, too. Now there's nobody available to take all of you for weeks. A good number of weeks."

"I was told that you know every smuggler in this country," I countered.

"Maybe so, but the most trustworthy are booked in advance. These Dutch people can't possibly stay in the attic that long."

I was both flattered and bewildered that he had chosen to confide in me. "Perhaps you could move them to a safer place," I offered.

Andre frowned. "You yourself have learned how difficult it is to find a hideout in Antwerp. And you're only one person, mind you."

I nodded. That was true. But why was he telling this to me? I shifted a bit nervously in my seat, waiting for him to continue.

In an impassioned voice, he said, "Here's what I'm thinking. Naomi, you might be able to save the lives of those four Jews! If you did that, you would know the most blessed feeling of accomplishment a human being can experience. In my opinion, no deed can be more noble. On top of that, you'd be paid a nice sum of money."

I gaped at Andre. "I don't understand what you're asking," I stammered. "The Dutch Jews...my escape... What are you talking about?"

Andre looked straight into my eyes. "My instinct tells me that you would be a capable guide, that you have what it takes to lead these people on a trip to the safety of the unoccupied French zone!"

"Me?" I shouted. I shot to my feet. "You're mistaken! Never in a million years would I be able to do it. You picked the wrong person!"

"Please, don't surrender to impulse. That's the easiest way out," Andre pleaded. He motioned for me to take my seat. "Think carefully before you reject an opportunity to engage your courage and fight back. Here's your chance to save four lives in addition to your own."

It took me awhile to recover from the astonishment caused by Andre's proposition. I took out my handkerchief and wiped my face. The suggestion was so outrageous I would have laughed if it hadn't been so pathetic. I hardly had guts enough to save myself, and Andre wanted me to smuggle a group across singlehandedly! Still, I owed it to Andre to at least consider his offer. Soberly, I replied, "Since you put it that way, I'll think about your offer. By tomorrow, I'll try to have an answer for you, one way or another!"

That night, in the mattress store, I gave my friend a detailed report of my conversation with Andre. On her way over, Helene had bought plums from a vendor — a rare treat. She washed the fruit and served it on a paper plate, and we both enjoyed the juicy plums while sitting on our beds, talking.

Helene was unable to hide her astonishment. "Wow! That's some tall order!" Yet it didn't take long for her attitude to change. She stepped off her bed and came to sit with me on my mattress. "If Andre shows that much confidence in your ability, then I believe you could bring it off," she said in a firm voice.

"I wish I could be as sure as you are, but I don't have the self-confidence. Oh, Helene," I moaned, "I simply can't decide what to do."

Helene took my sticky, plum-stained hand in her own. "Just think," she said. "You'd be leading four Jews to safety. They may not have another chance if you refuse. And you yourself will escape with them."

I averted my eyes from Helene's frank gaze. In truth, I was deeply ashamed of my cowardice. In my dreams, I had often concocted scenarios where I bravely saved my brethren from mortal danger. But now that I'd been asked to rise to the occasion, I simply wanted to crawl under my blankets and pretend I had never heard of Andre and the four Dutch Jews.

I withdrew my hand from Helene's and distractedly began to stuff paper plates and plum pits into a plastic bag.

It was a fact that I spoke Flemish and French as fluently as any non-Jew. I would blend in perfectly. Young as I was, no one would suspect me of smuggling people across the border. Perhaps the mission really was within my grasp. On the other hand, if any of the Hollanders would open their mouths to speak, their heavy accents would give them away as foreigners and, therefore, as Jews.

"It's too much responsibility — four lives depending on me!" I said the words aloud. Immediately, I clapped my hand over my mouth.

Helene had started to straighten out her bed, folding back the covers. Now she stopped.

"Since none of them speak Flemish or French," she said, as

though she hadn't heard my outburst, "someone has to do all the talking for them in Belgium and in occupied France. They're doomed if left on their own — and also if they don't move on soon!"

I stared resentfully at my friend. Didn't she realize I knew all that? The fate of those four Jews already weighed heavily on my heart. Did she have to rub it in? If I felt I could handle the mission, I would certainly have done so. I was, at bottom, terrified for my own skin!

"How I wish I had more courage. I'm just plain chicken!" I wailed. And, covering my face with both hands, I burst into tears.

"Hush, hush, Naomi. No need to make yourself miserable," Helene said soothingly. "Let's sleep on it. You may see things in a different light after a good night's sleep.

But if Helene thought a peaceful night's rest awaited me, she was mistaken. All sorts of fears assailed me. Just a few days ago I had witnessed a man on the tram very politely asking the conductor at which stop to get off. He had Jewish features but would have passed unnoticed had he not spoken. The moment he did, however, his foreign accent became the only sound the other passengers heard. It was clearly the voice of a Dutchman. Unwittingly, he had led himself into a trap. Remembering, I trembled inwardly.

At once, two men in black shirts — pro-Nazi Rexists — moved close to where he sat. As the Dutch Jew stood to get off at the next stop — my own stop, actually — the black shirts were immediately at his side, asking for his identity card. When he refused, they held him fast. "You'll show your papers at Gestapo headquarters, Jew!" one of them barked.

Appalled, I ran along but stopped at the corner. From there I saw them march the man off, flanked by the two Nazi collaborators. The poor man never stood a chance. It was that image of the Dutch Jew struggling feebly, protesting in vain as he tried to escape the grip of his abductors, that haunted me throughout the night.

Then another image came to mind, adding more torment: the *Judenrat* seated around a table, signing papers that would seal the fate of their own relatives, all to save their own skin. I had expressed deep scorn for them, but what about me? My actions showed a concern simply for myself. Was I any better than they?

Dear God in Heaven, what was I supposed to do? How much was I obligated to put myself at risk? If only Leon had been there to counsel me. I always respected his religious opinions, and, most importantly, he knew me. I wondered where I might find Rabbi Freigut. I sensed that he had understood me and would have the insight to guide me appropriately. What a relief it would have been to submit to the opinion of such a wise man and scholar. I could have consulted with Daniel, I suppose, but the latest I'd heard, he'd finally been admitted to the hospital. Thank God, he was at last getting treatment for his TB.

The next morning did not bring me the clarity and peace of mind I so desperately sought. If anything, I was in even greater turmoil.

Once again I found myself facing Andre across the desk in his study.

"Look here, Naomi. Time's running out. The dragnet is closing in on our people," Andre said, his voice distraught.

"The Gestapo must have gotten orders from the higher-ups in Berlin to get rid of all remaining Jews in their territories — to finish the job!"

I rubbed my temples, trying to quell the pressure in my forehead. "I understand what you're saying. We're sitting on a time bomb. I know you're right," I told him. "I'd like to help, believe me! It's just that I'm not sure I can do what you expect of me."

We had arrived at a stalemate: Andre's passionate conviction stacked against my immobilizing insecurity. There was fire in the black eyes that bore into me. It was impossible to remain untouched by the immensity of the predicament. Seconds, and then minutes, elapsed in a tense silence. Then something shifted inside me. A certain resistance crumbled. I was ready to submit, to do whatever Andre thought I should do. I opened my mouth to speak.

As if he were reading my mind and following the direction of my thoughts, Andre said, "All right, I'm going to put you through a test. You could call it a trial run of sorts. If you succeed, you will gain the self-confidence you're missing now."

Quickly, he outlined my assignment. I listened carefully to every detail, as though my life depended on it — which it did!

THE TRIAL RUN

Two days later, on a train headed toward the province of Hainaut, I reviewed Andre's instructions. My assignment was to travel to a small border town, Momignies, to locate Andre's contact there and hire this person to guide us across the border into France. The contact's name was Marie Gregoire, and she owned a farm.

However, Andre didn't know her street or house number. It was my task to plan the entire trip, find the woman, and make the necessary arrangements without arousing suspicion. This was to be my trial — a test to boost my confidence and acquire the skills for the more dangerous mission that awaited me.

It wasn't much to go on — the name of a woman and a farm. But at least I was somewhat familiar with Momignies. That was the town where the glass factory was located, which I had visited over a year ago to see about the missing shipment of *flacons*. Eric and Sarah, my employers, had been so proud of the way I had successfully managed that trip. And here I was, taking the same train route. If I had done well then, I would, I hoped, certainly succeed now.

Mama had packed sandwiches with sardines, white cheese, and jam, along with hard-boiled eggs and a piece of cake. She had provided me with enough food to last me at least two days. She made no secret of the fact that she was happy to see me making a move in the right direction.

At the outset, halfway between Antwerp and Brussels, the train made its regular stop in Malines. The man facing me in the compartment put down his newspaper and turned to the passenger at his left. He began talking about a Jew who had escaped from a nearby camp, only to be caught by SS troops on the open road. They discussed the man's fate with glee.

"That Jew must have broken out from Breendonk," the second man offered. "I heard they really finish them off there. They practice torture like they did in the Middle Ages; that sort of thing."

The conversation made me feel sick to my stomach. I swallowed hard and sat up straight. I silently warned myself: No matter what I hear, I mustn't lose my composure. I have to blend in.

The first man turned to a page in his newspaper depicting a caricature of a bearded Jew with sidelocks and an overly prominent nose. He handed the paper to his neighbor and pointed to the derogatory caption. The two men burst into raucous laughter. They held up the paper to give me a glimpse of the caricature. Expectantly, they waited for me to join in the hilarity.

With great effort I willed myself to display a smile. This appeared to satisfy them, and they settled back in their seats, talking among themselves.

Upon leaving Brussels, the countryside gradually turned bleak and gray, dotted with mounds of dug-up coal and heaps of anthracite. As the train passed through Charleroi, Belgium's coal-mining district, black dust settled over everything, including the people who worked in the region.

When the train reached the Ardennes, the scenery gave way to green hills, grass, and shrubs. Finally a wealth of trees appeared, forming the dense forests for which the Ardennes were renowned. I gazed at manicured lawns and castles with moats interspersed between the forests.

Once I had felt such pride in these beautiful, natural settings. My Belgian citizenship had given me a proprietary feeling that let me boast of these lands as my own. The events of the last two years had very neatly and effectively destroyed that myth. The many decades of our family's residence in Belgium meant absolutely nothing. My brothers Nathan and Eugene had done their military service. My brother Charles had left Mama after World War II broke out, when he was called up to join his reserve unit in Rouen, France. Their sacrifices and patriotism, as well as my own, had been misplaced—wasted on a worthless, idle value, I'd soberly come to realize.

The moment I stepped off the train in Momignies, I sensed the change that had occurred since my first visit. Two Germans in uniform and armed with rifles stood guard at both ends of the platform. Their penetrating stares scrutinized each traveler with suspicion.

Without looking to the right or left, I walked straight into the waiting room that led to the street. I sat down on a wooden bench and glanced casually at the passersby. It was crucial that I did not approach the wrong person for directions to Marie Gregoire's farm. Asking a Nazi sympathizer could land me in deep trouble.

But was it possible to detect intense prejudice and hatred merely by examining someone's features? For instance, that woman by the door holding a chicken by the feet, her expression slightly bored and harmless — would she turn on me, snarling, if she discovered my real identity? Or the teenage boy smiling down at a baby in a pram, twirling his cap to make the baby laugh — was he a Rexist in disguise? What were the true faces of the people around me? With a sinking sensation, I realized how hopeless this business was of ferreting out the good from the bad.

Suddenly, crossing the waiting room, I saw a familiar face. Under the visor cap, I recognized the ruddy cheeks and lively blue eyes of the stationmaster who had so kindly directed me to the glass factory on my first visit to Momignies. Why, he'd even walked me part of the way.

I stopped in front of the man and smiled at him. A glint of recognition appeared in his eyes, and I said without a moment's hesitation, "Remember me, monsieur? You were so helpful the last time I arrived here. I'd be ever so grateful if you would once again give me directions to my destination."

"Did I really?" he said, puzzled. "I don't recall meeting you before."

I reminded him how he had showed me the way to the glass factory.

"Aha! Yes, now it comes back to me. I remember it all right," he exclaimed, grinning. "How can I help you today, mademoiselle?"

He stepped outside with me, and we stood in front of the station. "Please, tell me how I can reach the farm of Marie Gregoire. Is it far from here?"

His brow creased as he pondered the question. "Marie Gregoire, eh? All the farms are somewhat remote. It's quite a distance if you're thinking of going by foot." Lowering his voice he added, "And now there are more Germans around town than ever before."

Just then, a young man in overalls and work boots passed us on the sidewalk. "Hey, Jean Claude!" the stationmaster called to him. "Are you driving your truck?"

The young man stopped and nodded. "It's parked over there," he said, pointing to a flatbed nearby.

"Here's a young lady who needs a ride to Marie Gregoire's farm. Is that much out of your way?"

The fellow removed his straw hat and said, "Not at all! It'll be my pleasure — if Mademoiselle doesn't mind joining me in the cab of my old rig."

"I'm really thankful for the lift," I told him, considerably relieved by what I recognized as an unexpected stroke of luck. "Thank you, dear Father in Heaven," I silently intoned. It was the kind of chance I'd prayed for.

I climbed into the front seat of Jean Claude's truck. In a matter of minutes we'd left the town behind us and entered a rural road. At the sight of the first farmhouse, no more than one kilometer along the road, Jean Claude stopped the truck.

"Here you are," he said with a sweeping motion at the flock

of fowl populating the front lawn. "This is Marie's chicken farm."

After I thanked him and he drove off, stirring a cloud of dust in his wake, I stepped carefully among the cackling hens and strutting ducks and moved toward the house. I noticed an open side door and was about to enter it when the roar of an engine made me turn around. On the previously deserted road, four Germans in uniform were approaching in an uncovered military vehicle. My heart gave a jump. What was this?

A woman emerged from the house, moving with easy grace. Without a word she came and stood beside me. She was slender and bright-eyed, her hair a honey blond, and she appeared to be in her early thirties.

The car slowed down and I thought it was coming to a halt. Instead, the four soldiers grinned at my companion and shouted, *"Bonjour, Madame! Une belle journee!"*

The woman returned their greetings as if they were her good friends. She continued smiling and waving at the Germans as their engine picked up speed and they drove on. Then she turned to me. "Hello there! I'm Marie Gregoire."

I gaped at her. This was Marie Gregoire, the woman entrusted to smuggle Jews out of the country? Ugly thoughts assailed me. What I had just seen made me wonder if she was really a Nazi collaborator. Perhaps she handed over Jewish fugitives to the authorities after they paid her. How could I possibly know?

"I believe you were sent by Andre to discuss business with me," she said crisply.

I nodded in reply.

"Let's go inside where we can talk. Or perhaps you'd like

to rest after your long journey."

Still upset by what I had seen, I welcomed a respite to sort out my thoughts and make up my mind about this Marie Gregoire. "Yes, I'd like nothing better," I said, and followed her into the house.

Hours later, when I awoke lying on a bed, I saw Marie with her back against the wall, looking at me. She held a gray-white speckled hen in her arms and kept stroking its feathers. In her paisley peasant skirt and black cotton blouse she looked surprisingly smart.

"You've been sleeping for the past one-and-a-half hours," she remarked with a smile.

I blinked my eyes a few times. I sat up, stretching my arms and legs. "Did I really sleep that long?"

"Oh yes." With her free hand, she picked up a towel and cake of soap from a bureau and gave it to me. "Why don't you join me in the front room when you're ready?"

She seemed very pleasant, but I was still on my guard after her behavior a few hours ago. After I freshened up a bit, I went into the front room, which was a dining room, sitting room, and kitchen all in one. There was a fireplace with a stack of wood all prepared for the first signs of winter. Two levers for pumping water hung over a massive, blue stone sink. In the center of a long wooden table lay a loaf of dark farmer's bread and a big knife and cutting board. Next to it stood a pitcher of milk. "I thought you'd like a snack," Marie commented. "Do help yourself."

Apparently Andre had not informed her about my religious status. He had not found it necessary, and I thought it was just as well. Why make matters more complicated?

"Thanks," I said casually. "But I brought more sandwiches than I could possibly eat." I unwrapped the cake that Mama had packed for me and turned aside to discreetly recite the blessing. The last thing I wanted was to enter into a long, involved explanation about my religious practices to this gentile woman who might be a collaborator.

Marie sat down sideways next to me. She spoke softly, all the while stroking the speckled hen. "I hope you didn't get the wrong impression when you saw me responding to the Germans earlier this afternoon. They pass the farm every day. My show of friendliness is nothing more than a ploy to throw them off."

I coughed, and some cake crumbs flew from my mouth. "You mean it's only a pretense?" I sputtered. "You sure seemed overjoyed to see them."

"*Les Boches! Salauds!* I hate their guts!" she said passionately. "But the game I'm playing works. It wards off the least shadow of suspicion that could endanger my job as a *passeur*. After all, I guide people across the border right under their noses."

By her own admission, Marie was a good actress. How could I be sure she wasn't acting now? I kept staring at her in silence.

"You're a stubborn one, all right," she said with a little shake of her head. Then she looked me frankly in the eye. "I ask all the people I take across to write to Andre from Paris. Most of them did send word to him after they arrived in France. So if you still have doubts about me, you can ask Andre to show you these notes, which attest to my credibility."

I let out a deep sigh. "Well, I must say, you nearly had me fooled! I suspected you of being a collaborator."

Marie smiled ironically. "Yes, that much was clear. In the future, you'll do better not to make your skepticism so obvious. In this business, we must camouflage our feelings."

I nodded contritely. Apparently, my acting wasn't up to par.

"Let's get down to business, then." She placed the hen on the floor, then spread her hands flat on the table and said, "What's Andre got lined up for me?"

I told her about the people in hiding who needed her to get them across the French border.

"That can be arranged," she replied without a moment's hesitation. "My conditions will be the same as for the last crossing."

I felt reassured by her strong, confident manner. It was clear that I was speaking to someone in command of the situation. If I was any judge of character, this woman had leadership qualities. Suddenly, though, her poise and know-how made me doubt my own abilities.

I told her, "After you've completed your part of the passage, there will be four lives depending on me to get them to Lyon. That much responsibility really scares me!"

Marie reached for the pitcher and poured herself some milk in a bowl. She said, "You came from Antwerp by yourself and found me way out here with no given address without a hitch during the whole journey." She stopped and drank from the bowl. "Believe me, you'll make it into Free France. Take my word for it. Just tell me when I should expect you with your group."

Marie's vote of confidence had its effect on me. She believed I could do the job! The clouds of doubt cleared. Without deliberating further I answered, "God willing, next Tuesday I'll be back with my group."

I spent the night at the farm in Marie's spare room. After hours of sleep I was awakened by the call of a rooster. The clucking and cackling sounds that followed were a novelty to me. I listened to the talk-fest of the barnyard fowl as I lingered in bed before rising. But the day started early on the farm. When the coffee aroma pervaded my room, I quickly dressed, prayed, and joined Marie in the kitchen.

Breakfast was a quick affair. I gulped down one of Mama's sandwiches and finished it off with some cool water from the pump. When Marie offered to drive me to the railroad station I gladly accepted. Her old jalopy sputtered and belched as she started the engine. Once we were rolling, it rumbled and shook to no end. Yet I arrived at the station unscathed and had only a short wait before the local for Chimay came lumbering in.

The return trip, with all the changing of trains, seemed shorter than the voyage to Momignies had been. Perhaps the fact that I'd resigned myself to the inevitable made it feel that way. Since my decision was irrevocable, pondering and weighing the risks involved was obviously futile. A quotation sprang to my mind: "Whoever saves one life, it is as if he saved an entire world."

In years past, when my brothers were having discussions or debated what they had learned in classes, I'd often heard them cite that quotation from the Talmud. It had been many years since I'd last heard it. Then it occurred to me that its resurgence was a good omen — a promise that I would succeed in my undertaking and actually be instrumental in saving people's lives.

When I arrived back in Antwerp, I headed at once for the Farkasz' house. Andre and Magda were unable to conceal their pleasure on seeing me.

"We're so happy to have you back, Naomi," Andre said after greeting me. He scrutinized my face, then smiled broadly and added, "I have a feeling you accomplished what you set out to do. Tell me that's true."

I nodded, smiling back. "I've arranged to leave here with my group next Tuesday. Marie expects us in Momignies later that day."

"It's exactly what I had hoped for!" Andre exclaimed. "And it won't be a day too soon, because there's no denying it — the heat's on."

I looked at him nervously. "Just what do you mean by that?"

Andre turned to Magda. "Why don't you tell her what happened last night?"

"Please tell me," I said. I looked at Magda's somber expression and was gripped with alarm.

Magda wrapped her arm around my shoulder. "First of all, Andre would like you to stay here with us until you leave Antwerp," she said firmly.

"Oh, is that necessary? Please don't misunderstand," I said quickly. "It's really generous of you, but I'd rather be with my good friend, Helene, in the mattress store."

Andre and Magda exchanged glances. Magda said, "You have no choice. They raided the mattress store last night. The building was sealed off and confiscated by the authorities. It was an act of God that you were out of town!"

I gasped. Then it dawned on me: "Helene! What about Helene? Where is she?"

"I cannot tell you for sure. We haven't heard from her."

There was a tightening of my stomach muscles. I closed my eyes and thought I was going to faint. Mustn't give in, mustn't give in, I willed myself. I held on to the back of a chair.

"When did it happen? Can't you tell me anything more?" I pleaded.

"I wish we could," Magda said to me, her arm still around my shoulder. "We don't know the details, but apparently the Nazis found the evidence that you girls slept there with your meager belongings, including your suitcase."

I plunked down on the chair. "Oh, Helene! Helene!" I cried. I shook my head. "She's so clever. She must have eluded those evil beasts! Those demons from hell!" I paused and drew a long, painful breath.

"You know, there was a ladder the store owner kept standing against the back wall of the house. He showed us how we could reach the roof of an adjoining building where his friend lived," I rambled on. "The owner promised us his friend would help."

Magda nodded. Seeing the tears I was unable to keep back, she said in a warm and sympathetic voice, "Chances are that Helene made it into that house and that they're hiding her."

I wiped my tears, then closed my eyes and silently moved my lips in a fervent prayer: "Oh, God! Dear God in Heaven! I implore you from the bottom of my heart, please let my dear friend, Helene, be safe and stay free of the clutches of the Nazis. Almighty Father, hear my prayer and protect us all from our evil persecutors. Amen!"

TEARS AND FINAL DETAILS

The Three Weeks came and went uneventfully. The pleasures we normally had to forgo, such as catching a swim on a hot day and going on an outing or to the movies, were anyhow forbidden to Jews.

But observing Tishah B'Av, the culmination of the period of penitence, was a different story. On the eve, we ate a hard-boiled egg with ashes and sat shoeless on the floor as we listened to *Kinos* and the reading of Lamentations. Andre's brother, Herman, who lived a few houses down the Mercatorstraat, came over to conduct the service. Mournfully, in a silvery voice, he recited the traditional heart-wrenching prayers that initiated our saddest and longest fast day of the year. In this summer of 1942, Tishah B'Av fell on Thursday, July 23, less than a week before I was to escape.

Numerous details had to be worked out. Yet no matter how busy I was, Helene remained constantly on my mind. Where was my friend? If she wasn't caught in the raid on the mattress store, why hadn't we heard from her? I had gone to see her mother and found the apartment locked. The thought that Helene's mother and sister might have been deported as well made my heart ache. I grieved for the entire family.

On the other hand, the optimist in me kept clamoring to be heard. Unable to subdue the voice, I eventually gave in and listened repeatedly to the message: "Helene is safe. Her mother and Gerda are safe, too." Subsequently, I ended up believing what I wished so ardently to be true — that somehow I would see my friend again.

Andre sent one of Herman's young sons to Evelyn's house with a message for Mama to let her know how much I longed to see her. Within the hour, my mother arrived at Andre's with Evelyn and my nieces Rachel and Lili. Hugs and kisses and laughter were, needless to say, interspersed with tears. I endured the separation from Mama and my other family as a dire punishment. Had I not known they were in Antwerp, I think my yearning to be near them would not have been so strong.

"Aunt Naomi, Mommy is taking me and Lili along to the hospital. We're going to see our Papa," Rachel blurted, unable to suppress her excitement.

Evelyn stroked her daughter's hair as she explained, "They haven't seen Daniel since he was admitted at the Stappaerts Hospital. Whenever I leave the house to bring him kosher food from home, the girls beg to go along. Today I finally consented to take them regardless of hospital rules." She smiled sadly.

"They should at least get a glimpse of their father now and then."

After they had filled me in on all the news and about an hour had elapsed, Andre briskly entered the room. He cleared his throat, then announced, "I'm sorry to break up this family gathering, but there's a number of things we need to do to get Naomi ready for the trip."

I threw Andre an imploring look. "Can't it wait?" I asked him. I was showing my nieces a trick — how to make a mouse out of my handkerchief.

Mama, who was seated at my left, pointed an admonishing finger at me. "Naomi, listen to this man. You must follow his every instruction." Then she turned to Andre. "Please guide her as best you can. She's my youngest daughter. I beg of you, prepare her as if your life depended on it."

Andre looked down at my mother, his dark eyes filled with compassion. "Believe me, madame," he said firmly, "five lives do depend on this. Naomi is getting the best possible training from me."

Reluctantly we said our goodbyes. Mama hugged me and stroked my face, her fingers lingering on my cheek. "Till we meet again," she whispered. I could not see the expression in her eyes, but an immense sadness seemed to emanate from her fingertips. I kissed each one of her fingers and then, feeling as if my heart would burst, we parted from one another.

After they had all left, Andre presented me with a leather briefcase. It would be my only piece of luggage and contain all the worldly possessions I could take with me.

Magda called me over to her sewing machine and said, "Let's not waste time. I have to make a long corset for you with a panel that will hold your papers: Your legitimate I.D. imprinted with the black *J*, your birth certificate, and other items."

It would also be necessary to carry the fake, blotched I.D. in my purse. I prayed no situation would arise that would force me to show it.

Magda went to work with her tape measure and jotted down on a scrap of paper the various measurements of the projected undergarment.

"I suppose this will add a few inches to my waistline," I remarked wryly, hoping to get a smile from her. But Magda was all business. "When the corset is finished and you've inserted your documents, we'll arrange the papers so they lay as flat as possible."

I needed to buy a few personal things, but Andre was reluctant to let me go out. "Danger lurks on every street corner these days," he said. "God forbid, you should be recognized by a former neighbor and get arrested now."

This time Mama wasn't there to intervene on his behalf. I listened to Andre's arguments and shot back with some of my own counter-arguments. Eventually, despite his protests, I ventured forth to shop at the Innovation department store. Though I adopted a carefree façade I was trembling inside, well aware that department stores were off-limits to Jews. I made quick decisions so as to leave the store in a hurry.

A summer skirt and blouse would fit into the briefcase. I could also manage to squeeze a pair of lightweight pajamas inside. Fortunately, I had on sturdy, leather walking shoes and expected them to withstand a great deal of punishment on the road.

I couldn't help recalling the last time it had been necessary to consolidate all my possessions into one suitcase — the day the Germans invaded Belgium. Mama, Leon, Benny, and I had been heading for France. Compared with my briefcase, that suitcase now seemed huge and capacious. Then I'd even found room to sneak in a photo album. This time, no such luck. Any address or picture might identify my Jewishness.

Andre asked me to join him in his upstairs study. He locked the door behind me before sitting down at his desk. Then he opened a drawer and brought out a stack of paper money that looked foreign to me. He began counting bills, licking the index finger and thumb of his right hand every so often. Next he divided the money into smaller piles and placed some of them in envelopes.

"Here's one envelope I want you to give to Marie Gregoire right after you get to Momignies. In this business, it's payment up front," he said with a grin. Then he handed me another envelope. "This is your payment — four hundred American dollars. You'll have to hide it on your person or in the clothes you'll be wearing."

I had never seen American dollars. I studied one of the bills. "I know it's worth a lot more, yet it's so much smaller than the Belgian hundred-franc note," I remarked.

He nodded. "It sure is. And it's interesting that an American one-, five-, ten-, or twenty-dollar bill is the same size as the one for a hundred dollars." Andre suggested that I fold my American money so that one bill could be slipped between the inner lining and leather covering at the back of each of my shoes. Alternatively, the bills could be sewn into the shoulder pads of my lightweight spring coat.

Later that day, a trader in foreign currencies came and changed all my Belgian money into French francs.

"I'm going to show you something," Andre told me when the trader had gone. Sitting down at his desk, he produced a tube of toothpaste and cellophane. He pried open the bottom of the tube with a screwdriver, releasing some of the paste. "Let me have your largest French bill — one thousand francs."

I gave him the bill, and after he began folding it, he said, "Let me have another one."

I handed him a five hundred franc note. Folding both bills together, he reduced them to less than the width of the tube. Then he wrapped the money in protective cellophane. After inserting the packet into the tube, he refilled its bottom with the paste that had run out. Finally, he rolled the bottom part up so that the tube looked as if some of the paste had already been used. I watched every detail, wide-eyed with astonishment. What other tricks did he have up his sleeve?

"Here you are," he said, handing me the tube. "With your toothbrush next to it in your briefcase, nobody will suspect what's inside."

It was reassuring to see his expertise, but all these preparations had a way of making me face up to the reality of the upcoming journey. "Do you think I'm really going to make it across?" I asked him frankly.

"Let me put it this way," Andre said. "The smuggling guides were successful in their enterprises as long as they were obscure and unknown. Once they became openly successful they had a struggle on their hands. They often lost in the very end."

I gazed at him thoughtfully. "What you're telling me is that as a new guide you think I have a real chance..."

"That's exactly what I believe!" he said with conviction.

Just then the bell rang — three rings followed by one short one.

"Oh, that must be Pierre," Andre said absently. "I suppose he got hold of those items I asked him for on the black market." He began clearing away the cellophane, wiping up a bit of toothpaste that had strayed onto his mahogany desk. "Naomi, would you mind getting the door?"

I went down the flight of stairs and opened the front door. For a second or two, Helene and I stared at each other. Then I let out a scream, and without uttering a word we fell into each other's arms.

Magda and Andre came clattering down the stairs. "What's going on?" Magda called. "Is something —" She stopped in mid-sentence.

Andre looked over her shoulder. Then he threw his arms up in the air. "She's alive! She's safe!" he shouted. "Thank God, praise God!" Magda rushed forward, fumbling in her pocket for a handkerchief, then joined in our embrace.

Finally we pulled apart to examine each other. "Guess those mattresses were getting tired of our company," Helene said gaily.

We were both overcome with a fit of giggling. Wiping away our tears, we slowly walked to the dining room, where we heard a blow-by-blow account of Helene's escapade.

She had been getting ready for bed when she heard the rumbling of an approaching truck in the night. Not waiting for the vehicle to stop, she darted out the back door and climbed the ladder that had been placed there for just such an eventuality. Following the shopkeeper's instructions, she landed on the roof of his friend's house and lowered herself inside the building through a trapdoor.

"You must have made some noise. Didn't that scare those people?" I asked.

"Apparently they heard something," Helene said cheerfully. She took a sip of the coffee Magda had placed before her. "Monsieur Le Duc stood on the second floor in his pajamas with his mouth wide open. He soon caught on to what had happened, though. He and his wife have kept me hidden this whole time."

"I take it they're treating you right," Magda said.

"Oh, they're real fine people. They begged me not to go out for days after the raid. This morning they went to Sunday mass, so while they're in church I decided to slip out and let you know I'm still around. Monsieur Le Duc went to tell my mother that I'm safe. She's still hiding in Gerda's room in Berchem. Anyway, they've told me I could stay as long as I wanted. Their twelve-year-old son is away in a Jesuit boarding school."

"Oh, Helene! I can't tell you how relieved I am for you," I exclaimed. "You've found a safe haven, at least for the time being, with decent, kindhearted people." The raid had turned out well for her; now she was more or less protected.

"And you know what?" Helene said. "Nadine Le Duc offered to bleach my hair. Said I'd look more Aryan that way. She'd even like me to wear one of her crosses on a chain." She shuddered delicately. "So far, I can't bring myself to do either of those things."

"Be careful," I warned. "Sometimes the kindness of strangers isn't so innocent. They might have some missionary designs on you, you know."

"I'll be careful," she promised.

My friend's visit ended as we tearfully bade each other farewell. "Pray for me, Helene," I whispered in her ear. "The day after tomorrow, I'm starting out with four Dutch Jews in my charge. Pray that I don't fail." With heart and soul I implored the Almighty to help me make it to the unoccupied French zone.

Helene smiled through her tears. "I'd bet my last franc on you," she said. "How I wish I could be your fifth charge. Knowing you as I do, there's not a shadow of a doubt in my mind that you'll succeed."

I knew she meant every word she said. But Helene had told me earlier that her mother had exacted a promise from her that Helene would never leave her.

"Thank you for having such trust in me," I said softly. "May God be with you always, Helene!" I called after her as she walked out the front door.

On Monday, I expected to see Mama, embrace her, and — the unthinkable — take leave of her. Instead, Evelyn arrived with my nieces to offer their final goodbyes. Michael and Sabine had already been settled for some time in a small villa in Brasschaet, where nobody knew they were Jewish.

I could tell at a glance that something was amiss. My sister's eyes were red and puffy, and I'd never seen such sadness on my nieces' faces.

"What's happened to Mama?" I immediately demanded.

"Nothing happened to Mama," Evelyn reassured me. "She wasn't up to coming today, but she wanted to make the trip anyway. I had a hard time persuading her to stay put."

I looked at her, dumbfounded. "Not up to coming?" I repeated.

"Mama has a violent headache. I gave her aspirin and left her sleeping peacefully in my house," Evelyn explained. "Trust me, it's better this way. You'll spare her additional tears."

I sat down, the air knocked out of me. "I know you did what you thought best," I said after a few minutes, "but I cannot undertake this journey without seeing Mama once more. It's out of the question. I must bid her a final *adieu*."

Magda and Andre, who had been listening on the sidelines, began to argue with me. I stared at them. "Don't you understand? The disappointment is more than I can bear. If she can't come to me, I'll go to her myself. I must hug and kiss Mama one more time!" I rose shakily from the chair.

Andre followed me out in the hall where I went to fetch my spring coat from the portmanteau.

"Don't try to persuade me not to go," I said with stubborn resentment, lifting my chin.

"Naomi," he began quietly, "don't think for one moment that I'm unfeeling. I sense the mental anguish you're suffering." He paused for a few seconds. "In spite of that, I can't let you go out on those treacherous streets and risk getting arrested just one day before your escape from Belgium. There's too much at stake. If, God forbid, they should capture you, it would break your mother's heart for sure."

I stopped groping for the coat and swung around to look him directly in the face. "But don't you see, Andre? Only God knows if or when I'll ever see Mama again."

"That's true," he replied. "Yet we can't let our emotions obliterate our purpose. Common sense dictates that we avoid pitfalls where the consequences would be disastrous. In this case, not just for you alone..."

My hand dropped. Andre had reminded me of the four Dutch Jews whose fate was now decidedly linked to mine. Not only was I putting myself in danger, but four others as well.

"This is the end of July 1942," Andre went on softly. "Every day, the chances get slimmer for a Jew to return home from a walk on our city streets."

I sighed profoundly, forcing back tears that welled up. "I hate you for this, but you win," I yielded unhappily. "I'll stay put in your house, Andre, till tomorrow." At that, limp and sorrowful, I rejoined Evelyn and her daughters in the dining room.

Evelyn came toward me. "Look here, Naomi. Mama asked me to give this to you." She produced a ring from her purse.

I recognized my mother's engagement solitaire — a mere half-carat diamond set in a white-gold mounting on a yellow-gold band. How Mama used to stress with pride that Papa had chosen a flawless blue-white gem for his intended bride.

Knowing how Mama treasured the gift she'd sent me, I was intensely moved by her gesture. The ring fit my right middle finger perfectly. After I slipped it on, I vowed never to take it off. "Please, Evelyn, thank Mama for me, will you?" I whispered in a husky voice. "Tell her how miserable I am that I can't thank her myself for this precious gift, which I'll always cherish. And tell her that she'll be forever with me in my thoughts."

I hugged Evelyn. As I kissed her cheeks, the taste of salt startled me. Tears were trickling from her overflowing eyes. At once, the girls' sobs surged in sync with their mother's weeping.

"What is it?" I exclaimed. "You say Mama is safe, thank God. Michael and Sabine are settled in Brasschaet. And my leaving isn't the end of the world, after all. There's no need to cry like this, is there?"

"It's Daniel," Evelyn cried out, her face distorted with pain. "Oh, Naomi, they've deported him from his hospital bed! When I came yesterday to bring him food, he was no longer there. And I've not been able to find out where they've taken him."

Suddenly I felt faint. My legs seemed to be made of rubber, and I slumped down on the nearest chair. What I'd just learned was too horrible to accept as reality. I kept shaking my head. "No! No! This can't be. It's all a mistake," I muttered.

"When I last saw Daniel, his weight was down to forty kilos," Evelyn wailed.

This remark solidified my final image of Daniel. I saw him lying with utter frailty in bed as Nazi troopers came to carry him away. The cruelty of this scene hit me deeply. The next moment, I, too, was weeping bitterly.

THE DUTCH REFUGEES

That evening, in spite of a tranquilizing bath, I slept fitfully, tossing and twisting, tormented by erratic dreams that made me break out in a cold sweat. Oh, why did these dreams have to rob me of the beneficial sleep I'd hoped for on my last night in Antwerp?

When I awoke at dawn, I attempted to recapture the fragmentary visions, but to no avail.

I slipped off the bed and, still groggy, walked to the window. I watched the faint light breaking through the darkness of the night sky growing ever stronger and more lucid. It was going to be a clear and sunny day. My lips began moving as I recited "*Modeh Ani,*" thanking God for returning my soul to my body. I said it with great feeling, for who knew what the next day might bring?

Turning away from the window, I went to wash my hands and get dressed for the journey, not forgetting to don the special corset, with the papers inside, that Magda had sewn for me.

Afterwards I stuffed my pajamas into the bottom of the leather briefcase Andre had given me. From the Turkish towel, soap, and toothpaste to the extra pair of socks, nothing compromising had been packed except for my forged I.D. and the Micheline road map of France. Should the authorities inspect my briefcase on Belgian soil, the map might alert them to the fact that I was about to cross illegally into France. But a ground plan indicating the route we were to follow seemed indispensable, so I felt compelled to take a chance and prayed that no inspection would befall us.

Despite the early hour, signs of downstairs activity reached my ears. The weariness caused by lack of sleep lingered on, and I decided to join Magda. On my the way down, the aroma of coffee and baking bread made me queasy. If I were to eat anything at all, I was certain I'd choke on every bite.

Pierre, Andre's gentile contact from Brussels, had come in on the first morning train from the capital. In the dining room, he was savoring a breakfast of fried eggs and freshly baked white bread. All the while, Andre briefed him on his task for the day.

"To begin with, you're going to bring four Dutch refugees here. They're waiting in an attic at 124 Provinciestraat. Be extra careful. The streets are crawling with Gestapo."

"Okay, Andre, I got that! By the way, these eggs taste really fresh. Magda must have cooked them with that Hungarian culinary know-how of hers. Never had a more delicious breakfast!"

I stared at Pierre, marveling at his ability to relish the food that — on this day — was downright nauseating to me. He cheerfully finished his meal and went off to fetch the Dutch Jews.

All along, I'd given no thought to what the refugees would be like. As we waited for Pierre's return, I began to wonder whether these people were young or old, obviously Jewish-looking or light-complexioned, confident or apprehensive. Were they well-mannered, or would they attract unwanted attention?

Presently I let out a vast yawn. I climbed the stairs to my room to bring down my luggage. While there, I stretched out on the bed for a moment — or so I thought. When I awoke, I realized I had dozed off for forty minutes. Alarmed, I quickly raced down the stairs with my luggage, expecting to see four refugees and Andre's scolding face. Instead, Andre was alone, and he hardly noticed me as he paced back and forth, stopping now and then to peer anxiously out the window. "Where are they?" he kept muttering.

My heart sank. It was far too early to have a glitch in our plans. The tension mounted in the room. We had a train to catch; this was going to throw us off schedule.

Suddenly Andre shouted, "There's Pierre. He's coming this way!"

The next instant, Andre reached the entrance hall and was opening the front door. I ran after him, Magda keeping pace with me. Through the open door we saw Pierre crossing the street with one travel bag in hand. Before he set foot on the doorstep, he announced, "They're coming. All's well. I kept them at a good distance. Just don't shut the door behind me."

Within minutes Annie arrived — a brunette of about

twenty-two — followed by her tall husband. Soon after, Annie's sister Lena tumbled into the room with her cousin Jacob, a nineteen-year-old boy with green eyes and a mop of shaggy blond hair. Their pallid faces showed considerable strain. Too overcome to exchange words, the sisters hugged and embraced.

"Thank God, you're all here!" Andre welcomed them. "Whatever caused that frightful delay?"

Pierre drew a long breath. "We eluded a Gestapo raid by a hair. No sooner were we on our way than the *Wehrmacht* trucks came swooping down and blocked all entrances to the street we were approaching." He paused, letting his gaze rest on the Dutch Jews who stood huddled together near a corner. Pierre went on. "People were running in all directions, some bumping into each other. In the general scramble to escape the raid, I got our four people to backtrack, scurrying close to the houses, while I shielded them as best I could. By the time the whistle blew to line up the victims in the center of the street, my charges had disappeared inside the house they'd come from."

It seemed Andre had been right again about the wisdom of staying indoors. "Did you have to show your papers?" I asked.

"I certainly did. But they didn't want an Aryan like me," he said, grinning. "Eventually I rejoined our Dutchmen. And when every last trace of the raid vanished, we set out again. Hence the delay." He shrugged. "Wish we could've arrived sooner."

"Never mind that now," Andre said with a dismissive wave of the hand. "We have reason to be overjoyed with the outcome. And we owe a bundle of thanks to you, Pierre, and your good judgment."

The others in the room nodded and voiced their recognition of Pierre's merit in a chorus of appreciative murmurs. He accepted the praise with a duck of the head that was both bashful and smug. Andre took this moment to introduce me to everyone.

I looked closely at the four Dutch Jews who were to be my charges. One could tell at a glance that the couple, Annie and Nico, were newlyweds. Eight months of marriage under the most trying circumstances apparently had not dimmed the stars in their eyes. They were good-looking, intelligent, and seemed to possess a certain refinement. My guess was they wouldn't attract any undue attention on the road.

Annie's sister Lena, who seemed to be in her late twenties or early thirties, also had a pleasant demeanor. Andre had told me that she had a husband who'd left Holland soon after the war broke out. He ended up in Buenos Aires and had paved the way there with the intention that his wife would join him.

Their cousin Jacob, whom they called Koba, was a talented musician. At nineteen he'd already achieved a certain amount of success with his band and was heading for what he hoped would be a promising career in music. All of them belonged to a family of wealthy merchants and were socially prominent and part of Amsterdam's Jewish elite.

I learned that they were all members of a secularized religious congregation. They had enough Jewish feeling to attend services on the High Holidays and to practice a few customs and laws.

Magda was circulating with glasses of lemonade and took

orders for tea. Soon afterwards, Andre turned to me and said, "Naomi, come with me to my study right away." He beckoned to Pierre, too. The three of us went upstairs.

Inside the study, Andre handed Pierre money and sent the young man to the railroad station to purchase our tickets. "Hurry back," Andre called after him.

"Tell me," I said as the door slammed behind him. "Can we stick to the planned train schedule? We've lost a good hour because of the delay."

Andre took two railroad schedules from a desk drawer and handed one to me. We studied the departure times of our connecting trains. Andre checked his wristwatch repeatedly. At last he declared, "Yes, if we step on it, you can still make it. So let's go down and start things rolling."

Like a captain in total command of his ship, Andre reentered the dining room. The four Dutch refugees looked at him eagerly, awaiting his directives. The tension rose as he bade everyone to sit down and seated himself at the head of the table. Andre addressed the assembly: "This morning we had a loss of time that hadn't figured in our plans. In spite of it, you should be able to catch your connecting trains as scheduled." He glanced at his watch once more and then went on. "In a short while you will be on your way to Vichy, France. We all know the dangers involved and prayers for Divine guidance are certainly indicated."

Lena shuffled in her seat. "I don't really know any of the appropriate Hebrew prayers, at least, not by heart," she admitted.

Andre's eyes flickered. "There's a Chassidic saying: 'God understands the language of the heart.' You can pray using any words you like," he told her. "With Naomi as your guide and spokeswoman, I truly believe you have the best possible chance for a safe journey. Her mastery of the French language is nothing less than superb."

With surprising warmth, Lena said to me, "The four of us are very fortunate to have you as our leader through occupied France. You were probably told that none of us speaks a word of French."

"I'm fully aware of that," I replied quietly. I could well appreciate her dread of the journey that lay ahead. I added emphatically, "With God Almighty on our side, I'm prepared to meet the challenge!"

Pierre returned and delivered five railroad tickets to Andre. Destination: Momignies.

"Everything looks okay," he reported. "The Nazis don't bother with inspections at Berchem's sub-station. Not important enough, I guess."

Andre gave each of us a ticket and explained, "At the central railroad station, Gestapo agents are posted at the track area. They study every traveler at close range. Nervousness is a sure giveaway. Lately many Jews attempting to flee the country have been arrested on the spot to be deported."

Behind me I heard a gasp. I turned and saw Koba sitting with his mouth hanging open and his pale green eyes riveted on Andre's face. "If any SS were to eye me, I'd break down. I know I would become a bundle of nerves," he murmured.

"Have no fear," Andre said evenly. "We won't be going to the Central Station. At the Berchem station, which is just a ten-minute walk from here, there aren't any Nazis posted."

He looked at each of the refugees, his eyes resting a bit longer on Koba. Finally he said, "You're in competent hands. At all times, pay careful attention to Naomi and follow her instructions."

Then he stood up and signaled for me to follow him. Standing in the entrance hall he went over our itinerary. He finished, "You've got time to leave the house by 10:20 — exactly fourteen minutes from now."

"That should present no problem," I replied, feeling the adrenaline surge up in me. "Everybody is ready with one piece of carry-on luggage to take along."

"Remember, Naomi, never travel in a cluster!" Andre warned. "On your way to the station, Pierre will walk with you, well ahead of the others." He handed me a small package with three cards. "They're the French equivalent of our stamped postcards. Please, mail one to me from Paris right after you arrive."

"I definitely hope to do that," I said fervently.

"One more thing," Andre added. "Should you ever have to change your route and pass through Metz, you must know this: From the buffet and bar at the railroad station there's a door that leads directly to the tracks. The Nazi inspectors are posted at all the other entrances."

"I shall remember your every word," I assured him.

Andre appeared satisfied. Suddenly, I experienced an irrepressible urge to start out at last. As we were about to reenter the dining room, I couldn't help blurting, "I only hope Koba doesn't turn out to be a problem. That young man strikes me as overly sensitive and the most vulnerable of the group."

Andre's eyes looked reflective. " *'Hashem yishmor tzeischa uvo'echa mei'atah ve'ad olam* — May the Almighty guard your comings and goings until eternity.' " He carefully mopped his forehead. "You'll do fine," he said quietly.

Finally it was time to go. I embraced Magda. In these last few days she had been a kind of sister-mother to me, providing the warmth and guidance I so sorely needed. As I thanked Andre for all his help, a thought occurred to me: If Andre had been single and younger, he would have been the kind of man I'd have liked to marry. He had the same dynamism and personable qualities as Elie Tischler, but he was a committed Jew, someone who valued the Torah and scholarship. And Andre was fiercely dedicated to helping the Jewish people.

He had dealt well with my fears and devised a plan that had truly increased my confidence. Though he came across primarily as a man of action, he also possessed a deep understanding of people. Compared to him, Elie, with his attachment to the Yiddish theater and his inability to settle down at the age of thirty-two, seemed painfully shallow. Meeting Andre clarified for me the kind of man I was seeking. It was reassuring to me, in the little I'd seen of the world, that people like Andre existed. I stood there, struck with these thoughts.

Again I thanked Andre, and inexplicably my eyes filled with tears. With my head lowered, I turned away.

The five of us had boarded the train at the Berchem sub-station and landed in Brussels's *Gare du Nord* without incident. From the doorway I surveyed the interior of the station's buffet, where food and drink were being served. I counted a number of empty tables and decided we could all wait inside for our planned connection. The express for Charleroi was scheduled to leave in half an hour. In Charleroi we would board the train for Chimay.

I chose a small table, situated so that I could overlook most of the room. Out of the corner of my eye, I watched Lena, Koba, Annie, and Nico sit down at two separate tables. Then I took a postcard from my briefcase and with my Waterman fountain pen began to write to my mother. How I wanted to pour out my heart to Mama! But the message had to be carefully worded; all mail was rigorously censored. Also, I couldn't allow myself the luxury of emotion right now. I could not afford a moment's distraction.

Although addressed to Evelyn, I wrote mainly to tell Mama that I missed her and to reassure her that I was in control of the situation. I wanted to convince my mother and sister that they need not worry about me, that I felt confident and anticipated no problems. After all, hadn't the trip from Berchem to Brussels gone as smoothly as could be?

I looked at my watch. Fifteen minutes to go. I glanced furtively at each of the four Dutch refugees. They were respectably sipping the Schweppes lemonade they'd ordered. My assessment that they wouldn't attract attention on the road had certainly proved correct. What lovely people, I thought. I desperately wanted to believe there wouldn't be any trouble ahead.

I had noticed a mailbox outside, near the entrance to the buffet. I walked over there, dropped my postcard into the slot, and was about to return to my table when a station attendant in uniform approached. Holding a postcard up in his raised hand, his eyes caught mine, and he shook his head.

"I found this card on the platform near the tracks," he said in a confidential tone. "Most likely some Jewish girl on a train of deportees threw it from the window."

My heart froze. For a second I wondered if it could be my postcard. But that was absurd; I had mailed mine. And the man said he had found this postcard near the tracks. Why, then, was he speaking to me?

The station attendant continued. "They all pass through here, you know. Lately I have seen train loads of Jews coming from Holland and France. These transports are increasing in a way you simply wouldn't believe!"

I kept staring at the man, unable to subdue the pounding of my heart. A lump lodged in my throat, making it hard for me to swallow.

Gazing at the card in his hand, the man sighed and concluded, "It's probably addressed to the poor girl's folks. I might as well mail it for her." With that, he let it fall into the slot.

I nodded, still incapable of uttering a word. Thoughts raced through my mind as, with great effort, I maintained my cool appearance despite my inner turmoil. Why did he have to mention a deported Jewish girl to me? Had he guessed, just by looking at me, that I was Jewish, too?

Seemingly unconcerned, I managed to get back to my table. I twirled my straw in the glass of club soda I had been drinking. Glancing down, I saw that my fingers were trembling. I put my hands under the table to prevent anyone — particularly my charges — from seeing the way they shook.

Suddenly I wished it wasn't such a long itinerary to Momignies. Marie Gregoire came to my mind, and this proved a comforting thought. Marie embodied the strength I so badly needed. She had guts. Her image would be an inspiration.

My gloom began to lift. The station attendant was no threat to me, even if he suspected I was a Jew. I took a deep, long breath, which helped to calm me down, and resolved not to become so easily frightened or discouraged.

Before long, we were on our way to Charleroi, then Chimay, and finally Momignies. The entire trip passed uneventfully.

When at last the train pulled into the Momignies station, I immediately spotted Marie Gregoire standing on the platform. I also noticed the sentry booth and the armed German guard pacing up and down. The minute I stepped off the train, Marie ran toward me and hugged and kissed me with unexpected warmth. Before I had a chance to ask what this outpouring of affection was all about, she whispered into my ear, "You're my cousin. That's what I told this Nazi animal when he questioned me earlier. So please, act the part."

Ah, Marie the actress. I had forgotten. With my voice lowered, I remarked, "Yes, he stopped to watch the two of us embracing. And the way he stares! He exudes sheer hostility."

From the corner of my eye I saw Annie and Nico standing near the exit, pretending to search for something in her travel bag. On the other side, Lena and Koba were milling about. Good. They were keeping their distance from me and each other. Even so, Marie said quietly, "I instinctively recognize the four who make up your group. Come, let's get out of here and have your people follow us."

But before we could depart, the German guard came closer and stood in front of us. His gaze bore into me, and I knew he was about to ask questions. "This is my cousin," Marie volunteered. "She's come for a visit." The next instant she disarmed him with her most dazzling smile.

The guard was momentarily transfixed. He nodded, grinning slightly, then, without uttering a sound, turned on his heels and resumed his pacing.

Arm in arm, Marie and I walked out of the station. "How was the trip from Antwerp?" she asked.

"All right." I peered over my shoulder. My charges were nonchalantly following, still at some distance behind us. "Forunately, my people have behaved properly and don't draw attention to themselves. They act as if they belong. You'd hardly believe they're foreigners."

"That's some lucky break for you!" Marie replied. We continued to walk side by side. "You'll spend the night at the Auberge du Lion d'Or. Jean, the proprietor, is a good friend of mine. He'll take special care."

I raised my eyebrows. "Why can't we stay at your chicken farm?"

"Walking that way is far too risky. It's crawling with German patrols these days."

"How safe are we at the village inn? Usually the SS have lodgings in these places," I asked.

"You're going to be put up in a separate wing at the Auberge. Nowhere near any Nazis."

"What about the other guests?" I persisted. "They might get suspicious, you know."

"Don't worry so much!" she retorted with a shake of her blond head. "You'll be safe there. I promise. And you'll be served a delicious dinner in your rooms."

I frowned and bit my lip, walking along silently. It was easy for her to say, "Don't worry." It wasn't her skin the Nazis were after!

"Come, we're close cousins, remember?" Marie said to me. "We can't appear too angry on the streets."

I immediately plastered a smile on my face. Inwardly I wondered if Marie was in this purely for the money. With her acting ability, it was hard to know what she truly believed or thought.

A minute later, Marie spoke in a conciliatory tone. "You can trust Jean as much as you trust me. What's more, Jean will be driving you to the rendezvous near the border when we start out before daybreak tomorrow. It's even closer from his place. Believe me, it makes the most sense to stay at the inn."

I nodded and could think of nothing more to say. She had a way of throwing me off balance. One moment she seemed facile and flippant, the next, truly committed and sincere. Or perhaps my own apprehensions magnified every nuance of her behavior. I remained quiet, preoccupied with the various thoughts that did not stop crossing my mind.

TOWARD THE SUN

When we arrived at the Auberge du Lion d'Or, Marie led me to an inconspicuous side door. There we waited for my four charges to catch up with us. We were whisked inside the entrance and found ourselves in the spacious kitchen.

Marie introduced everyone to the proprietors, Jean and his wife, Adrienne. Soup ladle in hand, he greeted us warmly. He was in shirt sleeves, and his chef's hat billowed out over a well-nourished face with ruddy cheeks. The sparkle in his small eyes revealed a fun-loving disposition.

Adrienne was pleasantly plump and appeared to be as jovial as her husband. She took a minute to greet the entire group, then returned to her preparations. Dinner was being served in the inn's dining room. Wearing a big apron, she flitted between stove and counters, supervising the dishing out of the evening meal.

"I'm leaving these five hungry travelers in your care till

tomorrow, Jean," Marie announced. "I expect you to treat them as well as you've always treated me!"

"Go on, Marie! Back to your chickens," Jean responded. In jest, he showed her the door.

Marie laughed out loud. "I'll be out of here in two minutes. But first I need your office, if you don't mind." She beckoned me to follow her as she led the way to Jean's private office. As soon as the door was shut behind me, she said, "Payment up front is the rule in this business. I'm sure Andre told you that."

"Yes, he did," I answered crisply. I took off a shoe and pulled out a wad of bills I'd hidden there. The rest of the money was still concealed inside the toothpaste tube and in my specially made corset, which also contained an I.D. and birth certificate, as well as an official paper attesting to my good behavior, a document I would need to acquire a visa for the United States. It was Mama's wish that I should ultimately join my brothers in New York.

Marie counted the money. She was pleased with the amount. "Everything will work out just fine tomorrow. You'll see!" She parted from me with her usual self-assurance.

By the time our group was shown to our rooms, Marie had left the inn. Adrienne assured me that our true identity and purpose was unknown to the rest of the staff. In addition, our accommodations would be in a secluded part of the building, accessible only via a back stairway; no other guests were lodged in our section of the inn. My spirits rose. Score two points for Marie, I thought.

Nico and Koba shared a room for double occupancy. Right near theirs, Lena, Annie, and I were given a much larger room with three beds. Its decor boasted fine furniture, and we also had the privilege of a connecting bathroom. The men joined us and settled themselves into the rich upholstery of a couple of armchairs. Nico stretched his legs, exclaiming, "I must say, at least they're trying to make us comfortable this memorable night."

Before long, a knock on the door startled us. For a moment, we all simply stared at each other.

"Don't open it," Koba whispered agitatedly. "Don't open the door!"

After the second knock, I decided to investigate. When I moved toward the door, Koba leapt up and stopped me. I stood still, and then I heard a woman's voice from the hallway. "I'm the chambermaid with your dinner. Please let me come in."

"Just a minute," I called. "I'll be right with you!"

Koba signalled to me frantically. I stared at him. His shaggy hair was in even greater disarray, and the wild look in his eyes made him appear very alarming. "It's all a trick," he hissed. "I bet SS men are standing behind that door. For God's sake, don't open up!"

I considered this. Then I said, "No, Koba, it's not a trick. We were told that dinner would be served in our room. It's part of the arrangement. Really."

Lena's features softened as she tried to soothe Koba. "Naomi is right," she said gently. "There's no reason to be alarmed. Come on, darling. You can relax for now."

He relented, but he took refuge in the bathroom while the rest of us waited in the large room.

I unlocked the door, and the maid wheeled a laden serving table into the room. She was accompanied by a boy of thirteen or fourteen. He carried a stack of plates, which he placed on the big table against the wall. He stepped outside and returned with cutlery, water glasses, napkins, and two bottles of Vichy Celestine mineral water. Then the girl skillfully set the table, and all of us watched her, almost hypnotized by the quick, clever movements of her hands. I complimented her on her adeptness. Meanwhile, Koba rather sheepishly emerged from the shelter of the bathroom.

"Well, you'd better start eating before your dinner gets cold," the girl told us. "I brought you five pork chops with mashed potatoes and gravy — a rare treat these days. I'm leaving now. Enjoy your meal!" With that, she and the boy were gone.

We each took a step closer to look at the dinner for five on the serving table. A complete menu at any time, it was decidedly a feast by wartime standards. Starting with cabbage soup, the meal ended with a dessert of Brie cheese and fruit. Even a bottle of wine, a red Beaujolais, was included, compliments of Jean and Adrienne. None of it, however, was kosher. Contrary to what I had expected, the smell of the nonkosher food didn't make me want to gag. My mouth was watering, as was everyone else's.

Clearly these people were not of Orthodox background. I wondered how they would react to this bit of temptation. Annie finally said with a sigh, "What in the world are we going to do with all this nonkosher food?"

Nico, a strapping six-footer with a hearty appetite, turned his head away from the spread on the table. He had once told me that his grandparents had been observant Jews. He said resolutely, "I may not eat strictly kosher food, but I've never eaten pork in my life. I don't intend to start today." He looked at everyone in the room. "None of us here are going to commit the grave sin of eating pig meat, or any of this stuff!" We vigorously nodded our assent, though I did see Koba cast a longing eye at the French wine and cheese.

I was astonished. After being cooped up in an attic for three weeks, hardly receiving proper nourishment, how could these people resist this veritable feast? Then I berated myself: Who was I to be surprised at the greatness of our people? A warm feeling stole through me. We were going to make it to Free France; I was convinced of it. Suddenly I sat up straight. A thought struck me, filling me with alarm.

"If we send it back, we'll be openly giving ourselves away! Everybody knows Jews are forbidden to eat pork. The chambermaid and that boy could easily inform on us to the Nazis around here."

Lena's fingers drummed the coffee table. "We'll have to dispose of it," she announced. "Make them think we gobbled it all up."

"But how?" Annie asked with a worried expression. "How could it vanish without arousing suspicion?"

Everyone started pondering the problem at hand.

"I have an idea. We'll slowly flush it down the toilet," I proposed at last. "The bones won't go down. We'll cut them off and leave them. Who eats bones anyway?" Then I added, "It's a good thing they gave us a private bathroom."

"Perfect solution!" Nico exclaimed. All of us began to breathe easier.

"You know what?" Lena spoke up, getting into the spirit. "Let's soil the dishes so it will look as though we ate from them."

Nico remarked, "Very clever. We'll fill the plates and empty them one by one into the toilet bowl."

"That's all well and good, but now there's nothing to eat," Koba lamented. "Ooh! Am I hungry. I don't remember ever being this hungry!"

I felt everybody's eyes on me, as if I was not only their guide but also their newly elected rabbi.

"Look at those delicious grapes and apples," I pointed out. "There's enough for everyone. And we can wash it all down with the Vichy water."

Nico, Lena, and Annie nodded their assent, while Koba let out a prolonged sigh. I grinned to myself. A Koba who was peevish was preferable to a Koba who was high-strung and anxious. I did have vague misgivings about him, though. Hopefully, if another tense situation presented itself, Lena would be able to calm him down as she had done earlier.

After eating the fruit, we went to work. Soon the last bit of cooked food had gone down the drain by way of the toilet. Five soiled plates, each with a pork-chop bone on it, lay scattered on the table amid bread crumbs, apple peels, the residue of grapes and crumpled napkins. Thus we created the impression that a sumptuous meal had been consumed.

When the chambermaid and her young helper came to clean up, she beamed. "I see all of you appreciated the famed cuisine of the Auberge du Lion d'Or. Not a scrap of food left over," she said with satisfaction.

I nodded and smiled back at her. Little did she know!

Before long there was another knock on the door. "It's us, Jean and Adrienne. We must talk to Mademoiselle." We recognized their voices and immediately opened the door.

Entering the room, Adrienne said in a solicitous tone, "I hope you've enjoyed your dinner and are pleased with the accommodations."

Jean broke in, "I'm afraid none of you will be getting much sleep tonight. We have to move while it's still dark. My van will pick you up at four o'clock in the morning for the rendezvous with Marie. We'll wake you up in time to get ready." He let his small, twinkling eyes wander, to rest briefly on each of our faces. "Are there any questions?"

"No, nothing I can think of right now," I replied.

"Well, then, let's call it a day. You all look dog-tired, and I need all the shut-eye I can get." With his wife in tow, he walked out the door.

Nico and Koba retired to their room. Lena, Annie, and I prepared ourselves for a few hours' rest, too exhausted even for small talk. I virtually fell into my bed. My last thought before I drifted off to sleep was about Koba and how he would hold up under the stress of our journey. Perhaps I was overreacting to his jitteriness, just as I had done with Marie. But I was too tired to probe this any further and soon dropped off into deep slumber.

Under a black sky illuminated by a galaxy of stars, Jean drove us in his van past the outskirts of Momignies to the rendezvous with Marie Gregoire. It was five past four. Koba looked bleary-eyed and kept running his fingers through his hair. Annie and Nico were continuously holding hands and murmured little comments to each other. Lena looked wide awake and alert. Earlier, just as I had woken, I'd found her seated at the edge of her bed, expertly applying makeup. I watched in astonishment for a few moments, then rushed out of bed to get ready myself. Now, some half-hour later, we were all sitting on benches inside the slow-moving van.

As my eyes became accustomed to the darkness, I perceived how the main artery ahead slowly shrank into a narrow dirt road. Finally, there was no path at all. We had reached the edge of the forest we had to traverse.

In the glare of the van's headlights, I could discern tall trees with notched leaves and a dense underbrush. What hidden dangers awaited us within? I prayed with fervor: Oh, God Almighty, please let these woods become the threshold of our salvation!

Presently, Jean brought the van to a halt. He shut off the headlights the moment he spotted Marie standing near a parked car. She looked remarkably calm and elegant with a gauzy scarf wrapped loosely around her neck. We all dismounted from the van. Jean rolled down his window, stuck out his head, wished us *"bonne chance,"* and then promptly drove off.

Lena, Annie, Nico, Koba, and I huddled together in the eerie stillness of the night. The forest loomed ahead like a menacing blackness waiting to swallow us up. All my senses seemed heightened, like those of an animal poised for danger.

As Marie approached us, I looked back at the parked car. I didn't recognize it as hers. There appeared to be someone inside. The leaves rustled as Marie came closer.

Finally, she stood facing me. The others drew back. She said quietly, "There's a trail inside the forest that you are going to follow. I'll show you where it starts. It leads to a clearing with a small chapel, where I'll be waiting for you."

I was astounded. "Aren't you going to be our guide until we reach the other side? Until we enter France?" My voice hiked up high with incredulity.

"Yes, but not for this stretch," she replied, while her hands played casually with the scarf. "I've been offered a car ride, and I'll arrive at the Chapel of St. Catherine ahead of you. The route I'm taking wouldn't be safe for you."

I lowered my head, mulling over what I had just heard. Marie Gregoire was choosing a convenient opportunity to make her trip easier — at our expense. Since she possessed a legal I.D., traveling by car posed no danger for her should a border patrol stop them. We obviously did not have that option. A surge of anger welled up in me as I realized that Marie really did not intend to start out with us.

In a tense voice, I whispered fiercely, "That's not how it's supposed to be. I'm not prepared for this!"

"Oh, come now," she protested. "You'll be just fine! We'll meet at the chapel, and from then on I will lead you. That's when it really matters."

From the corner of my eye, I saw Nico and Annie look over at us. Annie looked worried. I resolved to appear calm for the sake of the group. I said in a calmer voice, "You have no right to abandon us at this critical moment."

Marie eyed me as if from a distance. "My dear, you are exaggerating. I assure you, you'll be fine."

She's too glib, I cried inwardly. Easy for her to say, "You'll be just fine." Her self-confidence was always at someone else's expense. "It's not right. You've been paid to do this job from beginning to end," I insisted, forcing back my tears. But I saw from the set of her face that her mind was made up. She had a core of steel. It was clear that further words would be futile.

We rejoined the Dutch foursome and together walked silently to the entrance of the wooded area. I could barely detect the beginning of the narrow path.

"Here you go!" Marie instructed us. "Step lively. Keep your eyes and ears open. And remember, no talking. Not one single word!"

She returned to the car. Bitterly, I watched her take off. Then a wave of cold fear washed over me, transcending all other feelings. I dug my knuckles into my cheeks and breathed hard. My charges had to be protected from my fear. They were relying on me. I placed myself at the head of the group. With a pretense of bravery, I exclaimed to everyone, "All right! We're at the gateway to France. Here we go! Just follow me!"

The slender, winding trail forced us to walk in single file. Nico and Annie kept right behind me, with Lena and Koba following them.

Deep in the dark woods, we were oblivious to the sweet song of the nightingale or the chirping of crickets. Instead, we listened anxiously for any strange sound that would disrupt the natural order of the forest. Time and again, the lonely rustle of a tree or the crackling of branches startled us. Tension ran high as we imagined the enemy lurking behind every tree or bush, ready to leap out and confront us.

We continued to heed Marie's warning not to speak. Yet an impulsive "ooh" or "augh" would occasionally escape Koba's throat. Each of these utterings jolted me and made my stomach cramp with fear.

Was it only two days ago that I had regarded Marie's courage with admiration and held her up as a role model? Well, she had let me down badly, and I would have to seek my inspiration elsewhere... Suddenly, an alarming thought struck me. What if Marie would not be waiting at the chapel? After all, she had nothing to lose. She'd already been paid in advance. We'd be lost without her!

I tried to think rationally. Would she do such a horrible thing? I didn't think it was possible, but what did I know anymore? I steeled myself. Calm down, I thought over and over. Get control of yourself.

I had no idea whether the Chapel of St. Catherine stood on French or Belgian soil. I dreaded the border guards of either country as much as the German patrol. Meeting up with any of them would spell our doom.

Suddenly an image rose up in my mind. I saw Papa sitting at the table at twilight as Shabbos came to an end. He was singing *"Mizmor L'David"* with a pure, simple yearning that filled me with awe. He had once explained, "When I sing, 'God is my shepherd; I shall lack nothing,' at that moment I believe that even if the whole world were against me, as long as my attachment to the Almighty is strong, I truly lack nothing. Nobody can hurt me."

I had not recalled my father singing in years. Now, at the memory of it, a shudder went through me. "God is my shepherd; I shall lack nothing." It was as if Papa had gathered all those precious moments of his attachment to the Almighty, condensed them into a single moment, and given it to me. He offered the gift of true confidence — confidence in the Almighty. " 'God is my shepherd; I shall lack nothing,' " I repeated to myself as we trudged through the dark forest for an hour or more.

At length, a small, gray stone chapel came into view. Everything brightened under the starlit sky, and we blinked as we emerged from the black forest.

There stood Marie Gregoire, leaning against the chapel wall, her little scarf blowing about her neck. The sight of her evoked in me a moment of near ecstasy. Behind me, sighs of relief came from the Dutch refugees.

Then I checked myself. This woman might smuggle us into France, but she was not the source of our salvation. That claim belonged to the Almighty, and only to Him.

From the chapel, we continued to walk. Marie guided us, moving with light, sure steps. At long last we reached the end of the woods. Grasping the reality that we had arrived in France, my eyes filled. Koba let out a little yelp of joy, but he immediately quieted when Marie fixed him with a hard look.

"Remember," she said sternly, "we're still in Nazi-occupied territory. You all have yet to reach the demarcation line. You must cross it — illegally — before you can enter the unoccupied French zone."

"Yes, of course," I muttered.

Taking our first steps on French soil, we felt exposed and vulnerable. I could smell the scent of danger with every breath I inhaled. Though not as dark as before, it was still difficult to see. Fortunately, at six o'clock in the morning, there were no people milling about.

We had exited onto rough and rather rugged terrain. Marie led us across the open expanse as quickly as possible. The five of us strained to keep pace with her.

We soon reached a bistro. The white-haired woman behind the counter stopped drying dishes when she saw us. "Ah,

Marie! I knew you would be coming one of these days," she cried. "You brought five this time, eh? I just brewed some fresh coffee — the best ersatz you can get."

"*Tres bien,* Madame Therese!" Marie said, smiling. "And with it we'll have some pastries. The ones we can get without rationing coupons." When the woman raised her eyebrows in innocence, Marie continued, "The kind you're hiding under the counter."

Madame Therese guffawed. Everyone climbed onto a bar stool at the counter. After changing Belgian francs into French money, we were served right away. Greedily, we drank the steaming hot brew. The others devoured what seemed to be slightly stale *brioches*. Nico paid with French francs, leaving a generous tip, which delighted the woman.

"Tell me, Marie, what time does our train leave for Paris?" I asked.

She glanced at her wristwatch. "It is scheduled to depart in forty-seven minutes." She turned to the woman. "Madame Therese," she said in a low voice, "we must wait here."

"That's all right with me," Madame answered. "As long as we have no company. You know what I mean." She winked.

I repeatedly turned my head to look out the window. Suddenly I gasped. Two of the tallest gendarmes imaginable were coming up the road in our direction. I gulped. "Uh-oh. Trouble! The police!"

"Quick! All of you — out the back!" Madame Therese hissed. She rushed the group through a door behind the counter and out into a corridor. There she herded us into a relatively large broom closet.

Marie, however, remained seated on her bar stool. She had

nothing to fear. Her Belgian I.D. permitted her to cross the border into France. Earlier, Marie had mentioned to me that, should the authorities question her presence in the bistro, she would answer, "Madame Therese is my aunt, and I like to visit her."

In near panic, the five of us stood packed together in the small, windowless utility room. A bare electric bulb on the ceiling gave off the dimmest light. After awhile, the lack of oxygen made breathing more and more difficult.

Beads of sweat appeared on Nico and Koba's foreheads. Seconds and then minutes crawled by. I began to feel woozy, and I feared I was about to faint. I uttered a soundless prayer: "Dear merciful Father above, with heart and soul I implore you: watch over me and my four charges. Shield us from all that is evil. Let no harm befall us!"

Someone was gasping for air. "I am suffocating! I can't stand it another minute!" Koba howled. "Let me out of here!" Pushing and shoving, he managed to escape from the closet.

"Someone stop him!" Annie cried in horror.

"Catch him! Bring him back! Please," Lena pleaded hysterically. "That boy will be the downfall of us all!"

Without thinking, I raced after Koba. My heart pounding, I caught up with him at the entrance to the bistro. I growled into his ear, "Are you crazy? If you go in there, the gendarmes will interrogate you, and in one second, all of us will be thrown into a Nazi concentration camp!"

With eyes twice their normal size, Koba stared at me.

"Uh...I...I was choking in there. I thought I would die!" His face became distorted, and he mumbled between sobs, "Couldn't think straight anymore. You must forgive me. Please."

My urge to scold him died away immediately. I said in a low, urgent voice, "All is forgiven. But please, go back to the room. Move quickly!"

Koba took two steps, then paused, drawing a sleeve across his forehead. He looked fearfully at the utility room.

"You can leave the door open just a crack." Then I pointed with all the authority I could muster. "Now move!"

Koba darted back into the utility room like some chastened puppy. With relief I began to follow him.

Suddenly I heard the sound of a chair scraping the floor, and the tramp of approaching footsteps. Did they belong to the gendarmes? Had the noise in the corridor alerted them? I froze, trying to decide if I should make a mad dash for the utility room or, instead, saunter casually into the bistro.

There was no time to weigh the pros and cons. My feet propelled me toward the bistro. I knew I had made the right choice when the door flung open and a blond gendarme stood in front of me, his tall frame filling the doorway. Had I run toward the utility room, not only would I have been caught but the four Dutch refugees as well.

I walked toward the gendarme, my hands clammy. "*Bonjour,*" I greeted him before he could utter a word. "I see you have discovered the delights of Madame Therese's bistro, too!"

His pale forehead wrinkled, and he opened his mouth as if to object, but I walked breezily ahead into the bistro.

As I entered, the other gendarme, a darker fellow, was clambering to his feet.

The blond gendarme cleared his throat. "Mademoiselle, your presence here at this odd hour is very strange." He examined my face, and I realized, to my consternation, that it was covered with sweat.

All right, Naomi, I steeled myself. This calls for some superior acting. Get to it! I smiled and raised my hands in mock defeat. "All right, I admit it. You've caught me at my favorite exercise. Every morning I take a four-kilometer walk — at the crack of dawn." I fanned my neck with one of Madame Therese's napkins. "It's the only way I don't melt in this infernal summer heat!" I mopped my face with the napkin. "But I always work up a terrible sweat anyway." Unconcernedly, I plopped onto a high stool and said to Madame, "A black coffee, please."

The four of them — Marie, Madame Therese, and the two police officers — gaped at me in astonishment. Then Madame quickly got busy with the coffee preparation, and Marie resumed eating.

The darker gendarme came over to me. "An early-morning walker, eh?"

I took a deep breath. "Oh yes," I told him. "It helps keep those kilos off, you know." I patted my stomach, then added shamefacedly, "But those delicious cakes of Madame's always seem to undo my hard work."

He let out a chuckle, and for a moment I breathed more easily. My acting was working. From the corner of my eye, I saw that even Marie was taking note of my abilities.

Meanwhile, the blond gendarme's gaze had not left my face. He was sipping his coffee and watching me. Pure fear made me go clammy again. I reached for another napkin and dabbed at my temple and nose.

"It's hot in here," the blond gendarme remarked. I simply

nodded. "I'd like to see your I.D.," he said suddenly.

My heart skipped two beats. Then I gave him a blank, innocent look. "My I.D.?"

The other gendarme broke in, "Albert, is this necessary? Since when is taking an early-morning stroll illegal?" He gave me a grin.

"Of course it's not illegal," Albert said impatiently. "All the same..." He gave me an apologetic look. "I'm sorry, mademoiselle, to have to trouble you. Regulations, you know."

"No problem at all," I said hurriedly.

"Honestly, Albert," the dark gendarme said exasperatedly. "Why make her go to the trouble..."

I glanced over my shoulder to see if his friend's words had any effect. But Albert simply leaned on the counter, cradling his mug of coffee in his palm.

My fingers were trembling badly, and my breath was coming out in short spurts. To have come this far, only to be caught because of my phony I.D.! For it was as clear as day that as soon as he saw my I.D. with the blotched lettering he'd realize it was a fraud. Oh, Koba, why couldn't you have stayed put?

My fingers moved slowly, groping for the I.D. card, while my mind raced to think of a way out of the trap I had entered. An idea occurred to me, simple yet outrageous.

I spun around and walked toward the gendarme. "Here it is," I said, catching him unawares. I thrust my card so abruptly at him that his mug of coffee jiggled and overturned. The hot liquid spilled onto my arm and blouse, as well as on my I.D. card. "Oh!" I gasped, standing back. "Look what you've done!"

The blond gendarme gaped stupidly while I sputtered and

wailed, "I'm scalded!"

Albert finally found his tongue. "Mademoiselle, I'm sorry, terribly sorry!" he said over and over again.

Madame Therese fussed and fretted. "You poor dear. There, put some butter on your arm. Is that the only place you got burned?"

I sniffled and nodded. "And my I.D. card is all wet and ruined," I lamented.

The blond gendarme hung his head. "Please, mademoiselle, don't be angry. I was only following regulations. If there's anything I could do to help..." His words trailed off.

I thought quickly while I pressed the slab of butter against my arm. It really did hurt. "Perhaps you can," I said. "Till I receive my new I.D., it may take some time. Could you please just write a little note, explaining what happened? Just in case I should be asked to show my I.D."

"But of course," Albert said promptly. "It's the least I can do." With a flourish he took out a pen, while Madame tore off a sheet of paper and handed it to him.

"Here," he said finally, presenting me with a signed note. "This will help, should a situation arise."

"Another cup of coffee?" Madame Therese offered him.

"Oh no," Albert said hastily. "We have already extended our stay. We'd better be off." He raised his cap, and the two quickly retreated, shutting the door behind them.

Marie and I stared at each other, holding our breaths as we listened to the *click-clack* of their boots against the pavement growing ever more faint.

After a minute passed, I let out a soft whoop. Madame

Therese and Marie congratulated me on my quick thinking.

They listened, wide-eyed, as I explained the circumstances that had brought me back to the bistro. Suddenly, I clapped my hand to my forehead. "Oh no! My refugees!" I dashed back to the utility room to fetch them, and once again we assembled in the bistro. Annie and Lena hugged me tightly. They thought I had been arrested. It was a poignant moment for everyone.

Still shaken by the close call, I turned to Marie. I was anxious to catch that train. "How much longer till we can go to the station?"

After looking at her watch, she jumped off the stool and announced, "Time to go! You'll be catching the express to Paris, and I am traveling in the opposite direction. Back to my chicken farm in Momignies."

When we'd first entered the bistro, it was still dark outside, but in that half-hour of waiting in the broom closet, the sun had begun to rise. Marie led the way out of the bistro, all of us blinking and rubbing our eyes in the strengthening light of a new day.

We were approaching the station. Marie turned around and beckoned us to walk faster. Lena, Koba, Annie, and Nico were behind me.

We heard the long, drawn-out whistle of the oncoming train in the distance. This was it, then. We were leaving. Standing on the platform, I glanced down at the pavement and the steel tracks glistening in the sun. Soon the express would be hurtling along them, propelling me and my four Dutch fugitives to our destination. All the events of the last few hours receded to the back of my mind.

I touched my cheek. It was wet. Then my tears were everywhere, streaming down my cheeks, falling on my wrists and arms. Mama! Michael! Evelyn! I was being wrenched from the ones I loved. A feeling of profound sadness came over me.

This earth, these lands, had betrayed us. They had carried us for so long, but now they were spitting us out — or, worse yet, turning into a graveyard for the souls I loved best. I pressed my hand against my heart. The ache was unbearable.

As if from far away, I heard Marie say with quiet excitement, "We're just about there. You're going to make it!"

I glanced at the train before me, and then my gaze was drawn upward to the sun. It gave off a light so soft it was almost translucent and shot through with specks of gold. I moved quickly. Nico had just helped Annie onto the train and was now boarding himself.

A strange sensation came over me, something I had never experienced before. I had the oddest feeling that each step I was taking was not only bringing me closer to freedom but toward the forming of a whole person — me. For the first time I felt a complete readiness to marry and bring other souls into the world. Fantastically, I could almost sense those souls hovering about me, beckoning me: "Come, Naomi, step lively. So much depends on you. Come forward, so we, too, can be born."

"Hurry up!" Marie whispered urgently, jolting me out of my reverie.

I glanced at the dusty ground, then up again at the sun. I was pulled by those two images — the souls I was leaving behind, and the souls that were yet to be born. I hugged my briefcase closer to me. Then, squaring my shoulders as Mama would have done, I went forward toward the soft radiance, toward the sun.

THE AFTERMATH

The names of the many people who appear in this autobiographical novel — relatives, friends, rabbis, and acquaintances — have been changed for reasons of privacy. It is the author's hope, however, that their deeds and the fates that befell these men and women will remain forever as a testimony to their lives. Below is a brief account of what happened to them as a result of the war:

MAMA: In September 1942, an ad appeared in a local newspaper: "As an act of benevolence, additional food stamps for sugar are being distributed to Jews at the borough hall in Borgerhout." Naomi's mother went to the borough hall, perhaps with the intention of surprising her daughter and grandchildren with a gift of that scarce commodity, sugar. At the hall, she was arrested, along with other Jews who had fallen for the trap sprung by the Nazis. After World War II, Naomi was informed that her mother had been killed in Auschwitz.

MICHAEL: While hiding with Sabine in a villa in Brasschaet, Michael had become good friends with owners of a stationery shop, the brothers Le Blanc. One day, the brothers urged Michael to join them at an important soccer match featuring his favorite team, the Beerschot. To make the suggestion even more tempting, his friends offered Michael a free admission ticket. Sabine pleaded with her husband to turn down the offer. He argued that his friends had assured him he was safe in their company. On the Sunday of the game, in February 1943, nothing could stop Michael from boarding the tram and joining the Le Blanc brothers. That day Michael was arrested. He was brutally beaten and tortured for refusing to divulge where his wife was hiding. By the time Michael was deported to Auschwitz, his body was ravaged by typhus fever. At the stop before the last on the transport, when all the children, the elderly, the sick, and the disabled were removed, Michael was taken off the train and murdered along with the rest.

SABINE: After Michael was caught, Sabine and her sister remained hidden in Brasschaet. Often they would sit on the porch, knitting. On one such afternoon, a gray car pulled up with two Gestapo agents inside. The sisters immediately ran to a nearby villa, where neighbors had promised them refuge. But as Sabine fled, holding on to her knitting, the yarn unraveled and trailed after her, leading the Gestapo to her hiding place. They were caught and taken to Auschwitz. Sabine survived the camps, thanks to the intercession of a girl from Antwerp, known as the "Angel," who secured her a job in the "sewing room" in Birkenau and risked her life many times on her behalf. Sabine returned to Antwerp, married a widower, and gave birth to a son.

DANIEL: From his sickbed in Stappaerts Hospital, Daniel was transported to the concentration camp in Mechelen. From there, he was deported to Auschwitz, where he died.

EVELYN: A collaborator living across the street denounced Evelyn and her children to the Nazis. When the Gestapo came to arrest them, Evelyn received permission to fetch a coat for the girls and herself. Once upstairs, she rushed with Rachel and Lili out on the roof and nearly succeeded in escaping through a special route another neighbor had devised. However, an SS man stopped them at gunpoint on the adjoining roof, and they were taken to the camp in Mechelen and from there to Auschwitz. At one point, all children were to be separated from their parents and killed immediately. According to witnesses' reports, when the Nazis attempted to wrest Rachel and Lili away from their mother, Evelyn got off the train with both of them. Holding their hands, she joined them in their final destination.

CHARLES: Charles led the most peripatetic existence of all the family members. He was initially drafted into the Belgian army, only to be released and told he was on his own. Slipping aboard a ship of unknown destination, he eventually arrived in Casablanca. After contacting his brothers Nathan and Eugene, he received a ship's ticket. Destination: New York. Point of departure: Portugal. When he landed in Lisbon, he arranged with a Portuguese grocer to ship food to his family in Belgium, as well as to distant relatives in Poland, promising that he would send the grocer money once he arrived in New York. The arrangement continued until the Nazis prohibited parcels sent from abroad. In 1946, Charles received a check for forty-three dollars from the Portuguese grocer — money left over after the prohibition.

On his first Shabbos in New York, Charles went to shul and was invited home by a man who would later become his father-in-law. He was warmly taken into the circle of former diamond dealers from Antwerp and became a diamond cutter. Soon he opened his own shop and employed a number of people. After achieving success in that area, he became a stockbroker for a prestigious brokerage house in New York. He is still active and successful in his profession. Charles and his wife have five children and twelve grandchildren.

LEON: Leon was arrested by the Vichy police in February 1941. After briefly working with a slave-labor detail, he managed to receive papers and a ship's ticket to escape to Cuba. Eventually he joined his brothers in New York and married soon after. In Brooklyn, he received a position as a rebbe and lecturer at Yeshivas Torah Vodaath and is the author of several books on Jewish history, which are used in many yeshivos in Israel and the United States. He has nine children and numerous grandchildren and great-grandchildren.

BENNY: In September 1942, Benny fled from Vichy, France, joined an underground, and was eventually smuggled into Switzerland. He remained in Switzerland, where he later became a teacher of orphans who survived the war. He also studied psychology at the University of Basel. After the war, he emigrated to the United States. There he married and started a successful insurance agency. He has two children and twelve grandchildren. He still likes to learn Torah and, with his beautiful voice, enjoys *"davening far dem amud."*

CLAIRE AND JULIUS: Naomi's sister and brother-in-law had settled in Free France in Montagnac. After the Germans occupied the Free French zone, Claire, with her Belgian I.D., was not persecuted and even gave birth to a fourth child. Her husband, however, with his German passport, was arrested and incarcerated in the infamous camp Les Milles. Claire's brothers, Nathan and Eugene, had sent one ship's ticket, which she decided to give to Julius. He was set free and allowed to leave Europe. Julius survived the war in Cuba, while his wife and children stayed in Montagnac. They were reunited in Cuba in 1946. Today they live in Brooklyn.

EUGENE AND NATHAN: These brothers were instrumental in first bringing Charles and Leon to the United States. When World War II ended, with Charles's help they also succeeded in bringing Benny and Naomi over. Eventually, Claire, Julius, and their children arrived in New York, also thanks to the brothers' assistance. For years, Eugene was a successful diamond broker. In due time, he secured the prestigious position of broker for the Beers Syndicate of London. He and his wife have two children and nine grandchildren.

Being single, Nathan was drafted into the American army and sent overseas toward the end of 1943. He landed in Algeria and married a lovely Jewish girl he met in Oran. His wife, Celine, became part of a contingent of war brides who were shipped to the United States. She was welcomed by the family in New York and lived in Charles's house until Nathan was discharged from the army.

Meanwhile, Nathan, newly promoted to the rank of corporal, moved on with his troops to fight in the invasion of

Italy. He went as far north as Florence, then was sent back to the States where he remained in service till the end of the war.

Nathan and Celine had three children. When all their children emigrated to Israel, the parents decided to make aliyah, too. They settled in Netanya, and Nathan continued his profession of diamond cutter in Ramat Gan's diamond center. Nathan and Celine have eleven grandchildren.

HELENE: Helene, her mother, and her sister, Gerda, were arrested in a daytime raid on their apartment. During the selection process in Auschwitz, her mother was sent to her death on the left, while her daughters ended up on the right. The girls were put to work unloading the coal that kept arriving in trucks — coal to stoke the ovens. One day, a truck veered, hitting Gerda and breaking her legs. A guard blew a whistle and shouted an order to carry Gerda away. She resisted with all her might and cried hysterically, knowing all too well where they were taking her. According to witness accounts, Helene took Gerda's hand and soothed her. Making the decision not to abandon her sister at this time, she accompanied her to the ovens, where both were exterminated.

ELIE TISCHLER: Elie and his brother were staying in a hotel in Lyon, where they were awaiting affidavits that would allow them entry to the United States. One day, Elie met an acquaintance from Antwerp in a café on the boulevard. The two men ordered coffee and pastries. Before the waiter returned with their orders, the establishment was raided by the Vichy police. Elie Tischler was arrested and incarcerated in the notorious camp Les Milles. From there he was deported to Auschwitz.

RABBI FREIGUT: After the yeshivah in Heide had been

devastated by hoodlums, the *rosh yeshivah* settled in an apartment in Antwerp, on the Stoomstraat. There he gave *shiurim* to a handful of boys who remained. Only after the last of his students departed did Rabbi Freigut decide to arrange for his own escape to the Free French zone. He shaved his beard and, with all his belongings in one bag, boarded a train heading south. On approaching the border, the train stopped. A Belgian border patrol and German SS men came aboard. Rabbi Freigut, among other Jewish passengers, was arrested and deported to Auschwitz.

ANDRE AND MAGDA: The Hungarian couple was caught in a raid in their house. The Gestapo disregarded Andre's protestations that he and Magda should be released because of their Hungarian citizenship. They were deported to Auschwitz and were never heard from again.

PROFESSOR DELBEAU: After the war, the author heard reports that Raymond Delbeau was on trial for his collaboration with the Nazis and brought to justice.

ANNIE, NICO, LENA, AND KOBA: According to witnesses' accounts, while in Lyon the four Dutch refugees were able to secure visas for Argentina. They left Vichy, France, in time, before the Germans occupied the Free French Zone.

NAOMI: Naomi was safely smuggled into Free France and neutral Switzerland, where she outlived the war. In 1946, she arrived in the United States and married in 1948. Her husband is a devoted Sadigora Chassid from Galicia who continued his Torah learning while becoming a successful businessman. They raised two children, a son and a daughter, and have eight grandchildren. She and her husband are involved in numerous *chesed* projects in Israel and the United States. After their children married, she took writing classes in Fordham University and then went on to participate in writing workshops in Columbia University. Naomi resides in New York City.